Blood Daughters

Blood Daughters

A Romilia Chacón Novel

Marcos M. Villatoro

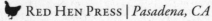 RED HEN PRESS | *Pasadena, CA*

Blood Daughters: A Romilia Chacón Novel

Book layout by Andrew Mendez

ISBN: 978-1-59709-177-0 (eBook)
ISBN: 978-1-59709-226-5 (hardcover)
ISBN: 978-1-59709-426-9 (tradepaper)

Library of Congress Cataloging-in-Publication Data

Villatoro, Marcos McPeek.
  Blood daughters : a Romilia Chacón novel / Marcos M. Villatoro. —1st ed.
    p. cm.
  ISBN 978-1-59709-426-9 (tradepaper)
1. Chacón, Romilia (Fictitious character)—Fiction. 2. Hispanic American women—Fiction.
3. Policewomen—Fiction. I. Title.
  PS3572.I386B57 2011
  813'.54—dc22
                    2011013316

The Los Angeles County Arts Commission, the National Endowment for the Arts, the California Arts Council and Los Angeles Department of Cultural Affairs partially support Red Hen Press.

First Edition

Published by Red Hen Press
www.redhen.org

When our daughters bleed
The hatred begins
—R.M.

To the students of Mount St. Mary's College

Marisa Jackson had a painful last name. Jackson. Unfortunate for Marisa. Good for the cause.

Karen Allende wanted to believe that Marisa's name might have saved the girl. It was so obviously American, like Andrew Jackson, or Michael. But Marisa's thick black hair and dark eyes and walnut skin called back to another country. And her mouth: Had Marisa's mouth tried to save her, pleading in Spanish and English for them to stop? No doubt. Marisa once spoke both languages fluently. She, like all her friends on her streets in Los Angeles, fell into the *vato* tongue, but they were just fooling around, like all thirteen year olds tended to do. Slang out a hot slur about boys, say something street-wise about the *putas* on the corner, those older girls who stared hollow-eyed at the children as if to say Your time's coming up child.

But there would have been none of that talk here, in her final moments. Only please, please, *ay no me corte señor ay no Dios ayudame Dios y la Santa María Virgen que me den auxilio* please I want my mamá.

Her Mamá. Now sitting in some stranger's home with people who promised they were doing everything they could, all the while keeping their eyes on a computer for incoming email.

So frantic in that makeshift office. So quiet out here, in the desert. A stone's throw from the Mexican border. A literal stone's throw.

Karen Allende had a job to do. So she stopped thinking about last names and bodies close to borders and a little girl's pleading voice. Karen flashed one of the Border Patrol agents her credentials, the badge and the card together in the same open wallet. He walked her around one of two Land Rovers. He was an American agent, Mexican descent. So was the

1

second fellow who had just arrived, the guy now on his knees, who was maybe twenty-five years old. Karen saw before he doubled over the name "Márquez" on his lapel pin. He had had time to consider the body. Márquez held the front fender of his SUV and tossed up his recent meal of eggs and chorizo and protein drink.

It was late afternoon and the air turned cool. Karen had been awake since way before dawn. Mid afternoon she had dropped asleep in the chair of a woman who worked for Justice on the Border, one of those fringe, left-wing groups that Karen had come to know. The woman, Mabel, had shaken Karen awake. "You'll want to hear this," said Mabel, and gestured to the police band radio on her kitchen table.

The missing girl's mother, Sasha, was asleep on the couch. She had hardly slept in the week since her daughter's disappearance. Karen let her sleep while she listened to the crackly report over the radio about a dead girl on the border.

Within forty minutes Karen was standing in the cooling desert, along with the vomiting Border Patrol agent and his colleague, who now walked Karen to the body. "So," he said to her, "FBI. This must be part of a bigger case, huh?"

"Yes," said Karen, "it is."

"Have to do with the Desert Women?"

"Maybe," said Karen, then thought better of it. "But that's a Mexican issue."

"Yeah. But still, she's so close to the border . . ."

"Excuse me, Agent Darío, right?"

"Yeah. Robert Darío." He tried to smile, but he had already seen the body. His voice rattled. Perhaps he was new to his job, and had yet to see just how many dead people there were spread over the border. Still, this one was more than just dead.

"Who found her?" asked Karen.

"Old man, lives in that arroyo," said Darío, saying *arroyo* like a gringo and pointing to a dip in the desert. "His dog, actually. Wouldn't come in when the guy called him. The old man went looking. The dog did some damage," Darío spoke with apology. "But, well, dog didn't do most of it."

Spiked nopales and saguaros grew in the loose gravel and sand. Karen stepped carefully around one of the cacti. Her tennis shoes crunched over tiny stones. Márquez and Darío had managed to hammer three wood stakes into the desert around the girl. They had wrapped yellow tape around the stakes, forming an awkward corral, low to the ground. It was a pitiful endeavor, Border Patrol agents marking a crime scene. But she liked the men for that. She barely had to raise her leg to step over the tape.

She looked down at the naked girl and the damage done. A girl who had just begun to bloom into womanhood, something no one could see now, not with those two slices into her chest and the one below. The doubt rose over Karen, doubt about being able to change the world one naked, dead kid at a time.

Darío might have thought she was praying, the way she stood there.

Karen pulled out her cell phone, flipped it open, shot pictures. She took over a dozen, though not from many angles. Just full shots. She speed-dialed a number and sent the photos on.

"So," said Darío, meandering close behind her. "What else needs to be done? We're here to help, if you need anything, though I expect you've got your own people, prints and all."

"Yes. They're heading out. Right behind me." She looked at the screen on her phone, checking the brightness of the final shot.

He looked over her shoulder. "That thing takes clear pictures for a camera phone." Darío was searching for things to say. "You sure got out here quick. This Desert Women case been open a long time?"

"Ten years now," said Karen. Then she got quiet. Ten years. When she had been thirteen herself. The same age as the dead girl.

"I'm sorry, I didn't catch your name . . ." Darío was polite, his awe over the Bureau turning ostentatious. Perhaps Border Patrol had been his second choice. Or third.

"Detective Allende."

"Oh. Like the actress?" Darío smiled. "She's great, isn't she?"

Karen could not help but smile. "Yeah. Really great." Then she looked at Marisa Jackson again and stopped smiling.

"Man, I remember when I first saw Rigoberta Allende," said Darío. He pronounced the name with a certain boyish reverence. "I was just a kid. I sneaked into *Generation Gap*, my first R movie. She played the Mexican maid to the rich guy. She was beautiful. Already an older woman, maybe in her thirties. But gorgeous. I fell in love with her right then, especially when she did that one scene, showed a little bit of, you know. She's a lot older now, but she's still good looking." He laughed.

Karen turned and smiled at him. The desert got quiet again.

And in that silence rose a question. "Hey. Did you say 'Detective?' Aren't you FBI?"

Karen heard the question. She also heard another car drive up, its two doors opening and quietly being shut down the hill from them. Her own car was uphill.

"Yes," she said. "We call ourselves 'detective' now. On these special murder cases."

That was a lame lie. He had caught the slight tremble in her voice. Darío was looking hard at Karen. Not just hard: he was a young guy talking with a pretty young woman who was supposedly a Fed and he now doubted her.

One of the men who had stepped out of the car called out. He was angry, his shout gave that away.

Karen glanced back. She knew him, African American, tall, a real hunk, someone she had avoided before. She snapped her phone closed. She stepped over the yellow tape. "Okay, I'm done, Agent Darío. Thanks much for your help. Those two gentlemen will take over from here." She barely gave him a glance, and no handshake, as she headed toward her car.

"You're not an agent."

She turned and walked back to him, huddling close so the two tie-and-jacket men could not hear. She lifted a card to his face. "Could you do me a favor?" Her voice, though nervous, also turned slightly flirtatious. "The person on that card? I promise you, she's with the Feds. Give her a call for me please. I'd do it, but I might be incommunicado for a while."

"What the hell . . ." He looked at the card. "Who's Romilia Chacón? Lady!"

But Karen was running now. It happened quickly. Darío's words were more a yelp. "Wait, you're one of those nutcase women, aren't you? That extremist group, I'll be damned. Márquez!" He stared at the card with the FBI seal. It looked legitimate. And more, there was the little girl at his feet, which he felt wrong leaving alone.

The real Feds behind Darío took over. They ran across the baked ground in their polished leather shoes and yelled for Karen Allende to stop. A cholla spike tore through the first man's pant leg. He cursed, worked the barb out, lanced his thumb. They did not draw their guns. His partner, white and overweight, headed Karen off, which made her switch back toward the body. He tackled her at the hip, snapping any fear right out of her. She loved that: the loss of all fear. She fell, her face hitting the sand, just five feet from the dead girl.

She stared at the horizon of Marisa Jackson's body over the desert while the sun settled and a slight wind flapped the yellow tape above Marisa's head like a long, twisting flag.

Karen reached into her pocket, snatched the phone out and slammed it against a stone. It shattered beneath her small, thin palm.

"We'll get the phone records," said the white agent, a hint of the South in his words. He actually smiled, as if appreciating her bravado.

"Wouldn't want to make it too easy for you."

The other agent, with the throb in his thumb and the rip in his pants, remained formal. "Karen Allende, you're under arrest for Cyberspace crimes as well as for impersonating a Federal Officer." He handcuffed her, then lifted her from the ground.

Darío looked at the two men. "What, you're not here for the little girl?"

The two real FBI agents said nothing. They carried Karen away. "They've never been before," said Karen. "Why change now?"

"That's enough, Ms. Allende. Your people keep our people from doing our work." He stuck his thumb to his lips, sucked at the pain.

"Careful," said Karen, "those cholla spikes are poisonous."

He popped his thumb away, looked at it, then at her.

The agent who had tackled her turned to Darío. "Detectives from San Diego Homicide will be here soon," he said. They took Karen away, leaving Darío and Márquez alone with the dead girl.

Darío took the card and its name, Romilia Chacón, along with its Los Angeles number and a second number scrawled on the back, to the squad car, where he kept his own cell phone.

Chapter 2

I'm losing him. Or maybe it's the other way around.

The thought rose up from under the weight of three drinks. Three whiskeys on ice. Little ice. I had already discarded the add-cubes-with-each-shot routine. Now I just added the Wild Turkey. No use fooling myself; I didn't necessarily want it cold.

"That's a man's drink," one of the guys had said to me earlier, on one of those rare Friday afternoons when a few of us Feds decided, What the hell, there's a decent Happy Hour nearby. Part of it was flirtatious, at least for a couple of the boys. The rest of us just wanted to loosen up.

"So what are you doing, putting down a man's drink?" His name was Lenny. Not the quietest guy in the L.A. Field Office. He was in his late thirties with a wife and kids at home, which I would remind him of if he kept up this callus pick-up.

"Who said men have the market on bourbon?" I took a big gulp from the tumbler.

"Look at Pearl over there," said Lenny, pointing to the blonde agent on the other side of the table. She ate pretzels and nursed a glass of red wine. "That's how a lady drinks."

"You are not winning points."

"I'm just saying, maybe it's not so good to hit the hard stuff." He looked at me with a real attempt at empathy. "You two girls went through a lot last year. So I could see, putting back a few shots. But she doesn't seem to need it anymore." He motioned toward Nancy Pearl again.

"Yeah well some of us didn't take a year off for a cushy job in D.C. to calm our nerves. One of us stayed here and did real work."

I was mad. Lenny just laughed. He lightly touched my shoulder, then casually turned to the conversation on his left. He stayed with that conversation and away from me for the rest of the Happy Hour. They talked about the Oscars. So: no pick-up here. Maybe Lenny was firing little warning shots at me: who in their right mind would want to go out with a liquored-up Latina?

Though I knew better than to give too much credit to Lenny. He was too loud for wisdom. Too idiot to be savant. And besides, now I had my eye on the target of Lenny's praise, Pearl.

Agent Nancy Pearl. She had recently returned to our West Coast Bureau after time off. Supposedly she was a victim of post-traumatic stress, brought on last year when a drug lord had kidnapped Pearl and me. Our boss, Special Agent Leticia Fisher, had sent Nancy off to work in a quiet DC office at Quantico until Nancy's nerves calmed. Now she was back in L.A., all healed in the head and ready to work for us again.

All a lie. Nancy had nerves of titanium. You could launch the Space Shuttle off her stone-cold, lying face. Nancy Pearl isn't even her real name. I knew that. And she knew I knew. She looked at me, but not with worry over my blowing her cover. More of a "You okay?" look, which pissed me off even more.

I drained the glass of a bad, watery gulp, stood up and said goodnight to them all. One fellow offered to call a cab. I swirled and told him I was fine, thanked him and walked easily to the door, got in my old Taurus parked in the Bureau's section of the Federal Parking lot and shook my head like a dog after a cold bath. I took Wilshire toward home. 405 North to the San Fernando Valley into Van Nuys, to my little three bedroom on Woolf Avenue, surrounded by fellow Salvadoran Americans and Armenians.

Mamá was in the shower. Sergio played a game on the computer. He greeted me without turning his head. Maybe that was it, what sank in as I poured my third drink (the first at home, the first as far as my family could see) and looked at him. It may have been then that I thought *I'm losing him.* I'm not sure now.

It had been a bad year. Problem was, we all had accepted that.

Sergio was nine now. A smart kid. They had put him in honors classes after his first year at the school on Kester Avenue. During one of our parent-teacher conferences one of his teachers had proposed the idea of putting him in gifted classes, but I wasn't sure about that. The pressure and all. I still wanted him to be a kid. "Besides, I think he's had enough . . . pressure on him lately," I had said to Miss Lauderback.

She understood, for she knew my line of work. Miss Lauderback also knew how Sergio had suffered: That a man named Carl Spooner had held Sergio and my mother, had put a gun to my boy's head and threatened to kill them unless I delivered to Spooner an infamous drug runner who had mutilated him.

To be honest, I started losing Sergio the day I lost Tekún Umán.

Which I've learned to stop thinking about. And certainly have never talked about, with anybody, including Mamá. Nothing good could come of it. Nothing at all.

Chapter 3

Mamá was out of the shower and drying her hair. From the couch I asked if she wanted something to drink. "No thanks. Oh, before I forget, you got a phone call from someone. A man."

"Who was it?"

"Here's the name and number." She handed me the paper. Darío. I didn't know him. Which bothered me; why would someone I didn't know have my unlisted home phone number?

"Did he say what it was about?"

"Just that he wanted to talk with Agent Chacón. He did ask if you really were an FBI agent."

I dropped the paper on my chest. The whiskey was moving nicely now. I'd call tomorrow. Or Monday. No, I'd call sometime soon, later tonight. Just not now. I looked down at my legs. They felt tight in these slacks. Suddenly tight, like I had gained weight in an instant. Shit. Though it had done some good to my chest, which I could see better through the eyes of the men at the Bureau.

Mamá sat down on the couch to my right, still scrubbing her long wet hair with the towel. She looked over at Sergio, then back at me. "You off tomorrow?"

"Yeah."

"Why don't you take Sergio out to the movies?"

"That's a good idea."

She glanced at the drink in my hand—No. That's not true: she stared at it. Then she looked back up at me. She said what we all knew.

"Too much. Again."

She had to add that final phrase, *otra vez,* to her statement. This had happened before, during the days I was on the case of my life: hunting my sister's killer. Once I had dealt with the murderer named Minos, Mamá could have told me I had no excuses for dancing with the bottle. But she hadn't. She let me enjoy my one or two *tragos* after work, to take the edge off. I had gotten shot in the leg last year, and complained of pain for weeks afterwards. The whiskey helped loosen the muscles. Mamá had allowed for that. But obviously she monitored me, just like she had my father: she could tell by the look in his eye, the way he spoke, just how many drinks were in him.

The strange thing was, I answered her. "Yeah. I know." Then I took another sip. I pulled at my slacks to free up my thighs.

She saw that and tried a hurtful ploy. "I noticed you haven't worn those designer jeans I got you last year. Not your style anymore?"

Sometimes living with your mother is a real bitch.

We sat there, both of us quiet for a while. Mamá picked up a book, a memoir by some poet from Nicaragua, Gioconda Belli. Sandinista revolutionary woman. Sometimes Mamá talked about the book and how brave Belli was, yet still very humble while working in the revolution to overthrow Somoza. Mamá spoke as if Belli would be the ideal daughter.

Sergio walked in. He said to his grandmother, in Spanish, "Abuelita, may I please have a Gogurt?"

She pretended to ruminate. "It's a couple of hours before supper. Go ahead, *mi corazón.*"

"'Ey," I said, "hombrecito, you haven't kissed me yet." I lunged forward from the couch.

He smiled a tired smile. He moved toward me, bent over to kiss me on the cheek. I grabbed him a bit too hard and stumbled. We knocked against each other. I grinned at him, right when a warm, brown wave licked right through me. I meant to compensate: I mouthed something about him and me going to a movie tomorrow. He said okay, but without enthusiasm. That should have been the warning, right then.

He walked away to the frozen yogurt in the fridge. I looked at my mother. She read the book as if she were alone.

Chapter 4

Before I knew that the phone call from the guy named Darío was about Karen Allende, I had already been thinking about her. It had crossed my mind to give her a call to see how she was doing.

But I knew she was doing fine. A hell of a lot better than before. While Mamá kept Sergio from going after a second Gogurt before dinner, I closed the door to my bedroom and looked through a pile of photos and papers. Pictures of Karen Allende and me. Pictures of me alongside her mother, Rigoberta Allende, and my mother, who looks giddy in the photo.

Considering how many movie stars my mother had met these past four years, you'd think she'd be used to it. Her little brother's very successful, very lucrative company, Cipitillo Cuisine, Inc., had made its mark in the movie industry. Uncle Chepe made the actors anything they wanted. His motto: we treat you like the President of the United States. You want crépes fresh from the pan? You got them. Sometimes Harrison Ford had a hankering for a seaweed salad with bacon, and Uncle Chepe got one of his workers to drive fast to the Farmers market on Fairfax for the ingredients. Charlize Theron wanted fresh portabello mushrooms in a thin pesto sauce? She got them. Chepe had an entire kitchen on wheels. Of course he made Latino food, his specialty being Salvadoran cuisine. Once word got out about his pupusas, "Can you make those?" asked Angelina Jolie. "Man, I love them! I ate them once in a little place in Culver City. Delicious! But they can be a little greasy." To which Chepe proclaimed, "For you, Ms. Jolie, I will make fat-free pupusas." "Really? How about vegetarian?" "*Por supuesto!*"

That day Mamá and Chepe sweated over making such a miracle. Vegetarian, okay: anybody can take a ball of corn masa and shove lightly sautéed veggies and cheese into it. But fat free pupusas is in itself an oxymoron. Yet somehow Chepe did it, all for Angelina Jolie and then, for all those secondary actors who lined up behind her to order their own.

His service got him in the door; accidental marketing made his name. The stars simply loved Chepe Chacón. He was not flirtatious nor histrionic. Chepe was simply Chepe. Honest as the day is long. Escaped refugee from El Salvador, fleeing from death squads, brought to the United States by his big sister Celia, my mother. And a fantastic cook. Jolie got the publicity ball rolling for him the day she asked on set, "Chepe, what does 'pupusa' mean?"

Chepe's brown skin turned, if not red, a slight orange.

"Oh goodness, did I embarrass you?" she said.

He muttered something, but she couldn't hear him.

My mother was nearby, laughing. Ms. Jolie turned to her. "Did I say something wrong?"

"Ay no, not at all." Then Mamá pulled Jolie to the side and explained the word pupusas, along with the appropriate hand movements that showed how a pupusas is formed, and what it looks like right before cooking: the perfect image of a vulva. "Well no wonder they're so popular," said Jolie. Both Mamá and she had a good, raucous laugh, while my uncle turned more orange.

That story, along with the translation of my uncle's company title, "Cipitillo" ("Bad Little Boy"), got him in *Los Angeles Magazine*. They quoted Jolie, "Oh no one makes pupusas for me except for my Bad Little Boy, Chepe Chacón." The magazine reporter followed that up with a slightly angry quote from Russell Crowe, "I'm not Hollywood's bad boy, mate. You must be talking about me cook."

It became chic, saying, "My cook, Bad Boy Chepe Chacón." Which made Chepe's business more popular. Which meant he could raise the prices. Which meant Hollywood wanted him more. For Chepe, it was all terribly embarrassing; he turned orange all the way to the bank.

None of this addled my mother. She spoke with the stars as if they were her sons and daughters. We have photos of Mamá pinching Tom Hanks' cheek. Mamá pulling Brad Pitt's head to her shoulder. Meg Ryan giving my mother a big smooch on the forehead. And in every photo, my mother smiles with the serenity of a woman who's just so proud of her little starlet children.

Except with Rigoberta Allende. With Rigoberta, my mother turned terribly giddy.

But only at the beginning. They first met on the set of *Miles to Go,* a drama in which Rigoberta Allende plays the Italian mother brought to Los Angeles by her aspiring screenwriting son, played by James Caviezel. That was when someone took the photo, before any real conversation began between the two. It happened four years ago, just a few months after I had captured the serial killer named Minos. We had recently moved to Los Angeles, and Uncle Chepe had hired Mamá to work the books for the company, along with making her one of the site managers. After the photo and the hugs, my mother said to Rigoberta, "At last I meet my idol, the first Latina to win the Oscar."

"And I," said Rigoberta, with a drama that she did not feign, "I have the honor of meeting the mother of the woman who saved my only daughter's life."

A panged expression crossed over my mother's face. I've never been sure how to interpret it: was she humbled that this world-famous actor saw me as a heroine? Or maybe it was a certain regret, that this moment, one that should have been light and star-studded and purely delightful, locked itself up with our own past, knotted with blood and my career of choice.

Still, Mamá was graceful. They hugged each other once more and started talking in Spanish, which allowed the crew members and other actors to move on. I couldn't escape; I can't remember which of them grabbed me and pulled me into their little huddle. It may have been both. "You've got a brave angel for a daughter, Señora Chacón." "Please, call me Celia." "And I am forever Rigoberta, and forever in your debt. This girl of yours has true cojones." Neither laughed at that, for it was not a joke, it was high Latino praise. I just nodded my head, trying to figure out how to look humble.

Karen, of course, had not been there.

Rigoberta Allende had succeeded in keeping the paparazzi from her daughter in the weeks after I found Karen and the five other lost souls, all strapped to redwood trees in the middle of a California national park. All of them naked and drugged, all ready for Minos to start a living dissection on each of them. It was to be his masterpiece. But it didn't happen. I stopped him. Karen Allende, along with the other much lesser known Angelinos, were delivered back into the trembling hands of their families.

But the story had gotten out, that before the kidnapping, Karen had called a suicide hotline. Why she was ready to kill herself, no one understood. She was the kid for whom everything was going perfectly. She was a senior in high school. Smart, popular, and the daughter of one of the more famous stars of Hollywood, an actor who was no less than a saint among most Latinos. When Karen's mother showed up on the screen, you just felt warm inside. Even when she played the obligatory Latin cleaning lady taking care of somebody like Jack Nicholson, you loved her. She had a look in her eye that showed she was not going to be your usual "Sí señor" maid.

Then came the day years ago when she made headlines by announcing, in an interview with a *Los Angeles Times* reporter, "I will never play a maid again. I'll become a real maid and clean my neighbor's house in Encino before I get in a black dress and white apron for the camera." It was bold. It was also before she won the Oscar. There was a little simmer of animosity toward her among some of the Hollywood elite, who said she won the Academy Award only because she had said something so politically charged. None of us believed that. She had announced her moratorium on maid roles four years before walking across the stage to receive her Oscar.

Since then, Rigoberta Allende and her daughter had moved from Encino into Brentwood. And that's where Karen's depression and suicidal tendencies began.

The entertainment media had a field day, as did the yellow newspapers found in the grocery check-out lanes: the Allende family was a Latino Mommie-Dearest phenomenon. Some speculated that Rigoberta had abused her daughter. Others figured it to be simple neglect.

It was much more basic than that. It was the shake-up that fame can bring to a family. It was being the daughter of divorced parents—a couple divorced due to the husband's bouts with clinical depression. All this drove Karen to call that suicide hotline. A phone call that Minos answered.

Karen and the others did not remember their time with Minos. They have no memories of the days held inside a storage facility in the San Fernando Valley, nor of later being tied naked to the trees, not even of Minos taking a black marker to their bodies to map where he would insert and pull the scalpels. Minos had given them Midazolam Hydrochloride to keep them unconscious and limp and unable to fight. Midazolam Hydrochloride, like its date-rape cousin Rohypnol, erases short term memory. At first we all saw this as a hidden blessing.

Later, for Karen, it became a curse. And that's when she and I became friends. More than friends.

Weeks after the day Mamá and Rigoberta met, Rigoberta called me. "Please," she said in Spanish, "I don't know who to turn to. I have to be careful, the media, they'll eat this up."

I started meeting with Karen. In the beginning it was clumsy. She didn't want to talk with anybody. She would blow up at me, much like with her mother. She was not drinking or taking any drugs. But she looked worn out, an eighteen year old who had slipped partially into the grave, and who wasn't sure how to feel about that.

At first, I wasn't sure why I stuck around. I'm a federal agent, not a psychologist. But I did stay, and later I understood why: it had to do with my sister.

I had lost my only sister Catalina to Minos years ago, when I was in college. Now, with Karen, I was the older sister. I was taking Catalina's place. For some reason this soothed me.

Karen said, "Tell me what happened. What he did to me."

I did. Someone more in tune with these things may have admonished me for being so direct with Karen about her near-murder. But no one was around; and I know how the absence of knowledge can gnaw at you like some feral, rabid animal. So I told her everything. How Minos had trapped her by promising to help her. How I arrived, with an FBI squad.

Then she wanted to know what had happened to Minos. So I had to tell her, but I did so partly, as those are my memories, not part of her forgetting. "I got him. You don't need those details."

She was satisfied with that and asked no more about my final dealings with the killer. But she did ask, "That scar on your neck. Did he do that?"

A look must have crossed over my face, as if I could see the reflection of my eyes in hers. I reached up to the left side of my neck instinctively, covered it loosely with my fingers, an old habit—an informal, casual hiding of the large, thick scar. "No," I said. "That was . . . it was some other shithead who did that."

The curse didn't hide the tremble in my voice. I hate talking about the scar, hate how it clings to me like some ugly ghost, a fucking *duende* that messes with my looks. It's true: men look at me, then, when they see the scar, they look away.

Karen said, "You know, my mother knows a plastic surgeon in Beverly Hills. He could take care of that."

"What, take it off?" I may have laughed, the way a hopeless clown laughs.

"Maybe not completely. But yeah, they're really good. They can do just about anything."

"Wait a minute. You mean to tell me your mother's had plastic surgery?"

"Well duh." Karen walked over and sat next to me. She lifted the curtain of my hair from my neck, which I had forced to fall there—again, another habit. She touched the scar. Ran her finger over the rough edge of the Keloid. "Yeah. He's good. He could take care of that."

"For a fortune," I said.

She was thinking. "Maybe Mom could get him to cut a deal for you." She smiled at me.

We became friends. Something I had not enjoyed in a while, since college: a friendship with another woman. At the time Karen was still a teenager. I was near thirty. Much older, from her point of view. I became the surrogate older sister. Something she never had, something I once had and lost. After eating at her home with her and her mother, or going out with her to a movie at the Promenade in Santa Monica, or her coming out to my blue collar home in Van Nuys for pupusas, we kissed each other on the cheeks. "Buenas noches, hermana," she would say, practicing her Spanish on me, something her mother had not taught her. *Good night, sister.*

I would go to bed, thinking of my older sister, but in a way that I had not felt before. Not of distance, but of a letting go. In the first slips of a dream, I watched Catalina drift away from me. Strange, but she was smiling.

Chapter 5

After those first weeks, talking with the famous Rigoberta Allende became commonplace. Whenever she left town for a shoot in Toronto or Italy, Rigoberta would call me. "Just, if you have some free time, Romi," she'd say, "if you could give Karen a call." I happily obliged.

They invited me to Karen's major events. I attended her graduation from the high school in Brentwood, and that same year, in the fall, accompanied Karen and her mother to the Catholic women's college, which was not far from her house.

At first I had misgivings about their pick in colleges. Why was Rigoberta sticking her daughter in an all-girls school? But Karen corrected me. "It was my idea," she said. "And it's a college for women. Not a girl's school."

On a Saturday we drove through Brentwood and entered the campus. It sat high on a hill, overlooking all of Los Angeles, the Getty Museum and the Pacific Ocean. Beautiful, yes; but it was cut off from the city. You could see the city, but couldn't touch it; and it certainly couldn't touch you. There were statues of Mary, and nuns walking around, some with habits and veils and some with nunny street clothes, and all I thought about was getting off that mountain and taking Karen with me.

We were less in touch after that. She had new friends on campus. She also joined some group called Peace and Justice, which I supposed had something to do with, well, peace and justice. She was changing. And I missed her. But she was not my sister, really; she was the child of a world famous actor. She had her own life. And I had mine, in the Bureau.

Then came the day when Rigoberta called again, this time with a panic in her voice. "Karen's been arrested. During a protest. They picked her up with a bunch of other kids."

"Okay," I said. "Where is she?" I picked up a pad from my desk and was ready to write down the address.

"Georgia," Rigoberta said.

Rigoberta bought me the first class ticket to Atlanta. She paid for the rental car. I drove quickly through Atlanta, knowing my hometown well and not worrying over the three whiskeys they so generously offered in the front row seats of the plane. I made my way to Fort Benning and showed my credentials. This was an army base. Though I worked for a federal department, I didn't have much latitude here.

There was Karen, her eyes swollen and puffy, along with her cohorts, all their eyes swollen as well. They had rushed the premises of the School of the Americas and had handcuffed themselves to the inside front gate. The soldiers had used a pepper-based emollient called capsicum on them, smearing their eyes with the oil. It makes the protestors less protesting, makes them beg to get the handcuffs off and be taken away so they can wash out their eyes.

I worked my way as deeply as possible into the base. I spoke with one officer who moved me down the hall to another officer who finally introduced me to someone in charge. Some phone calls were made. The Commanding Officer, after half a day of keeping me in a waiting room, walked out of his office. His last name was Alberts. "You're Special Agent Romilia Chacón," he said.

"Yes, I'm here about Karen Allende . . ."

"Stopping those terrorists on the Golden Gate last year. That was you, wasn't it?"

The respect in the soldier's eyes worked in my favor.

I got Karen out of there on my authority. I was her official warden, her probation officer. "She's all yours. Karen Allende is now officially a case for the FBI."

Which meant we would have to open a file on her. Nothing big about that, I thought. I could keep her under friendly surveillance. The most important thing was, I could get her home. I almost skipped out of Officer Alberts' office, right to Karen, whom I had never seen so pissed.

"What about my friends?" was how she thanked me. "Who's going to get them out of here?" Followed by "No way, Romi. No way I'm walking out of here and leaving them. We're in this together. Jesus, you should be in here with us! Don't you know what the School of the Americas is? It's a training ground for death squads, sent all over the world. Now they're in Haiti and Colombia, and God knows what they're doing in Iraq, but it wasn't long ago they created the death squads of El Salvador."

That was meant to move me. "Come on," I said, "we're going home."

"Like hell we are."

So I did what I had to do: I threatened her. "What you don't understand, girl, is that you have no choice in this matter. You're in my custody, not as a friend, but as a suspect for the FBI."

She actually smiled at that. "Oh I get it. Now you're the advocate for the Feds. The party-line gal. Have you forgotten you're Salvadoran? Or do you just eat pupusas and talk the talk?"

That did it. I slammed her hard, in Spanish, with my arm raised Fidel-Castro-style, "*No me digas esas babosadas de ser Latina, cuando apenas hablas el idioma cipota, y a la gran jodida saliste de la cuna de diamantes de Hollywood y ¿Cómo te atreves a acusarme a ser una vendida? Jodido!* Get your fucking ass in the car."

She didn't get it all, but nobody in the room could have missed my pissed-off-ness. She obeyed. We flew home without saying a word. Both of us hurt and pissed at the other. I drank whiskey and ignored her. She drank a beer and watched the movie. I almost said something, but the moment I was about to, the sting of her words set in. So I stayed silent.

We stayed silent for the next year. No more invites to the house in Brentwood. Rigoberta called us a few times to say that Karen was doing fine, focusing more on her studies. I could hear the apology in Rigoberta's voice.

Of course, I knew Karen was doing fine. The agent in charge of Karen's new file kept me updated. "She went out with a fellow last night," said the young Agent Banks, a new guy in the Bureau whom I had given the file to, something to cut his teeth on. "Boyfriend's name is Jason Bright. Scholarship kid on his way to Harvard. They played Lip-Hoovermatic in his car in front of her house. But nothing much, she wouldn't let him get far."

"Good for her," I said. All good: she was studying, not getting arrested, and necking on a Friday night. Not even smoking grass. All good signs. The

Georgia protest was a blip. I wanted to believe that. I wanted to make hers a passive file, one we wouldn't have to worry about.

But I did worry about her. And I took her mother up on the invite to her college graduation. That huge crowd of families, most of them Latinos, proud, working class Mexicans and Central Americans, the fathers wearing ties that were knotted loosely and thick below their necks, the mothers in first-worn skirts from Target. Children everywhere. And there, among all the graduates, was Karen. She looked happy.

After the ceremony I looked for her in the crowd. She smiled at me, but it was careful. We hugged lightly. I said congrats and how wonderful it all was. Her mother was over to one side, signing autographs. A slight, kind ruckus was building up around Rigoberta, which made Karen and me rush our conversation. "Listen," I said, "I'm never good at knowing what to give as a gift." I handed her my Bureau card, with my name, office number, and (something I never give, yet something she already had) my home phone number scratched on the back, with the message.

She understood. She smiled. "Oh. So does this mean you've closed my FBI file?"

I nodded.

"Gosh. So what will I brag about to my radical friends?"

"There's a little note on the back," I said.

She turned it over, and read the message I had written. She understood the Spanish. "Okay," she said.

I probably couldn't have expected much more. But I filled in, "If you ever need me, I just want you to know that I'll always rush right to you. Anytime."

"Thanks."

And that was it. She was too proud to hug me again; and I was too old to take a risk. Too old. But not too old, in my car and driving down that Brentwood hill, to cry.

That was over a year ago. So at first, when the guy named Darío called, I did not connect the dots. I called him back later that night, after a fourth shot of whiskey roused in me that strange, false energy of the well-lubed soul. "Yeah Mr. Darío, Romilia Chacón here, FBI. Who the hell are you?" I laughed to soften it, to hide my drunkenness.

He told me about a young woman some agents had just carted away. "She asked me to call you. She your little sister?"

A sober thought cut through. "Does the back of the card say, '*Tú siempre eres mi hermanita?*'"

"Yeah it does. Listen, we got a dead girl out here, and no one from the Bureau has come to investigate."

"Why aren't your boys handling it?" This was making no sense; Karen at the scene of a dead body. Out in, where the hell did he say he was, the desert? Which desert?

He answered, "It's a Fed call. The Desert Women case."

"Oh. Oh. Okay." Yeah. Okay, *Not okay*.

"Wait a minute," said Darío. I heard someone speaking behind him. "Listen Agent Chacón, sorry to bother you, some agents from your San Diego office just showed up."

"Wait, wait, what happened to the young woman?"

"Like I said, they took her away. She pretended to be one of your agents, so they arrested her."

"Where'd they take her?" My head swam. I filled a plastic bottle with water, with the phone cradled to my shoulder. A couple of times the phone, then the bottle, slipped.

"Don't know."

I thanked him. We hung up. I quickly called the only person in the Bureau whom I could trust with this: the woman who had lied to me in one seventy-two hour period more than some people lie in a lifetime.

Chapter 6

This was what I could entrust to Agent Nancy Pearl:

"I'm drunk."

"Okay," she said. A television played in the background.

"And I need a ride to San Diego."

"Why me?"

"You drive faster than any white woman I know."

⊷✦⊷

This was desperation. Both Nancy and I knew it. We hadn't talked since the night of a birthday party some five, six weeks back, when I had smarted off a bit too much for Nancy's comfort. All I had wanted was some blunt honesty from her. I've played the little soap-operatic moment in my head a few times, knowing now how embarrassing it was to me and to all the other people at the party—the agents, their spouses, and others who were just friends of friends. Embarrassing to us and dangerous to Nancy. Still, Wild Turkey makes me honest.

"Come now, little miss Agent Nancy Pearl. Tell us, what's your real name, huh?" I had smiled to take the bite off it. And I had added, just to make it, I don't know, right: "Are you really who you say you are?" I laughed. Maybe a little too loudly.

Next thing I knew Nancy had a grip on my upper arm with that bony, muscular hand of hers. She pulled me into a bathroom and closed the door. Ooh I hated her then. Hated her height that was four inches over me and her tits that were smaller but perkier than mine and all that highlighted blonde that always gets every guy's attention the chela bitch.

"Romilia, what the hell are you doing?"

"What the hell are you doing coming back to L.A., girl?"

"My job."

"Which job?" I was really on a roll. I felt a Bogart moment coming on, "What, you work for the Bureau, or for Mr. Murillo's ghost? Or maybe you're not the kind that tells." I raised the whiskey to my mouth.

She snatched the glass from me and slammed it on the bathroom's countertop. "You say too much, Romilia, and you won't just sink me. You'll go down as well. Conspiracy theory: they'll figure out neither of us was kidnapped by Tekún Umán, and that you knew about me all along."

"I *didn't* know about you all along. And you *did* kidnap me."

"I was holding you. For protection."

"You were taking orders from Tekún."

"He's dead, Romilia."

That silenced the room. There was, way back in my head, a desire to weep. But I had drunk enough to keep that from happening, thank God. Still, my body moved, and I stumbled into her shoulder.

"You need to deal with that, Romi. I'm sorry."

She left the bathroom. Then the desire to cry won out over the alcohol. I sat on the toilet for a while. Some guy came by. "You okay in there?" I said I was fine, but tears can cut through whiskey.

⚶

In the car now, I wanted to ask her questions. We had a two hour drive ahead of us. Nancy called the field office in San Diego from her cell phone. A fellow on the night watch filled her in on the crime scene: pre-adolescent girl, Hispanic, found in the desert outside of the city, near a Mexican town called Tecate. Two San Diego Homicide detectives were already on the scene. Yes, two Federal agents had shown up earlier to pick up one Karen Allende, but they had come from the L.A. office. The guy in San Diego knew little more than that.

Nancy hung up. I drank water. It was quiet for a few miles. I looked down at a magazine on the space between us. *New Yorker*. It was turned to a poem, a large poem, but I was sure Nancy had been reading the article around the verse.

"So. Where were you?" I said.

"What? When?"

"After Tekún. After San Francisco. Where were you, really?"

"In D.C., Romilia."

"Doing what?"

"Very boring office work." She added, "And of course, therapy."

"Bullshit."

"Fine. Check the records. Talk to my SAC at Quantico, a guy named Barley. He'll tell you. I did inventory on the back log of hacker cases. I followed up on the anarchic wet dreams of about two dozen adolescent geeks. And I pretended to be upset about the kidnapping. Four months of faking PTS." She rolled her eyes.

Silence, for about five miles. "You didn't go up to the Bay?" I said. "Try to fish him out of the water?"

She sighed. "You know they did a search. You think too highly of my abilities. Also of his."

"So, what, you're a real Federal agent now?"

"I've always been a Federal agent." Her voice turned angry, like a warning. But then it softened, "Look, if it's any help, I miss him too."

I said nothing. I believed that. Tekún had not been her lover; he was Nancy's surrogate father. Ever since the day he had found Nancy and her mother living out of a cardboard box in an Atlanta alleyway, Tekún Umán had taken care of mother and daughter. He had put the two in one of his comfortable, clean homeless shelters. He had taken Nancy to a doctor who cured her of rickets. Tekún also took care of a homeless man who had tried to rape Nancy in a bathroom of the shelter; the man was never heard from again. Tekún sent Nancy to school and got her mother in a college business program. He gave Nancy's mother start-up funds for a small tourist clothing shop outside of Mexico City, funds the woman would never need to pay back, though she did. All his philanthropy, all Tekún's goodness, was funded by one of the best heroin, cocaine, and meth production systems in the Americas.

Of course she missed him. So I shut up about it for the rest of the drive.

Nancy asked about Karen Allende. I filled her in. "What in the world was she doing at a crime scene of a murdered child?" she asked.

"That's the first question I mean to ask her."

Nancy then called our L.A. office. Yes, they had sent two agents to pick up Allende. But they were going to take her to the San Diego office first for processing, since the incident occurred in San Diego's district.

"Where do we go first?" said Nancy. "The San Diego office, or out to the desert?"

"The office," I said. "The case isn't ours. It's either a local killing for the cops, or it's that Desert Women thing, which means it's a Mexican problem." I settled back against the seat and drank more water.

"Desert Women? Jesus." She looked down at the road. "But I thought the body was found on the State side of the border?"

"Yeah, that's right. That's what the cop said." I ruminated a bit, but drank more water and closed my eyes.

I was just about to catch some sleep when she said, "You know, you need to sober up."

"I'll be fine. I'll have this water finished by the time we get there."

"That's not what I meant."

Chapter 7

They had Karen in a holding room. I passed by the one-way mirror and smiled; they had given her what she asked for, a Hershey Bar and a Diet Coke. No woman on earth craved chocolate more than Karen Allende. And still she stayed so thin.

To be that age again.

On second thought, no.

Karen had been charged with cyberspace crimes, or doing something illicit over the internet, which was why our two specialists in computer hacking, Randall and Shrieber, had been called down from L.A. to San Diego. I don't know why everyone called Agents Randall and Shrieber Klick & Klack, except that they were always together, one always laughed at the other's jokes (while no one else did) and they finished each other's sentences a lot.

"So, what are the specific charges?" I asked.

Randall spoke first. He wore thin metal framed sunglasses all the time. "You had a passive file on her. We had to make it active again after some cops said a woman fitting her description had taken pictures of another crime scene. She's been impersonating a Federal Agent. But that's just the beginning."

"Or the end," said Shrieber. He didn't wear sunglasses. Just heavy, heavy aftershave from Target. "She's been connected to that left-wing computer hacking outfit, 'desertwomentruth.com.'"

"Only it's not really a dot-com," said Randall. "That's just a name for the computer virus."

"What virus?"

"A pretty sophisticated one," said Randall. "It's got lots of legs. It can start with an attachment, or sometimes it uses portals that other viruses have left behind."

I turned to Nancy. She cut to the chase for me. "It's got different ways of getting into your computer and infecting it. You know, viruses? They can shut down your personal computer."

"Yeah I know, I know. But why would Karen be involved in a hacking group? She's not the type."

"What's the type?" said Randall. He adjusted his glasses.

I wanted to say *You*. "She's never been interested in computer stuff. And she's not one to waste her time like that, playing on them all day."

"I don't believe this group thinks it's wasting its time," said Shrieber. He turned to his laptop on the table, a good one, with a beautiful liquid screen and a perfect image of Keanu Reeves in Matrix pose. He opened up a mail server. "We're still working on where she sent the pictures," he said. "But whoever received them, they worked fast to harness the photos to the virus." He typed away.

"What are you doing?" I said.

"I'm looking for a hookup, with desertwomentruth.com."

"What, you're inviting them into your computer?"

"Basically. We have hunt-and-route capabilities. This is a program that can take inventory on recent targets of the virus. This, for instance, see? It's the internal network of a medical practice in Denver. There are the names and emails of all the doctors. Big outfit. And there, Dr. Hank Becker has received an email from someone supposedly at the Mayo clinic in Minnesota, but it's not. The virus is riding the email address. Check out the Subject box."

I murmured it aloud, "'*So you like little girls?*' Wait a minute. You're telling me that you—we, can break into other people's emails without them knowing?"

Randall, Shrieber, and Nancy all looked at me. Was that embarrassment, or pity, in their eyes? Randall hit the keys some more. "I'll copy the email with our virtual lift program, so the good Dr. Becker doesn't have to worry about Big Brother nightmares . . . and then I'll isolate the email in my program, and . . . there. There's the attachment. Let's see what it says."

He opened the attachment. His screen filled with the face of a dead little girl on a desert floor.

Underneath, in a simple, easy to read font, was a message: "Click here to know the truth."

Randall clicked, and opened up a series of photos, along with columns of copy. In the corner of the first photo was today's date, and 6:17 p.m., posted just two hours ago.

Randall opened one of the photos. It showed the girl in her entirety. "Oh. Oh," he said in a low whisper. "What did they do to her chest?"

I looked. The girl was naked. Her breasts and genitals were gone. Flies filled the wounds.

We all got quiet. But I knew what we were becoming: four pissed off—no—enraged Federal agents.

"I need to speak with Karen," I said.

⇒◆⇐

Before I went into the holding room, Shrieber filled me in on everything they knew, including how they caught her at the site and how she had smashed her phone. "We should have the number that she called within the hour."

She smiled as I walked in. I'm sure she was happy to see that Officer Darío out in the desert had made the phone call. "Ah, mi hermana," she said, and her gringo accent, or lack of it, was pretty good. She had been practicing.

We started with, "How you doing?"

"Fine, fine."

"You okay?"

"Yeah." She looked at the one-way, to refer to the agents, that they had treated her respectfully. Then she lifted the cola and gestured to the chocolate bar. "Got everything I need."

"Your mom?"

"She's great, even though she didn't get nominated this year, which pissed her off rightly. She should have gotten the Oscar for—"

"No, I mean you. Does your mom know about you? Here? What you've been doing?"

"Of course not."

"And what is this thing you've been doing?"

"Saving women's lives."

"Through federal criminal activity."

"I'm just making more public what's already public, but ignored."

"And what's that?"

"The girl."

"What about her?"

"You know her name?" Karen took a bite from the chocolate.

"Not yet, but we're—"

"Marisa Jackson. Age thirteen next week, on Wednesday. You can get that from the police report filed in one of the east L.A. squad rooms. You'll even get her mother's name, Sasha Fernandez Jackson. And you'll find out that Marisa has been missing for over a week.

"But what you won't see in the police report is anything about Sasha almost killing herself with grief. How Sasha ran into the streets looking for her daughter. How Sasha, with her two other little kids in tow, went from precinct to precinct without getting one damn bit of help."

"Hang on, slow down, *despacito*," I said, wanting to add *Get off your damn high horse,* but thought better of that. "So, you know all about this girl and her family. But you're the one snapping lewd, inappropriate pictures of her at her murder scene."

"Why would you say lewd?" She acted confused.

"Some people will get their kicks off photos like that."

"Really? Maybe they're the ones we can rouse out of the shadows. Maybe they're the reason all this happens."

"Karen, what the hell is all this about? What is desert-women-truth? And why the hell are you involved in this? I thought you gave up left wing protests."

"Oh, is that what your little file keeper said about me?" She smiled.

I hesitated, then asked, "Why did you have me called?"

"I guess because you're my sister."

I didn't know if she meant that sincerely, or as some ironic stab.

Maybe it was sincerity. "Romi, remember that night, up in the mountains?"

I remembered. "What about it?"

"You stopped me from doing it."

"You stopped yourself. Only the person can stop herself from . . . deciding that."

"You saved me."

This shut me up. I wondered if this was the closest she would get to forgiving me for the embarrassment in Georgia.

"You could have had me put away, but you didn't. You took me home, stayed with me all that night and the next. You had your mother bring Sergio over, which was a real nasty trick. You know that boy of yours is the only man who can melt my heart. You know how to mess with my head in ways nobody else does, because you saved me from him."

She didn't need to explain Him. The killer who had taken so much from me, who had taken my real sister from me.

"Look Romi, don't think I'm a nut case. I've had ample therapy. Psychological counseling all through college. I'm fine. Well, as fine as you could be after, after what Minos did. But it shaped me. Yeah, it shaped me, what he did."

She looked over to one side of the room. She was not at all frightened, or so it seemed, of being picked up by the authorities. She seemed blind to fear. That scared me.

"Listen," I said. "I'm glad you're feeling all right. But all this, it isn't good. They've got huge charges on you. Impersonating a Federal agent, damn, girl. That's a lot of years. And this internet thing, I'm not versed in those laws, but what you sent out on the web, that's disturbing. I don't know what the legal repercussions of that are. I'm sure your mom can get you out on bail, but Karen, I've got to be honest with you. I don't think the courts will be sympathetic."

She wasn't listening to any of it. She was looking at me with a whole different conversation in her head. "Romi, do me a favor. Read the site."

"What, your virus?"

"The virus will take you to other sites. About the Desert Women."

"That's a Mexican case. The Bureau can't just jump in and get involved in a foreign murder investigation."

"It's not foreign, Romilia."

"Right. This girl, Marisa. One kid from east L.A., that's a tragedy. And that makes *her* a U.S. case. But just her. Come on," I said, and I actually laughed, "who's going to take on those border ghost stories?"

She looked at me in a way that was almost pitiful, as if I was one of a large group of very blind people. "Romi, this has been going on for over ten years. Hundreds of murdered women on the border. And now children. There's a connection. I'm not sure what, or who. But no one is paying any attention to it. Just check out a few things, okay?"

"All right. All right."

"The web virus. Read it."

"Okay."

"But first, go out to where Marisa is."

"Crime scene. Fine. I can do that now." Though I didn't want to; my heavy sigh might have given that away.

She ignored it. "Then go to an apartment building on Barrington."

"What, in Brentwood?"

"No, just south of San Vicente, north of Santa Monica Boulevard. Marisa was supposedly seen there when she first disappeared."

"How do you know all this? You a private detective now?"

"Please?"

"Okay, fine. I'll check it out. But whatever I learn, I'll have to hand over to San Diego Homicide. It's their jurisdiction."

Just me saying that word, *jurisdiction,* disappointed her. "Romi, when you caught Minos, did you do it by the book?"

"What's that supposed to mean?"

She smiled just slightly. "I guess, working for the Federal government, you've got to learn the hoops, right?"

I wanted to say something to that. Something angry, or maybe sad. Her words were simple and blatant. They were the words of a young woman, just recently out of college, still green. Green, and arrogant. I was thirty-two, and wanted to tell her something about the road ahead, that after a while, girl, you just realize how exhausting it is to ditch the book. To break the rules.

Last year I lost a partner in the Bureau and another man I loved while trying to protect him from my own Bureau. I can still see him at night, when I'm trying to unwind: there goes Tekún Umán, leaping from the Golden Gate Bridge.

So she was right: I had gotten more careful as of late. Because not being careful meant doing the wrong thing, losing too much. She would learn that someday, I wanted to say. But then her lawyer showed up and escorted her from the room. At least she didn't leave me sitting completely lost in the swill of my own guilt: she touched my shoulder while walking to the door.

Chapter 8

According to Agent Randall, the crime scene investigation in the desert was still in process. Since Nancy was driving, I asked, "Feel like checking it out?"

"Afraid so."

⚓

Karen was right about some things, such as me not being very enthused over visiting a crime scene, especially that of a dead thirteen-year-old girl. This, again, may have had something to do with age and the need to mete out my energy. One easy parameter: don't get involved in other jurisdictions. Work on your own turf. That didn't have anything to do with toeing the line; more, it had to do with wanting to go home at the end of the day.

Which I hoped to do today. It was just past midnight now. If we planned this right, Nancy and I could check out the scene and ask the detectives who took the call what they thought. We wouldn't get in their way, and I'd make sure to tell them that right off.

I thought Nancy would head toward Tijuana, but she took another set of highways: the Eight Freeway to the 125, then onto the 94, which quickly turned into a state road. I had no idea which way was east. Nancy, however, knew these roads well, and not only the roads: she knew the underground roads too, literally underground. She knew the routes Tekún Umán had once taken, or at least his cocaine had taken, from Mexico into the U.S. As his FBI mole, Nancy knew everything about his business, and could keep the Feds from finding it.

That information came in handy today. "Ninety-four will take us all the way to Tecate," she said, "which is close to the scene."

We passed through small, sleeping towns named Potrero and Dulzura. Not even the Taco Bells were open, which meant it was past midnight. Soon we were near Tecate, which was on the other side of the border. Guards stood at a guard post, not as many of them as at the border with Tijuana, but enough to stop the small flow of traffic.

Nancy didn't drive toward the crossing. The body was on this side of the world.

A twelve-foot-high sheet of metal fencing separated the two countries. The fence ran all the way from Imperial Beach in San Diego out to here, then stopped in the open desert. It had yet to become our Berlin Wall, petering out just fifteen miles inland from the ocean. The authorities figured the desert was enough to keep people from passing through here. They were partly correct: many Mexicans and Central Americans chose not to come to the States because of the desert. Many others did, and died out here from heat exhaustion. Still others made it, somehow.

My mother had made it, thirty-six years ago. Carrying my sister Catalina. They had crossed through the desert, along with my father. No doubt somewhere nearby. Though I've never asked my mother about it.

We had to circle around some small roads in order to find the crime scene. It was just beyond where the metal fence abruptly dropped off. "This is near Colonia Nido de Las Águilas," said Nancy. "That dried-out riverbed over there? That's the border."

"Looks easy to cross here," I said.

"Sure. Right into four hundred square miles of pure U.S. desert." Her headlights slapped up against the yellow ribbons. "There's the girl."

She parked. We got out. I shined a flashlight, more as a heads-up to the San Diego detectives already here. Nancy called out our credentials. I held up my badge. In the moonlight, upon a hill, stood the outline of a large cross, a good twenty feet tall.

We introduced ourselves, shook hands with the two detectives, whose names at first I did not remember. One was Latino, the other white. That should have been a sign, right there, about my drinking: I always remember the names of people present at crime scenes, memorizing them on the spot, a demonstration of clear thinking and control. It keeps me alert and welds my thoughts to the place. It shows that I care, whether I do or not.

But here was a body. A little body. You can't help but care about that.

Nancy talked to the San Diego detectives. "We're on the Karen Allende case, the woman they caught taking pictures here. Mind if we follow up with you? We'll stay out of your hair." She smiled. It was just a touch flirtatious, which worked nicely.

"Have at it," said the white guy. "I'll give you my notes too if you'd like."

Either he was flirting back, or he really didn't care about territorial issues. Either way, Nancy worked with him, while I walked to the body, toward the buzz of all of the flies.

"How long she been out here?" I asked.

"Since sundown."

I looked at the detective. "Sundown?" I said.

"Hey," he said, "we got here as fast as we could. There was some confusion, that woman out here taking pictures, then the Feds, then we got the call. It took a while. But the M.E.'s already come and gone, done his preliminary work, he's gone on back to wait for the body."

"So. Where's the transport for her?" I asked.

"They uh, I think they got lost. They don't know the desert much. They'll be here soon enough."

That was too much. I turned away from him, toward the dead girl who had been insulted by ineptitude for the past seven hours. I bent down and shined a flashlight on her.

The girl was twisted, her right arm over and above her head, her left arm to the side of her torso. Her legs formed the number 4, with the right leg straight out, the left bent and its knee pointing outward, the ankle underneath the right knee. She had no clothes. It helped that I had seen her before, in Karen's pictures. I could ignore, or try to ignore, or just pretend to ignore, the damage done to her chest and genitals.

I turned away, swatting at flies that I couldn't see, only hear. Then I forced my stare back at her wounds. And I thought that word, *wounds, they are wounds,* and somehow that allowed me to look again.

The edges of the incision were clean, as if a razor had parted the skin. Everything that would have made her a woman was gone.

This was a meticulous rage.

I walked away, asked the Latino guy if he had a cigarette. He did. I took it, took his light, thanked him and walked away. He knew not to follow me, nor try small talk.

For three minutes or so I stood in the deep night of the desert and smoked. Then I pushed the butt in the sand, pocketed the filter and returned to the girl.

Her head bothered me. No cuts to it, though there was a blood stain at the back of the head that soaked the hair and started to clot up bits of sand under her. Her head was cocked slightly, the back of her skull pushed shallowly into the sand. The position cocked her jaw open.

A sign that the killer may have dumped her here, maybe dropping her out of a car or truck . . . though that scenario bothered me. She wasn't dropped. I could tell that, once I shined my light on her elbows, her buttocks, right calf, and especially the heel of her right foot. Those curves in the sand showed that she had not been dropped, but launched.

Tossed. From where her feet pointed.

I looked up, toward a large white cross that stood upon a hill behind me. A cross, out in the middle of the desert. What was that all about? I had seen no churches anywhere on our drive out here. But there it stood, large and white in the moonlight.

In the opposite direction I could see the shadows of men, huddled together, walking around the desert.

Over to my left, Nancy was still talking with the white detective. She was asking if they had taken fingerprints from the body, or did the M.E. have any specific cause of death. "Excuse me," I said. "Nancy, which way is north?"

She and the detective pointed away from us, in the direction of the cross. "Why?" asked the detective.

I looked south, toward the dry riverbed that Nancy had pointed out to me, and to that cluster of men.

"How far are we from the Mexican border?"

"You're on it," the white detective said.

"But we're still in California, right?" I asked.

"Oh yeah," he said. "Can't pass into Mexico without permission. Not our jurisdiction, and a shitload of trouble if you do. These days, with the terrorist threats, the President's even cut off Mexico. That's why they're over there." He pointed beyond the riverbed to the group of figures.

"I thought they were with you," I said.

"Oh no. Not ours. Mexican police, from either Tecate or east Tijuana. But I hear they've called in La Policía Preventiva. The Mexican FBI."

"Oh." I was confused. "So, what are they doing?"

"Just checking out the area. Whenever a crime incident is this close to the border, both sides come out. It's an agreement we have, to help the other side check out the perimeter. But you can't cross. Gotta stay in your own playground." He laughed at his own little metaphor.

I said, "She was murdered over there."

"How you figure?" said the detective. He and Nancy walked to me and the body.

"She was tossed."

I showed them the ripples in the sand around her frame. "We're what, twenty, thirty feet away from the border? She got tossed over."

The detective, whose name I finally got—Somner—was perplexed and dubious. "How could a killer throw a girl that far? She's little, but still, she must weigh fifty, sixty pounds, maybe more."

"It wasn't one person. Two at least. Probably picked her up together and flung her."

"What the hell for?" said Somner. "We follow border rules, but killers don't. Far as they're concerned, this is just one big desert."

"I want to go over there."

"No way, Agent, what's your name?" His saying that made me feel better. "Chacón? Agent Chacón, you cannot go traipsing around Mexican territory as a U.S. Federal Agent."

I looked at him and wished Karen were here, to see me wanting to break a rule.

Nancy helped. "Come on," she said to him, "we're out in the middle of nowhere. Like you said, who knows where one country ends and the other begins?"

"They do," he said, pointing toward the cops who walked around and talked lowly to one another in Spanish. There were six in all. I walked a bit closer, just to catch their voices. Some of them spoke about the place, maybe they'd find some leftover cigarette boxes or something. Others talked about a recent soccer game. None followed a meaningful pattern: they all meandered.

I walked toward them. Somner, though trying to keep a gentlemanly demeanor about him, called out to me, "Agent Chacón, do not cross that border."

I turned to him, nodded, held my hand up in a "calm down" fashion, then walked right up to the edge of the dry riverbed. This got the Mexican cops' attention. They shined lights straight on me in a way that said, silently, the same thing that Somner had said.

I spoke to them in Spanish. Good, clear Spanish. Which at first confused them, me being a gringa Fed. But they talked back, figuring I was some other gusano Latina who worked for the American government. "Find anything yet?" I said, kindly, after making introductions.

"No, not yet," said one fellow. He introduced himself. Officer Saenz. "We're still looking. But it looks like it's an American killing."

"No, I don't think so." I told Saenz what I had found, the wake in the sand that her body had made. "She was killed in Mexico, and thrown away in the United States."

"You sound very sure of yourself." And though he was smiling (we held our flashlights indirectly toward each other, for sake of conversation), I could tell, by his inflection, that he didn't care for my theory. He was a young guy, very good looking. He worked out; he wore a short-sleeved blue standard cop shirt, even in this cool night. His chest held the cloth tight.

"Yes, I'm pretty sure," I said. "So I was hoping you could tell your men to stop stomping around like that? They may disturb the murder scene, if they haven't already."

This sudden, hardly subtle game of verbal cock-fighting riled him. He was Mexican, my mother would have reminded me; he could pick up on my Salvadoran accent. She wouldn't hesitate to remind me about the hostility between Mexicans and Central Americans.

After a long thirty-second silence between us, in which he crossed his large forearms over his massive chest, I said again, "Your men, please?"

"So what should they do, Agent Chacón?"

"Stand where they are. If they could quit moving, just for a moment."

He turned and told them to stop looking and moving.

"Okay," he said. "And now, señora?"

"Well, there's the body," I turned and pointed toward Marisa. "I measure about thirty feet. That's a long way for one person, but maybe two guys, and if they're really strong, you know, in good shape," and I turned to him and glanced at his nicely cut body and stumbled on to another thought. "The ripples in the sand around her body show a trajectory that starts from, well, about where you're standing."

I shined my light around him. Nothing much but scrub, sand, rocks, more sand. And him.

Nancy came over, stood beside me, and introduced herself in impeccable Spanish. We did not shake hands with him, as that would mean closing the ten foot gap between us, besides breaking some international law. But she was cordial. "Thanks for being out here with us," she said.

He smiled at her, but spoke to me. "So what should we be looking for?"

"Body parts," I said.

"I see," Saenz said. "So is that another reason you think this is a Mexican killing?"

Again, my mother would have warned me: no machismo quite as pure as the Mexican variety. "No, I don't think that. I do think, however, that it occurred in Mexico. So the body parts of the victim may be in your area. Jesus Christ, this is crazy, standing here like this." I said that last bit in English to Nancy. Which was rude to Saenz, I know, but I was getting frustrated by the glass wall of border.

"Then why don't you come on over?" said Saenz, in crisp, accented, but perfect English.

I said nothing. Was that an invitation or a threat?

Nancy spoke for me, in English. "Thanks Officer Saenz, but we've been read the regulations."

"I will say nothing, if you are quiet." He smiled. Then he added, "It would be my honor, to have two beautiful women such as yourselves on my Mexican soil."

"Careful, Officer," said Nancy.

"I mean no disrespect." He looked down slightly; he could have been averting his eyes in humility, or checking out our thighs through our jeans.

This was a chance. Though the air did not feel right; I sensed it, and I was sure Nancy did as well. Still, it was an opportunity.

Then Saenz raised his head, looked over us and shouted kindly to Somner, in English, "They have permission to come over."

Somner started walking over to us, leaving behind the car where he had been speaking to San Diego through a radio. "What the hell's going on? That's not possible." But by then, Nancy and I had shown our badges, as if they were passports, and had stepped across. "Fine," said Somner, sounding more than aggravated. "It's your alls' asses on the line, not mine."

Saenz laughed, a small, kind chuckle. "Don't worry, Officer," he said, then looked at us, "their asses will be fine with me."

Chapter 9

We were now in Mexico.

Nancy and I shined our lights in half-circles around us. Saenz stepped back, giving us room. "Don't move too far, please," I said, afraid he would walk over evidence.

"My pleasure to stay."

I ignored that. I turned and looked at Marisa's body, which had now been there too many hours. The sun was rising over both our countries. In a few moments I could flick off my flashlight and use the light of day. It helped the investigation; it didn't help beautify the scene. A naked girl, torn, lying alone in the waking desert, a chorus of flies thickening over her.

We were in the middle of the riverbed. Just a glance up, and I could see over the rim of the dead river, an embankment made during the wet season, when this bed flooded with water. Now the thick silt was dry, left smooth by the last rains months ago. The only things that disturbed the silt were where Saenz had walked—straight out of the shrubs on the riverbed's south side—and where Nancy and I had crossed over. Which told me it had been a long while since illegal immigrants had last crossed via this route. No doubt Nancy was right; most would be too frightened to enter the States through such a vast desert.

"Over there," said Nancy. She pointed to the east, toward the direction of Tecate, where feet had disturbed the silt. But not by immigrant feet walking one way.

We walked along the edge of the riverbed to where she had pointed. The mud was not smooth. It had been broken up, walked on, back and forth, by more than one person. Two people. Those were boot prints in the silt. And naked foot prints, small, within the circular patterns left by the boots.

They were chaotic. The child prints, with little toes and the turn of a small arch, went one way then another. The boots had moved more directly; the barefoot child was lost. There were other disturbances in the silt, blunt gashes, rounded indentations formed by a fallen body. And a small handprint. In the handprint, blood. It had mixed with the dust and had coagulated there, turning the dust into a patch of paste.

"We need a sample of that," I said, "to match it with the girl's blood."

Nancy pulled a small package from her fanny pack: a portable crime scene kit. She eased the package to the ground, placed it on untouched silt. She opened the flaps, pulled out a vial and got to work on the blood.

"You got a camera in that pack?" I said, gesturing to her hip.

"Got it."

"How about some plaster, for a mold?" I meant it as a joke. It fell flat, with all this evidence around us.

Nancy took pictures. I turned to Saenz. "This is the crime scene," I said to him. Then I gave him an excuse, "No doubt you missed it, in the dark."

"Are you Indian, Agent Chacón? A tracker perhaps? Lakota?"

"You see it. The markings. There was a scuffle here, some fight. Or a beating. Or this guy," I pointed to a bootprint, "did his killing right here. He let her stumble around a while before tossing her over the embankment."

"Why do that?" said Saenz. "Why come all the way out here, kill a girl, and throw her across a border that is not even marked?"

"I don't know," I said, then let some of my thoughts slip around, "It seems, just a bit symbolic . . ."

"Excuse me?"

I know it was thin, but I followed out the thought. "It seems like some sort of statement. Killing her in Mexico. Tossing her into the U.S. It doesn't make sense in a practical way. But maybe he, or they, weren't being practical. And that cross over there, maybe it's got something to do with it, since she was tossed in that direction. . ."

Saenz was listening. He was also smiling.

"You try to explain it," I said, and gestured to the evidence of the desert around us. "Then try to make sense out of ripping a little girl up like that." I wanted him to get it without me explaining it: symbols of misogyny, rage; symbols of things we all could agree upon as evil.

He looked around at the same desert. "Agent Chacón, it's hard to say where the border is out here. It's moved through the centuries. Most of this was Mexico. San Diego and Los Angeles were Mexico, for most of history. But now, who's to say where your country ends and mine begins?"

I didn't like his tone. He sounded like he held a grudge for past broken treaties. "I think our killers know where the border is," I said.

"And why more than one? There's no proof—"

"Yes there is." I turned and pointed to the low edge of the riverbank, where two sets of boots stood in tossing position: next to each other, their pointed toes facing California, with a small space between them. A space the size of a girl.

Nancy had already taken that picture. She was now circling the perimeter of the scuffled area, taking one shot after another of the scrub brush that ran along the Mexican side of the riverbed.

We worked for another half hour. Nancy filled the digital camera. I walked slowly, my hands behind my back, letting the sun and the shadows it made through the shrub be my guide. All the whiskey was gone from me, and I had drunk enough water to clean me out. I wasn't hungry yet, but I knew that, once we left this scene and I could put Marisa Jackson's face out of my head for a short while, hunger would come about. It would be welcome—for hunger meant my brain had fooled itself into forgetting all these images, at least for the time it took to eat.

I found another stain of blood, this time on a flat stone about the size of my hand. There was blood around the stone as well, on the sand. I told Nancy to lift it, as we'd want to check this sample against the sample in the small handprint. She took a bag of the coagulated blood in the sand for good measure. It was obvious that Marisa had been over here as well; she had stumbled around. Her footprints went back and forth, as if she were lost.

I walked away from the stone and that multitude of small prints. Near some scrub I found more boot prints. Numerous ones. But they could have been made by the clumsy movement of those damn cops.

Those cops, who just stood there, watching me. Collecting not one shred of evidence. Thoughts came to mind, ones I could blame my mother for had I not believed them so deeply now: Mexican cops, worthless, corrupt, lazy. Mexican cops who weren't lifting a finger to help Nancy or me. Just standing there.

Which I could have believed, except for the way they stood there: they looked pensive. One man had his hands up slightly as if he wanted to come over and give us a hand. But not one of them moved, as if they were afraid to move.

Saenz remained silent. He walked to the edge of the riverbed. On the northern side stood Somner, his hands in his pockets. He said nothing and tried not to watch us, as if by not seeing us, this international faux pas would go away. But he was still curious.

Sometimes Saenz glanced back at his own men. And those cops watched him. Carefully.

All this was wrong. But I wasn't sure what to do with it. So I did my job.

I thanked Saenz, shook his hand, and started to head back to our country and our car. Nancy was ahead of me. She did not hear Saenz call me back in a voice that was almost a whisper. "Agent Chacón. A word, please."

"Yes, Officer Saenz?"

"You should hand your evidence bags over to the Mexican PPF."

"I agree. I'm more than happy to give them what we just collected. But since they've taken their time in getting here this morning, and since the San Diego Medical Exam has yet to show up, I'll take the evidence to L.A. to keep it safe."

"You should leave this one alone."

I couldn't tell if that was a threat, a warning, or, by the look in his eye, worry. Concern for me? Highly unlikely, as we had just met; and he had been an ass-wipe with manners.

"Why?"

"Agent Chacón, none of this is good."

"I agree."

"No, you don't understand." That was worry in his eyes. He glanced back at his fellow cops. "You don't live here on the border, you don't understand that there is a third, country here."

"What do you mean *third country*, who, like the Colombians?" I was thinking drug cartels.

"No, that's not what I meant. Well, yes, drugs, of course, they are always . . . but this is, an invisible country. And it is much larger than either of ours."

"Who are you talking about, the Mexican Mafia? Why would they go around killing little girls?"

I knew the cartels and the Border Mafia were strong entities and had much more money than our own anti-drug departments in either D.C. or Mexico City. I was about to say this; but Saenz had gotten quiet. And he kept glancing at his colleagues, who had their eyes completely on us.

I whispered, "You in some sort of trouble, Officer Saenz?" then I risked it, "Your boys there, are they on the take? Getting paid off by one of the cartels maybe? Any of them guilty of this?" I jerked my head toward Marisa.

He said nothing. He turned, walked more deeply into Mexico. He entered into that dispersed group of cops. They moved away, to their squad cars parked on a back road that we could not see. And just like that, they abandoned the crime scene. In the distance, I couldn't distinguish Saenz from the rest of them.

Chapter 10

Karen saw things that Romilia has yet to see.

Had she been at the border with Saenz, Karen would have understood what the Mexican cop meant when he had said, *There is a third . . . country here.* No confusion. In fact, Karen might have complimented Saenz on his alacrity, his ability to say in six words what this was all about. How large all of this was.

Which is why she was not afraid. She sat in a second holding room, drinking a second diet soda and nibbling on the chocolate bar they had given her in San Diego. The drive to L.A. in the back of the car with the two FBI agents up front had not bothered her, though she was tired now. It had been a long day and was almost morning. Romilia was at the border. Romilia would catch things others had overlooked or covered over.

Karen knew that Romilia has a gift. Eventually, Romilia saw things the rest of us didn't.

Though Romilia would never say this. Or she'd chalk it up to simple obsession. "I just get something stuck in my head, I have to follow it out or I'll go nuts." This was said one night when they had stayed up late in Romilia's house, playing several rounds of poker with Sergio. The boy had cleaned them both out, and then had fallen asleep on the couch. Romilia and Karen stayed up, drinking wine and talking.

"So. It was just deep curiosity that led you to find me? Find us?" Karen had said. "Everyone else was looking through the hills in Malibu. You figured out Minos had taken us up north, to the Redwoods."

"No. That wasn't just curiosity, God no," said Romilia. "That was a countdown."

Then she shut up, as if the wine had let that slip out. But Karen knew what Romilia had meant: countdown to when Minos would have begun dissecting Karen and the others alive.

Much like the countdown a few years later, when Karen, a sophomore in college, had called Romilia out of a final desperation that meant to keep her alive. But then Karen had hung up. Still Romilia had found her, not on campus, but up in the mountain behind the college, tucked away in a crevice just a few feet off the side of the fireroad. Later Romilia gave a haphazard explanation on how she found Karen, "Oh, I just figured you weren't on campus, you had left the area, I just figured. . . ." Figured, no doubt, that Karen didn't want the bullet from her father's gun to go through her and through a window to hit another student. Didn't want to get her room messed up. Didn't want to disturb the faculty, the other students, with the gunshot report.

Romilia had kept Karen alive through the following months. She visited Karen every other day at the clinic in west Los Angeles. Brought her magazines. Sneaked in chocolate. In the psychiatric hospital, Karen took meds and sat in talk therapy for weeks. It was a meticulous, nerve-wracked stitching of spirit back onto muscle and bone. Romilia was a part of that. Karen once asked her, "Why do you keep coming here? Why do you care?" Romilia answered, "It's a sister thing."

Karen believed that.

But Karen also understood something else: since the day she had crawled into the crevice by the side of the fireroad in the Santa Monica Mountains, just behind the campus, and had pushed the barrel into her mouth and aimed upward into her palate, things hadn't been the same. The desire to die. That had not gone away. It had been there before she met Minos. Some thought Minos would have been enough to shock her out of her tendencies, but no. After the scare of being kidnapped by a psychopath, that intriguing tremor of thought, *You're still alive,* simmered through her once more.

"Come on Karen. Sister. Hey. Come on."

There is that image, always. The sky beyond the crevice, blue and bright over the Santa Monica Mountains. Then Romilia, how she filled that sky when she bent over and reached in, toward Karen. Romilia had smiled at her. She had reached in, her hand open, not to pull the gun out of Karen's mouth, but to give Karen the option of handing the gun over. So calm, like an angel. A brown, beautiful angel.

Though Romilia was not calm; she was all human. Karen knew this after uncocking the gun and placing it in Romilia's open palm. She crawled out of the crevice and fell and Romilia caught her. Romilia's whole body rattled with a human fear of loss. Much better than some angel.

So none of this was going to be easy. The desire to die had twisted into something great. The protests in Georgia had helped rouse this change even more. In Georgia she had been afraid, with U.S. soldiers slipping that stinging solution into her eyes, snapping the handcuffs and taking her and the others away. She had been terrified. Then Romilia had come along, and Karen had gotten pissed.

Georgia had helped her get to this: getting arrested by the FBI. Hauled to Los Angeles on some really big charges. Now she ate chocolate. And she thought about what she needed to do. The next step. A step that desertwomentruth.com wasn't so sure about. Her young colleagues believed it was over, that their group would break up now. They wouldn't show up at the jail; they would wait for her. Karen's mother would have to save the day, as only money can.

Right on time. There was Rigoberta Allende. Karen knew those eyes that peeked through the slit in the doorway of the holding cell. A day or so and a bail bond later, and Karen could get back to work.

Chapter 11

Nancy and I drove into Los Angeles just as the sun was coming up. We hadn't talked much in the past half hour, each of us in our own worlds. I had no idea what Nancy thought about. I was thinking about the To-Do list Karen had given me.

I had done one of the three requests, checking out the crime scene of the dead girl. Next on the list: the little web virus of desertwomentruth.com and an apartment building in Santa Monica. I was tired, and wanted to go home. I chose the web virus.

But not through a computer. Randall and Shrieber had handed me a half-inch thick file of multicolored hardcopy prints, all downloaded. Instead of infecting my own computer at home, I could flip through pages. I could study, on paper, the group's purpose, its mission.

They used hacker tactics to send the world these horrific pictures, ones that Karen had taken. Were they radicals? Was this some type of cyber guerrilla warfare? Showing us all of the horrors of the Mexican-American border? To what purpose?

It was eight o'clock Saturday morning when we drove around Long Beach. Bright sun now, so I picked up that *New Yorker* sitting on her brake lever. "You got a subscription?" I asked.

"Uh, yeah. I do."

That big poem didn't interest me, until I saw its title and read it out loud. "'A Venom Beneath the Skin.' Catchy." I read the first two lines to myself, *There is a venom beneath the skin/that cries at night.* I turned to the poet's name. Latin dude, Mauricio Rafielo. Didn't know him. And since I could never read in a car, I let the magazine plop back over the hand brake.

"You all right?" I asked her, looking at her.

"What? Yeah. Why?"

"Nothing. Just looks like you're worried about something."

"Nah. Just, tired."

Half an hour later Nancy pulled up in front of my house. "You got plans for today?" I said as she parked her car in front of my house.

"A hard-core date with my bed." She grinned.

"Ah but for the single woman's life."

"You?"

"Coffee with my mother. A date with my son. That new sci-fi pirate movie."

"Not too bad."

I opened the door. "You're right. Not bad at all. Thanks for doing this."

"What are ex-partners for?" She grinned at me.

"Right." I grinned back. My partner the Mole.

Mamá was awake. Sergio was not. Like a good nine year old, he had learned the patterns of school, and after a week of getting up early, he slept in on weekends. "Everything all right?" said Mamá.

"Karen," I said.

"Ay. What trouble is she stirring up now?"

"I'm not sure." I placed the file on the table, thanked Mamá as she handed me a cup of coffee, which, I thought, was a good sign. Maybe she wouldn't start preaching to me again.

I lay on the couch, put the coffee on the table and opened the file. I ignored the photos and went for the text. From the style of the writing, I could tell Karen had written most of these essays. I got about three paragraphs in, learning a general history of what some had named "The Desert Women," a catch-all title for all the women who had died in the desert that stretched between California and Texas in the past ten years. Were Karen and her group trying to solve the crimes of over three hundred murdered women? Four hundred, and growing, according to her report. That, in my mind, wasn't the work of one man; that was a killing field, with many killers to blame. A tragedy born out of the drug trade and the lawlessness of border towns. But as god-awful as this information was, I just couldn't keep my eyes open. After staying up all night, the sleep was thick, and I welcomed it.

I only woke to welcome my boy. Sergio stumbled into the living room, his pajamas on. He had his hand down his pants and was picking at his butt.

"Stop that," I said. He bent over and kissed me. Then he lifted the closed file off my chest, dropped it with a dramatic flair on the coffee table, and jumped on me. He buried his head into my neck, grabbed the blanket draped over the futon and pulled it haphazardly over us. "You're the aggressive type," I said.

"I'm still sleepy," he said.

As far as he was concerned, I had not been out last night and into the morning, studying a dead little girl at a desert crime scene. I had been in my own room, asleep, and had simply made the long haul from my bed to the futon for a morning nap. That image was fine by me. Besides, he was snuggling me, as if he had already forgiven my whiskey-stumble of last night.

"Hey, how about that movie?"

He looked up at me. "'The Pirates of the Caribbean," he said.

"Yep."

"Can we get popcorn?"

"Sure."

"Soda?"

"Whole nine yards."

"Hot dog?"

"That's a bit much."

"Pretzel?"

"We going to a movie or a cafeteria?"

"I want a pretzel."

"Fine."

"And popcorn."

"One or the other."

"Popcorn." He grabbed me tighter, which seemed impossible, but somehow he could manage such things.

It was a great day. A great day. I would look at the file later, along with all my other case files. And I'd try to find that damn apartment on Monday. It was the weekend. Karen would be held in a cell until Monday, where she'd stay out of trouble. No doubt Rigoberta would call soon, but all I could suggest to her was that she wait until Monday. That's all I could do.

We drove from Van Nuys to Sherman Oaks while Tom Petty sang about the Ventura Boulevard on the radio. I asked about school. "Fine," Sergio said, but little else. So I pried, about friends, bullies, any drugs? "Ben and I play a lot. Also a guy named José David, he's nice." This was good to hear. I took Sergio's words in like candy. Or better yet, food. The case at the border was not my jurisdiction. Right now, the only thing I wanted in my jurisdiction was my boy.

In the movie theatre, before the previews, he opened up more about a girl named Lea who had her eye on him. "But she's kind of weird," said Sergio. "She hangs around my desk but she won't say anything. Then, when I say something, like, 'What do you want?' she gets all mad. What's up with that?" I explained to him, some girls are shy, unsure of what to say. "Yeah, okay, but why the mad part? Come on."

"Do you like her?"

"No." He looked at me, trying to look serious. But then he grinned. "Yeah. Well, kind of."

"Yes or no?"

"Come on, Mom." He paused, but not for long. "Were you like that?"

"Like what?"

"You know. Stupid."

"Probably." I reached over, took some popcorn from the bag in his lap. "Love makes you stupid."

"Then I don't want to be in love. No way."

"Sorry, kiddo. It's bound to happen. You're going to get stupid on me."

He hit me in the arm. "What about you?" he said. "You ever get stupid?"

"Oh yeah. With your father."

To which Sergio did not know what to say. He has never known a real image of his father, dead from skin cancer when Sergio was one. He's only seen old photos. Sergio doesn't know that for a year I took care of his father, watched him die, tried to be a cop and a new mother while coming home to a man who was wasting away. Sergio did not know how, horrible as that year was, it was also a strange year—how focusing on my kind husband's death had taken my mind away from my sister's killer. For a year I focused on him. A man who loved me, who never raised his voice to me. A man who was the sane one.

Nor has Sergio ever felt a need to pretend to be sensitive around me being a widow. Which is fine by me. "Have you gotten stupid since then?" He giggled.

"Quiet. The previews. Oh look, there's Johnny Depp. I'd get stupid for him."

The lights dimmed. Sergio and I got lost in a world of pirates rescuing criminals from Mars for two entire hours, together.

At the Stone Cold Creamery afterwards, Sergio picked it up again. "So come on, you're not dating. Afraid to get stupid again?" He liked this love/stupid analogy.

"First of all, let's call it like it is. Love. Okay? And second, no. I'm not afraid of it. He'd just have to be somebody pretty darned special."

Ever since Sergio entered school, he and I have spoken more English, which infuriates my mother. She's always afraid the language, and thus the Salvadoran culture, is going to be lost. But I try to let go of some things, knowing my kid is fully bilingual and knowing there is a silent pressure among all his friends to speak English in school. While eating ice cream, we spoke pop-gringo. "So you're not tight with anybody now?" he said.

"No. Why, you want me to be?"

"Well, yeah."

"And why's that?" I licked my peanut butter chocolate swirl.

"Because, I don't know . . . I think you'd be happy that way."

I stopped licking. "I'm happy," I said, licked some more, looked at him. "What, you don't think I'm happy?"

He was embarrassed, according to that curling smile. "I don't know."

"Sure I'm happy. I've got you, cipote. You're the best man around."

"Come on, Mom. That's not what I mean."

"Look hijo, you might be surprised someday. I'll walk through the door with bedroom-eyes Johnny Depp holding me, and you'll get jealous."

"No I won't."

"What, you won't?" I shoved out my lower lip.

"No. I mean, yeah. Mom!"

"You are so easy to mess with, cipote."

That tone lasted all through the weekend. Sunday night I made myself a drink and poured him a soda. We watched television together, also a rarity, as Mamá and I pushed the books on Sergio. On Monday morning I sat with him and ate breakfast, made sure he had his backpack with all his books. His grandmother made his lunch of tortillas and peanut butter. I drove him to school. At the Kiss & Drop, where other parents volunteered to shepherd the kids through the gate, Sergio put his arms around my shoulders in the car, gave me a kiss on the cheek. "Bye Mom, see you later." Then me: "Te quiero hijo. Have a great day." He got out, slung the backpack over his shoulder, walked through the gate. Before disappearing around the corner of one of the school buildings, he turned and, through the wire fence, waved at me. It all seemed normal to him, which made me happy: as if Sergio had this every day. His mother here, with him, and not lost in other people's lives and deaths. I had jettisoned the file and the apartment building and Karen's choices from my mind for the entire weekend. I had been with my son. He had turned and had waved to me one last time, as if to add cream to the topping of the goodbye kiss. I sat there, forgetting to drive away, with a little punch of tears in my eyes and an idiot's grin on my face, in love with that little shit. Stupid, through and through.

Chapter 12

There were open files of cases on my desk; but it was Monday, and I had those promises to keep.

I reported my findings to my boss, Special Agent in Charge Leticia Fisher. She already knew of my San Diego road trip with Nancy. "Sounds like your Karen's in hot water. Hot and deep." Fisher has a baritone voice, like a gospel preacher's. Though still womanly, it was a tone of both motherhood and balls, born in her Mexican-African American bones. None of us messed with her. But I had come for permission.

"So," I said, "can I have the morning?"

She nodded. "The apartment's in our area. Check it out. But give San Diego Homicide anything you learn."

I left the office, took Wilshire west and headed to Santa Monica, then turned south on Barrington. I parked on the opposite side of the street, just up from the apartment building that Karen had told me about.

This was a nice neighborhood, though not wealthy. The apartment building was clean, its small yard and Birds of Paradise bushes well-groomed. In most areas, such as my beloved Van Nuys, the apartments are so run down, you don't expect much more than single moms with a slew of kids coming out of them, followed by the prerequisite heroin dealers, pimps, and gang members. If you could look for Crack Houses in the Yellow Pages, most of the addresses would be in Van Nuys. This made the homeowners' prices a bit more reasonable. I had bought my little house as snug into a neighborhood as possible, two streets away from the nearest apartment building.

But this one on Barrington, just on the edge of Santa Monica, was nice. New stucco, colored a Santa Fe brown. No fans in the windows; the place had central air. And all of the windows had a uniform set of cream-colored blinds. I could picture writers living in there, with stacks of screenplays on their desks. And actors: the ones we see weekly as extras on sitcoms.

Women and men walked in and out of the complex, most of them white. A few smokers. Young, most of them just around thirty.

I had brought files of other cases. Lettie Fisher had been kind the past several months. Since my final encounter with Tekún Umán last year, in which I had almost been turned into mincemeat, along with every other commuter driving over the hidden explosives strapped to the Golden Gate Bridge, Fisher had been easy on me. She took into account the bullet wound in my leg. She hadn't sent me away to Quantico, like she had Nancy; but Fisher had given me desk work: gang-related materials gathered by other agents to follow up on, profiles of young men who had been in juvie a time or two, who had a couple of drug raps on their backs, not much more. But they were young men who could be possible inside links to the well-organized gangs in the Valley and in East L.A. My work had drifted into the Valley, where the less formal BVN gang had been doing a bit more recruiting in my neighborhood. I saw their *Barrio Van Nuys* tags on trees whenever Mamá and I took walks.

I had everything I needed in the car: files on the gang members, my cell phone to call the office in case I needed more information, and a huge cup of coffee, freshly roasted and ground from the Coffee Bean and Tea Leaf just up the street on San Vicente.

And I had Karen's file.

It was yet another beautiful day in southern California, so I had the windows down. No one to bother me. No one to take me away from Karen's essays.

She was a good writer. These essays were clear, concise. She didn't rely on melodrama to stir the reader. But it wasn't pure journalism. The way she wrote, it seemed Karen cared for each woman who had died in the desert. As if she had known each and every one of them.

Which was impossible. There had been, according to these reports, four hundred and nine bodies of women found in the desert just across the California-Mexico border in the past decade.

I corrected myself: four hundred and ten, counting Marisa Jackson.

Though could I count her? She was found on this side of the border, not in Mexico.

Again, a fact that I had to remind myself of. The Desert Women were a Mexican problem that I had heard about a couple of times on NPR or read about in the *Los Angeles Times*. Women who had disappeared while walking to their jobs at the *maquiladoras*, their bodies later found in the desert, sometimes just their bones. Most of them had been raped before being killed. All of them murdered, usually with knives or some other sharp instrument, according to either puncture wounds in the skin of the newly dead, or nicks in the bones of the long ago murdered.

According to Karen's writings, the first body was that of a sixteen-year-old girl from Tijuana named Silvia Rodriguez, reported missing seven days before they found her, raped and dead in the desert east of the city. Since then theories had formed, everything from the possibility of a serial killer living somewhere on the border, to whether or not a drug cartel was responsible.

I didn't doubt that the cartels played some role in this. I wondered if the feds in Mexico had made any ties between the Desert Women and the dealers. What had the Mexican authorities found?

According to Karen, nothing. Her articles lambasted the Mexican police for their laxity about the killings. She also suspected that some groups of police were directly involved in the deaths. This, of course, made me think about Officer Saenz on the border.

Still, why did she want me to come here, to this apartment? Something about the girl Marisa being spotted here after she had disappeared. How would Karen know that? And who had the girl been with? Had she been by herself, or with her abductors?

And Marisa, a child. According to Karen's writings, most of the Desert Women were young adults, the youngest being eighteen. Women. Not children. Though horrible, Marisa's death did not fit the exact profile of the Desert Women victims.

I was about to call Karen's number, then remembered where she was. I called the jailhouse where our agents usually held suspects, then felt terribly guilty for not having visited Karen there over the weekend, as I was sure her mother had. But then again, I had been a mother all weekend dammit. I reminded myself of the need to be a mother, sometimes for whole stretches of time.

"This is Special Agent Romilia Chacón, FBI. I was checking in on Karen Allende, they brought her in Saturday morning." I gave the assistant my badge number.

The phone assistant crossed-checked my badge, though I knew he knew me. He was always the one at the front desk whenever I called, but I had forgotten his name. "Yes, Ms. Allende was released just about an hour ago."

"Really? On bail?"

"Yes. Her mother handled it. Caused quite a hooplah, seeing Rigoberta Allende walk in like that. I think every Hispanic in the cages stood up for her."

"So Karen's home."

"She better be. Bail was high, five hundred thousand. The judge handed that over earlier today. But for impersonating one of your agents, they'll make her stay close to home."

"Thanks, uh—"

"Jimmy, Agent Chacón."

"Right. Sorry Jimmy." I hung up.

I called Karen's home number, the one in her room. Her message machine answered. I said, "Hey, it's Romi, just checking in to see how you're doing. Call when you can," and hung up. I almost called Rigoberta, but decided not to. Rigoberta had been through enough. I figured she and her publicity agent were now having to fend off numerous media calls about her jailbird daughter. I'd call later.

Besides, the apartment building had just gotten interesting.

After two hours of surveillance, where there's enough pedestrian and automobile traffic, something's bound to happen. Though a quieter part of the street, this section of Barrington had its share of visitors. One fellow, a very young, tall glass of cold water who looked like he was from Des Moines, scored a packet of coke from a white kid who was definitely L.A. The kid's adroit moves on that skateboard showed him to be homegrown. A homeless woman in her fifties pushed a grocery cart up the sidewalk. Today was garbage day in this section of Los Angeles, so she did well with the aluminum cans plucked from the blue recycle bins. Another homeless person, a fellow who looked Vietnam Vet-age, scooted over the sidewalk, his yellow and brown stained tennis shoes never lifting from the cement. He spoke to himself in long, comma-less sentences.

Traffic pulled in and out of the area, vying for small parking spaces. A cop came by twice. The first time he stopped next to me, rolled down his window, and was just about to ask me why I was loitering when I showed him my badge. He nodded, waved, and drove on.

A van drove by and parked three cars in front of me. The driver did not get out. The young white woman with steel blonde hair, tight jeans and a tiny T-shirt riding on the passenger side did. She looked both ways on the street, crossed and entered the apartment building, and ten minutes later she came back out. I figured she lived there and had dropped by to pick up something she had forgotten.

Thirty minutes later the same van, windowless, big like the old vans but newly painted, drove by again. Again it found a parking space ahead of me. Again the driver did not get out, but the passenger did. A girl. A couple of years younger than the first young woman, who had not been a woman either, but a teenager, which made this girl a pre-teen even though she dressed in clothes straight out of a parent's nightmare.

This Latina girl looked both ways. She crossed the street. She almost went into the apartment building but stopped when a man started walking toward her. My window was down. "Hi Prissy!" he said, in a kind, somewhat shaky, wimpy voice. He was tall, white. He wore glasses and jeans that looked ironed. He had thinning brown hair, a short sleeve shirt that had weak, spindly-looking, pasty arms dangling out of them. A true ninety eight pound weakling, and the scariest thing that had walked down this street today.

Prissy was confused. She pulled her little purse up high on her little exposed shoulder and looked back to the van. She did not appear scared, not at all; more, she had the stare of someone who has to reorganize her thoughts, think over a secondary strategy. The driver, whose face I could not see, must have given Prissy a signal. Prissy nodded, walked to the white guy, and took his hand like a daughter takes a father's hand.

She led the way. Toward the apartment building.

I got out, walked across the street and onto the sidewalk. They were on the first steps of the apartment's front stoop. I had to move quickly. "Excuse me, hi," I said. I smiled. At first they ignored me. The man was the first to turn, but the girl did not. She had a bead on the door.

Pasty-Boy looked scared.

"Could I speak with you, sir, for a moment?"

"What for?" he said. And that said it all. Guilt in his gut sucked the blood right out of his face.

I pulled my badge and held it up. At that instant, the large motor in the van turned over. The driver gunned it. Prissy slipped out of the guy's limp fingers and bolted toward the van. A BMW screeched and stopped, almost hitting her as she crossed the street, which was enough for me: I ran after her. Prissy was confused. She ran toward the van but then saw me and judged the distance to the van too risky—I'd probably catch her. She ran down the street, away from the BMW as if afraid it would run her down. I bolted forward and got parallel with the van. The driver of the van, a Hispanic woman, much younger than me but rougher, aged, yelled at Prissy in English to get her ass back into the van. She looked at me, and I couldn't tell if that was fear or rage or simple hatred in her eyes.

I ran straight to the van, shouting "FBI!" She pulled out so fast that I barely had a chance to step back. As I made to unholster my gun the bitch shoved open her door and used it as a shield against me. I went flying. I rolled onto Barrington, tried to get up fast, and managed to get part of the plate but not all. A Lexus drove toward me. I jumped out of the way. The driver, cell phone to his ear, yelled at me, "Hey lady! Out of the way, jeez—!" The van was screeching down the street. It did not stop to grab Prissy. It turned left onto Iowa, no doubt heading toward the 405 Freeway. Prissy had bolted between two other apartment buildings.

White boy tried to bolt too, but he was out of shape. I ran, got him in a few strides, yelled for him to stop and clicked back the hammer. "Sit this one out, buddy."

He stopped. He was out of breath. He bent over, which made it easier for me to grab that limp wrist, cuff it, then cuff him to the metal banister of a bike rack.

I went after Prissy. But she was gone. I circled the block once, looking down every alley. But I couldn't leave the guy shackled for too long.

The cop drove through again. He stopped for me. "There's a girl, Hispanic, maybe twelve, thirteen, dressed like a whore, or a Jean Benet-Ramsey type. She's got a little purse, green, gold trim on the bag and the string. Also, a van, no windows, maybe an early eighties model, dark blue, Hispanic woman driving, age about twenty and looking really pissed. California plates PH 1, maybe a 4 after that, didn't get it all."

"On it," he said. He drove and spoke into his radio.

Back to the man at the bike rack. People walked by, glancing at him but not wanting to get too close, not to a guy sitting on some steps, his wrist cuffed right next to a very nice Schwinn. He was crying. Whimpering.

I hate whimperers.

"Okay," I said, "what was this all about? Why the hell did all of you bolt like that? Who's the girl? And that woman in the van?"

He didn't quite answer me. All he said was, "How'd you figure it out? I always used my ATM. My ATM!"

Chapter 13

There were no less than four ways to go about this. Take Whimpy Boy to a local precinct and have him questioned. Follow the van. Find the girl. Find out which apartment they were heading toward, and the landlord, and why the landlord would rent out a place for older men and little girls.

This meant the cops needed to get a warrant to search the apartment. They would do their part, tracking down the girl and the woman driving the van. And I didn't doubt they'd do a decent job shaking down this john, whose name was Rudolph Madson, but who from now on would be known in this precinct as Mr. ATM.

All of this leg work, and all of these hoops, such as the warrant, belonged to LAPD. I should have been thankful—one less job for me. But I wasn't. It was due to Karen that all of this had happened. Somehow she knew about the apartment house. I sat on the other side of the one-way mirror and looked at Mr. ATM as he sat there, rubbing his fingertips over the table. I tried calling Karen's cell and home phones. She didn't answer. I'd try again later, after hearing the cops shake information out of Madson.

He wasn't a stubborn shakedown, though in the wrong hands he could be lost. He had as many questions as the detective had for him. He wanted to know how I had found him, how I had known that he was arriving today. He talked quite a bit, though much of what he said was circular, as if he knew that he still had to toss up a fire wall. Some remnant of defense said to his milky self, Save your ass. Don't tell them everything. Back up. But another part of him wanted to confess to something, the part of a man that respected and feared the authority of law enforcement. That side of him, after confessing, may have breathed easier, as if having given over a secret that had haunted him for a long while.

The detective's name was Blaze. He was about my age, early thirties, a fairly good looking white fellow who wore a red tie rather than the conservative blue of the older detectives. Still, he had kept with a white shirt and coal-black suit. He was in shape, like a swimmer, lithe. He didn't take advantage of ATM's nervousness too quickly. Blaze didn't stumble, like a new detective might stumble, into yanking out a quick confession. Yanking, with a guy like this, could cause him to pull in, retract his words like a turtle pulling into the shell. Blaze got to know ATM. In the first thirty minutes, Blaze became Madson's newest best friend. He didn't ask about the girl, as if that were too obvious. "I was wondering Rudolph, if you could help us with the woman in the van. You know, the Hispanic lady?"

"I don't know who she is."

"Is she always the one who arrives?" (Not, "Drops off," not "delivers the child." Blaze was good.)

"Yeah. Yeah she's the one." Madson drank from the soda can.

Here was the tap-dance: at no point did Blaze ask "Do you know why you're here?" For Madson's final sliver of inner logic would have responded too quickly to that. The voice might have put a few things together, such as the fact that they had not read him his rights, for they so far had no specific reason to read him the Miranda warning, except for running away from me. But that voice was starting to work its way to the top of Madson's consciousness anyway, as if, in getting comfortable with Blaze, he was also getting less frightened. Fight-or-flight was easing off, enough for some logic to seep in. He said, "Officer Blaze, why are you holding me?"

"What do you mean?"

"Do I need a lawyer?"

"Do you think you need a lawyer?"

That made him pause. Here Blaze took a risk, "Mr. Madson, do you realize that the woman who brought you in is a federal agent? With the FBI?"

Madson crumbled. He recognized two things: he was caught in a federal crime, and he was fucked. He knew this. He knew that sex with little girls was a no-no, and that he was involved in something silent and wrong to the world yet oh so worth the risk for him, though a risk that needed planning. Like paying in cash. Like using your ATM to leave no paper trail, especially for your wife, or for your kid at home.

Which he had. A wife of fourteen years. A daughter, twelve, named Jessica. Rudy Madson had been assistant coach for her soccer team in the Valley, somewhere in Encino. Oh yes, he loved his wife, he did, Elaine meant the world to him, but sometimes, just sometimes . . .

"Sometimes you simply need something more, right Bill?" said Blaze.

Madson looked at Blaze, and nodded, and wept.

Slowly a confession formed. Blaze said, "Now, you know you have certain rights here, let me tell you what they are." Rudy nodded, still pouring out the tears. He waited until Blaze finished with the statement written for dear Miranda, then Bill opened his conscience wide.

How Blaze kept a priestly, counseling face, I'm not sure. What Rudy said came out in spurts at first, but soon broke into long flowing explosions of release. Blaze let him talk. I had seen this before. Men guilty of something, knowing they were guilty and desperately seeking absolution. They wanted someone to understand the why behind their actions, someone who would not only empathize but also respond with kindness. Which Blaze did. It started with that phrase, "Sometimes you need something more, right?" And Blaze was able to keep that up throughout, Oh sure, sure, marriage, sometimes things get stale, and yeah, my wife, she doesn't understand that a guy, he's got needs, you know? "Exactly!" said Madson, ecstatic that he had finally met someone who was in the same field of thought as he. No doubt he had forgotten about me in this sudden ejaculation of human connection, "Jesus, sex with my wife anymore, for her it's a chore. And sometimes I think Elaine looks at it as disgusting, which makes me feel, I don't know, guilty or something. Which I shouldn't feel, right? I mean look, I'm a good Dad. I do it all. I take Jessica to her soccer practices, and last year I was assistant coach, though I couldn't do it this year, our office has been so loaded with the upgrading of our computers. But I'm still there, at all of Jessica's games."

"They're on the weekends, right?"

"Yeah, Saturday mornings."

"What position does Jessica play?"

"She's a forward. Three goals so far this season."

"Sweet!" Blaze smiled.

Blaze got Madson back to Elaine; for talking about the wife would get him talking about the girl at the apartment. "Elaine. Remember in college, thinking yeah, you loved her, but like your buddies would say, you also got live-in sex, right? Room-and-board pussy, that's what my friend Sam called it. I hated it when Sam talked like that, but it's kind of true, isn't it? Sometimes that way of talking, those words, well, they're more on target than anything else.

"So, sometimes, you just got to go somewhere else." Madson sipped some Soda. He looked into the hole of the can.

"You mean, like, what was her name?"

"Priscilla. Well, they call her Prissy."

"Prissy. Right. What's she like?"

"I didn't ask for that young, you know."

"No? Oh. Gosh. That's good to know." Blaze wrote that important note down.

"Yeah, no, I asked for younger-*looking*. Someone young. That's all I said. They're the ones who pick them for you."

"That how it work? They do the choosing?"

"Yeah."

"So that's their decision."

"Right. Right!"

"So what happened, when you first got together with Prissy?"

"I saw her, and I looked over at the woman in the van, you know, I thought there was some mistake. But the van drove off. And there I was in the hallway with her. I didn't know what to do."

Blaze waited. Silent. Not a hint of judgment in his eyes.

"Well, Prissy just took my hand. 'Come on,' she said, and she took me into the apartment."

A pause of silence, which may have been a mistake, but Blaze then asked, "Then what happened?" Then Blaze did something that bothered me, for I couldn't tell if it was real or dramatized: he grinned. Just the slightest of grins.

A grin that Bill interpreted as brotherhood.

"She may look like a kid, but she's not. She's short. But I know a lot of short women. And the things she does? That's no child. It's a full woman, trapped inside a child's body."

Blaze leaned into the table. "Really? What did she do?"

Madson leaned in too, two men over a table, alone. And Rudy Madson made the mistake of believing, for a moment, that this world and this cop thought like him. "She opens her mouth real wide. None of this lick-the-flagpole stuff, you know, like Elaine, jeez, you'd think I was putting a gun to my wife's head. Not with Prissy."

The words hovered in the air like cold invisible fog. And Rudy Madson's face cut through that fog and he realized he had slipped. Oh to have sucked those words back into his throat and swallow them whole. Too late.

Blaze said, "So, how does this work, Bill? Bill? Tell me how it works. How do you pay? I mean, who do you pay, do you give the money to Prissy? Or the woman in the van?"

"What? No. No it doesn't work that way. There's a guy, he shows up at the door, right when we're done. He doesn't knock, he's got a key. The first time, I was still, we weren't finished. He told me to pay him, get out, my time was up, but it wasn't, I had brought money for an hour, and he had come in after thirty minutes. I gave him the wad of dough. 'Oh,' he said, 'My mistake.' And he walked out and let us finish."

"So you pay this guy."

"Yeah. I give Prissy the gum, then I give him the money."

"Gum? What gum?"

"Prissy likes gum. First time we were together, I went to Albertsons to get the cash. I bought a packet of Wrigleys, then asked for cash-back. The cashier thought I was crazy, asking for a hundred dollars with a packet of gum. But anyway, I had the gum on me, and I don't chew gum. So I gave it to Prissy. She really likes it. But the first time she didn't know what to do with it, you know, those Mexican kids, they don't have the things we have. She ate the piece. Tore it open and ate it like she was starving. I said 'No honey, don't eat it, you chew it like this, see?' And I took a piece and chewed it. So crazy, having to teach a kid how to chew gum."

"She's Mexican?"

"Yeah. Yeah I think so."

"She speak English?"

"Oh yeah. But I heard her yell back to that woman in the van, in Spanish. She's bilingual."

"The guy at the door. What does he look like?"

Bill looked around, as if still waking from a dream, groggy, but slowly recognizing he had blown it. Recognizing how he wouldn't be taking Jessica to any more soccer games. Maybe Jessica's own child someday, but no— Jessica wouldn't let old Dad near the grandkids, not after all this.

"Latino guy. Black hair. Kind of tall." His voice cracked.

"I'd like a complete description of him, please."

"Sure. Yeah. Yeah I can do that. If that will help. He's about my height, a little taller, and thin—"

"Tell you what Bill, I'm going to have someone come in who's an artist, they'll get you to give a really good description of the guy, see I can't even draw stick-men." Blaze got up to leave the room.

"Wait. Please."

Blaze turned back to ATM.

"There's uh, there's a little problem." His voice rattled hard, getting the words out. "The guy always warned me, not to be a . . . they called it, a *conejo suelto*. That guy, the first time at the door, he made me memorize that."

"*Conejo suelto*," said Blaze, pronouncing it perfectly, much better than ATM's beat-up Spanish. "Loose rabbit." What did he mean by that?"

"I think it meant he'd kill me, if I talked with the police."

"Oh." Blaze paused. "Well. Maybe we can put you somewhere, where they can't get to you." He turned and walked out.

Mr. ATM now understood it all. He also saw, as if for the first time, the camera in the upper corner of the room.

On this side of the glass Blaze looked at me. "I could use a shower. In Clorox."

"Good job," I said. "Really good job."

"Our friend is an isolated," said Blaze.

"What's that?

"Three general types of pedophiles. Closet, isolated and sharer. The closets, they stay home and whack off to pictures of coy children cut out of *Newsweek*. They don't harm anybody. Isolateds, like Madson here, go looking for kids. Sharers sell. Either pictures or, in this case, the kid. But this sounds more organized, some sort of pre-teen prostitute ring going on." Blaze wiped his face with his palm. "How'd you say you learned about this?"

I told him about Karen.

"What, you mean the daughter of Rigoberta Allende? Yeah, I read about her."

"What? Where?"

"*LA Times*. This morning. It's front column, about that kid murdered at the border. The Allende girl was taking pictures for that wacko feminist group."

I thought to call Rigoberta, see how she was doing, knowing how much the paparazzi bothered her. Just then a cop walked into the precinct with the girl. Prissy. She looked like a painted child manikin. She stared straight at me, as if blaming me.

I wanted to be the one to question her. But this was not my territory. To even mention the possibility would ruffle the LAPD feathers. Lettie Fisher had warned us more than a few times to play nice with local law enforcement. While they took Prissy to another room, I hit Rigoberta's private number. Before I could say anything, Rigoberta said, "Romilia. She's gone."

"Gone? Where? What happened?"

"Those damn reporters. I've been so crazy keeping them at bay."

"Rigoberta, where is Karen?"

The sigh rattled out of her. "I don't know. Her car's gone. She must have left in the middle of the night."

Which meant she had broken parole. Hotter water, and Karen was the one cranking up the gas. "I'm coming over," I said.

Before leaving the precinct, I walked by the room to look at the girl. I had wanted to see a girl; I had wanted to see a child who had been used, shattered, a little waif shaken out of a nightmare. But all I saw was Prissy, age twelve who, when Blaze walked in smiling a fatherly smile, leaned back in her chair, threw her arms over the chair to accentuate the bosom she didn't have, and crossed her legs to one side like a tiny mistress.

Chapter 14

Back at our offices I reported in to Lettie Fisher.

"So," she said, "what do you think?"

"I think we need to wrestle this one from LAPD. It deals with child prostitution. It could mean some sort of kidnapping of kids. It's more than just LA. Karen was down in San Diego. That's a wider region."

"And?"

"It's because of Karen that we found this ATM guy, and the girl."

It didn't take Fisher long to make up her mind. "I'll call Chief Paddin. We'll work it out. You want this? You're going to need a partner. And you'll be leaving the office more. Think you're ready?"

"Yes. It's mine."

"Good. I'll see if Agent Pearl's up for this as well."

Before I could put my two cents in on that, Fisher turned around and walked down the hall. I raised my hand up to make some vague point about being able to handle this one on my own, but she had already gone around the corner.

Within ten minutes Nancy stood at the opening of my cubicle. I filled her in, then told her what I had not told Fisher, that Karen had gone AWOL.

"Fisher's going to find that out soon enough. You heading over there?"

"Just to see if Karen left anything behind."

"Like what?"

"I don't know. A note."

"A note? What, like she's going to do something stupid?"

Nancy meant suicide. I said, "Maybe."

"What should I do?" she asked.

67

"LAPD's after the Latina woman in the van. Run the same details through VICAP, see if you can come up with anything." I stood from my desk, walked around her and headed to the hallway.

She followed. As we walked I gave her the partial license plate number. "All right," she said, "then what?"

We had all we could from Mr. ATM. We had Prissy, who we'd question once LAPD handed her over. The van and the Hispanic woman, gone. And a dead girl, Hispanic, around the same age as Prissy. "I'm going to Karen's," I said. "Meet me at the morgue in two hours." I walked ahead, toward the front door.

"So, you'll be there?" she said.

I looked back. "What? Yeah I'll be there, what do you . . ."

But then I knew. She was referring to the first time we worked together, long before I knew who she was: a fully-trained FBI agent who worked for a drug lord. A drug lord whose name, Tekún Umán, roused rage and hatred and fear out of my fellow federal agents, roused in me none of those emotions, and only one emotion in particular. Before all that, I had stood her up. At the morgue. I had worked on the case without her help, because at the time I believed her to be nothing but a wet-nosed rookie blonde who didn't know the first thing about procedure. Boy was I wrong.

"We okay?" she said, "you and me, working together?"

"What? Yes, of course, I can work with anybody."

"Yeah but it's not everybody who can work with you." She smiled.

"What the hell's that supposed to mean, that I'm hard to get along with?"

She smiled again and cocked her head.

I walked up to her, close, just five inches between our noses. Not to threaten, but to whisper. "Does anybody really know who you are?" I wanted to be angry. I wanted only to remember how she shoved an ether-soaked rag over my face, kidnapped me, dragged me to Tijuana. But those memories pulled up the others, of Nancy helping me save my mother and son from a killer. And then I had to think more recently, of moments in a bar, when she looked at me, when she said, with her eyes only, *You okay?* Like she really cared. Funny, but I remember my sister Catalina looking at me like that, whenever she saw what she called "*Las sombras*," the shadows, coming over me.

All that I had to think about. Which left me damned confused.

Then she added to the confusion with such clarity. "Romi," she said, using my pet name, "believe me when I say I'm your best friend." She looked straight into my eyes. Nothing fierce. Pure, I don't know . . . *cariño*.

I backed off a few inches. "In two hours," I said, "Meet me at the morgue."

⤝✦⤞

In Brentwood the newspaper, television and radio reporters stood on the sidewalk and sat in cars along Camelia Street. Some smoked. Others ate from small cardboard boxes from Carl's Junior, or from plastic boxes purchased at a Whole Foods Market, filled with eggplant Parmigiana without the cheese, just a sauce made from organic tomatoes. I knew the reporter who ate that: she was young and up-and-coming, and worked for one of the local news stations, though I couldn't remember which one. She had tried to become my best friend the days after the Minos case. Maggie, I believe was her name. A news-babe who liked hitting the streets.

She saw me before the rest of the media crowd did. My ten year old Civic driving through a Brentwood neighborhood was never mistaken as a neighbor's car. I slowed, then made the car crawl through the flock of reporters, each of them asking me questions through my closed window.

"Hi, Romilia, hi!" said Maggie. I kept driving.

In the house Rigoberta and I hugged and kissed each other's cheeks. "Have you heard anything?" I asked.

"Nothing. She's not called. No note. Nothing." Rigoberta looked at me as if hoping I had the answer.

"Got to get her back before her parole officer calls . . ." I walked into the bedroom.

Nothing there. Nothing that would lead me to Karen. Her bed was made, her drawers all closed, the clothes still in them. Nothing ostentatious, like a note. All her clothes were in the closet, still hanging. I remembered a large T-shirt, one I had given her, with the FBI seal on the front, dark blue with gold trim. She had liked that shirt; she had stenciled on the back of it, *The Feds Started a File on me, but all I got out of it was this lousy T-shirt*. That was a hoot among her friends. It was not here.

Her friends. Who were her friends?

I thought of my son Sergio. I thought about his friends. The girl who liked him, Lea. Those two boys' names, Ben and David, he had never mentioned them before. I wondered if Sergio had buddies that I did not know about. Which was a danger, one that too many parents slipped into.

Who were Karen's friends?

Rigoberta's young assistant was on the phone. She fielded media questions, looking as fretful as a family member but trying to stay calm. "I don't understand," said Rigoberta. "I thought it was strange too, that none of her clothes are missing. Her underwear's still there. No luggage is gone."

"She might be back soon, Rigoberta. Maybe . . . she could have just stepped out to meet with her friends. Do you know any of them?"

Rigoberta shook her head "No," in a way that showed she knew how big a parental mistake that was.

As much as I wanted to, I couldn't stay. Nancy was expecting me at the morgue. The case couldn't get too cold. "As soon as she shows up, call me, okay?"

"Fine Romi. Yes."

I walked out, looking back at a movie star who believed too deeply that she had failed as a mother.

From my car I called the main switch board at the Bureau offices on Wilshire and asked for Agent Randall's cell phone, then called him. "Randall, it's Chacón. Listen, do you have any information on the individuals who run that virus?"

"Just Karen Allende, and only because you had started a file on her."

What goes around. . . . Had I not begun that file, they would not have been able to match the description of the woman taking pictures of little dead bodies with Karen. Then again, why blame myself? If Karen had not gone off to Georgia and gotten her ass arrested for the good of some cause, there would be no file.

That's what this was all about. A cause.

A belief in something. Can you switch suicide for a cause?

If that were the case, I should have been thankful. But I couldn't be, not completely; for in the movement from depression to saving the world, Karen had not given up her ability to make rash decisions. Like jumping bail.

My cell phone beeped twice. Someone else was calling. I wasn't going to get much more out of Randall, though he was chattering on, no doubt surfing on his computer while talking with me. "Sorry Klick—Randall, I've got a call, better take it." I punched the send button. "Romilia Chacón."

"Romi. Have you found anything yet?"

Shit. "Karen. Where are you?"

"What did you find at the apartment house? You did go, didn't you?" That wasn't accusatory. She was hoping, like a kid, that I had stuck to my word.

"Yes. I went. We busted a guy." I gave her sweeping pieces of information, including the woman in the van.

"Who was she?" asked Karen.

"We're not sure. We've got an APB on her."

"Who was the girl?"

"Her name's Prissy, we think she was a kid caught in some child prostitute ring."

"Oh God. Is she all right?"

Karen sounded worried, like a mother. "Yeah. She's okay. They've got her in custody."

"Oh thank God."

"Karen, how did you know about the apartment?"

"There's this contact we have, with another group. They're working on border issues too. They told us about the apartment. This makes sense, doesn't it Romilia? This girl Prissy, and Marisa, out in the desert. There must be a connection, right?"

Karen, now playing detective. "Karen, where the hell are you? Do you realize how much trouble you're in if you don't check in? They'll slam your ass right back in jail, until they try you. And your mother—"

"I'm okay. And Mom will be fine." Her voice was crowded with noises around her. She wasn't driving, for she always drove with the windows up. Nor did I hear her car radio. I heard people, talking in the background. For that moment, while Karen talked about how fine her mother would be, I listened to the world behind her. Someone very close said, "Go on Sammy, see if you hands are as big as his." Sammy complained. That was a father talking with a teenage son. They sounded too Midwest for LA. The father said, "Hey, they do fit! 'Go ahead punk, make my day,'" and laughed. I saw an image, of a father from Iowa with a camera around his neck, ruffling his embarrassed son's hair. Standing over handprints in the sidewalk.

Grauman's Chinese Theatre.

I was on the 405, heading south, toward the morgue. It would take me a good twenty minutes, fifteen if I was lucky, to get to Hollywood. I could do it. If I could keep her on the phone. If I told her enough of what I knew, instead of talking about her mother, and how much trouble Karen was in.

Karen didn't care about trouble. She wouldn't hang up out of anger over my acting too much like a bitchy older sister. She would hang up out of boredom. But not if I talked with her about this thing she cared so much about.

"So," she said, "do you think there's a connection?"

"I'm sure there is, but Karen, why are you so involved with all this?"

"Because these are important issues. The Desert Women, we began with that. But then recently we stumbled into this child sex world. We started getting reports on other kids being taken from their homes in Mexico, and some in Eastern Europe. It's a child pornography ring of some sort."

"That doesn't explain why Marisa was killed," I said.

"I think she was a reject."

I wasn't sure what to say to that. The sudden silence let another background voice reach me, "Who you talking with?" Young voice, articulate. Male. Karen hushed him. "Man, you shouldn't be talking with anybody, come on," said the guy, to which Karen whispered to him, "It's just my mother, I need to calm her down." A lie. Why would she lie to her friends, to the other people involved in this? Then that young man spoke to someone else, still nervous, and the other person, a young woman, said to get a grip, the pick-up would be by soon.

A meeting was taking place, a meeting of the disbanded cyber guerrillas of desertwomentruth.com.

I had to keep her on the phone. "Listen Karen, I'm heading to the morgue. Where they've got Marisa."

"Oh good. That's good." She was happy that I was working the case. And in that happiness I heard the first, slightest tinge of worry.

"Yeah," I said, "what they did to her, it was inhuman."

"She's not the first, you know."

"The uh, the desert women?" I dodged around a Lexus. He beeped. "Do they all end up cut to pieces like that?"

"No," she said. "No, most of the women are just left for dead. Stabbed, raped, shot. Sometimes just their bones are found. But lately there have been a number like Marisa. I think it's some type of mark for a particular killer. That section of the desert, where Marisa was? Just south of that, it's a cemetery of women. It's a field of women, where they all are taken to die."

Her tone didn't sound good. Too laced with melodrama. "Yeah, that's horrible." But I had a hard time of hiding my real concern, which was losing

Karen's signal. I was on Sunset, past UCLA, cutting through Beverly Hills. I kept my voice calm, as if having an ordinary chat with my adopted little sister, all the while whipping by BMWs and Jaguars. "Karen, who are the women? Are they all prostitutes, do they have anything else in common?"

"Most aren't prostitutes, Romi. Most of them work in the maquiladoras, all along the border. All of the big corporations that have left the States for cheap labor in Mexico. It's all so ostentatious, when you go there. Juarez, El Paso, Tecate, all the way to Tijuana. A long line of companies. Many of the women work—worked—there. Most of them have long hair, and were all known as 'pretty.' Most of them are in their teens, some a little older."

I passed the Hustler store, which meant I had to take a right soon, to get on Hollywood Boulevard. I was close.

"This is horrible, Karen. It's a good . . . cause to work for. But I'm not sure how you're going to work for it from prison." I laughed, just a bit. I parked the car north of Hollywood, on Vine. In a red-line space, where buses pulled up. When the cops checked my plates in preparation for writing my ticket, they'd see my government sticker and would know I was Federal.

She had ignored my prison joke. "It's all horrible. I just, I can't rest until we find out more about it. Some think it's the drug runners, others believe it's the Mexican cops. I don't doubt it's both, along with other people who are taking advantage of poor folk who are crossing the border. Everyone's involved. So no one gets blamed. It's just, out of hand. Pure chaos. And you can't rely on the media or the Mexican government or even our government to do anything about it. And, no offense Romilia, but I don't see the Feds making any direct actions on this. It's poor women on the border, who no one cares about. So it was time to take some drastic actions, to get people to wake up to the plight of women."

The way Karen spoke, she sounded either prophetic or extremist, and I wasn't sure which of those two distinctions to fear more. "You're right Karen, we've got a long way to go when it comes to women's rights . . ."

"Where are you? It sounds like you're running."

"Yeah at the morgue here, the steps up the hill are a real killer." I looked down Hollywood Avenue, at the ornate Asian roof of Grauman's, then down at the sidewalk of stars: Bette Davis, Edward G. Robinson, Milton Berle. Then the handprints of Harrison Ford, the robots from Star Wars, George Burns' cigar. Now, just to remember, where in the hell Clint Eastwood had sunk his hands. . . .

Across the cement patio of Mann's Chinese Theatre, several flocks of international tourists walked about, looking down, sometimes bending down to touch the cement once touched by Hollywood stars. I looked over. Karen looked up. Our cellulars to our ears, our eyes now locked on each other.

I expected her to scowl at me, but she didn't. She grinned, and through the phone I heard the clarity of her surprised, beautiful laugh, "Oh sister. You're good. You're really good."

Her smile, across the patio, seemed to linger along with the laughter in my ear. But it was gone. I moved toward her. She turned and disappeared.

I ran, bumped into two then a third tourist, the last of who cursed me, "Hey bitch!" So I thought it was he who tripped me, who hit my lower shin hard enough to crack it. I fell, dropped my phone. Its lower flap popped off like an old jawbone. I grabbed the base, stood, looked for Karen, but she was gone.

Faces in the crowd glanced at me, then they looked away, some with disgust for my disturbing their tourist moment. Except one guy. He made the mistake of staring for one second too long, then jerking his sight away. Somewhere near me a car door slammed. The car screeched into gear. The crowd parted just slightly, and I saw it. Blue, dark blue. A sedan. But that was all. The guy bolted. I tackled him. We landed next to Humphrey Bogart's splayed fingers.

"FBI, you little shit. Where is she?"

He stuttered something about not knowing.

"Who's driving the car?"

"I don't know! We were just supposed to meet here, if things went wrong."

"Things have gone very wrong you little prick." I flipped him over, bent his left arm into the small of his back, pulled my cuffs and popped them over his wrists. "You the one who tripped me?"

"No," he said, ready to cry. His slobber dribbled into Bogart's palm. "That was Courtney. I swear."

⚜

The boy, Robert, cried in the back of my car. I called ahead to Fisher. "I'd like to have him," I said, loud, so he heard me. He did; he whimpered more.

"I thought you were heading to the morgue," said Fisher.

"I was. But this came up along the way. I thought—"

"Hand the boy to Klick and Klack," said Fisher. "They'll know how to question him about the cyber virus."

That surprised me, how she used their nicknames. Meant for some levity, I suppose, but I could tell, from her tone, that she was not up for me to argue with her. "Yes ma'am."

Shit.

I tried to keep the car that Karen had gotten into in my head. Dark blue, sedan, could have been a Honda or Toyota. Courtney had taken me down before I got any real look at plates or driver. And Courtney, the second of the trio, the one who had popped my shin, had gotten away.

But Robert hadn't. He sniveled in the back of my car.

At the Wilshire office I took him up our back elevator, though that wasn't necessary; he didn't need the padded elevator, nor did I; there was no risk of him attacking me, not the way he whimpered.

I took him into a holding room, where Randall and Shrieber were already waiting. They had been there a while, I could tell by the intensity of Shrieber's cologne. The way they sat there, side by side, with a thin file before them on the table and each with their hands together, the fingertips only touching. Randall had his sunglasses on. Perfect. "Robert. We've been looking forward to talking with you about the alacrity of your cyberspace abilities," said Randall. He pushed the sunglasses up with his index finger. He did not smile. Neither did Shrieber. I left the room, feeling better about going to the morgue.

Chapter 15

Today Dr. Dibbs was not his usual insecure yet smug self, the image that most cops and agents had of him.

All agreed, Dibbs did his job well. But he had a shadow hanging over him, the ghost of a living man, his predecessor: Dr. Noguchi, known popularly as the Coroner to the Stars. Noguchi had made such a name for himself that whoever had come in after his retirement was sure to pass through years of comparisons. Some wondered why it had to be Dibbs.

He was young for a Medical Examiner. I put him in his late thirties, maybe early forties. He was balanced overall, with a chip on each shoulder. He was good at his job; he just didn't have Noguchi's showmanship.

Today, there was little emotion in his eyes or his voice. I wondered if Marisa's body had gotten to him more deeply than the other cadavers that rolled through here. Perhaps his way of dealing with horror was to check all emotions altogether.

He handed Nancy a file, then turned toward his freezer room. "That's yours. It's a copy. I suppose you'll want to see her," he said, "so I went ahead, pulled her out, prepped her on the slab. This is the last day for that." Meaning, after today, the body would be prepared for handing over to Marisa's family.

Marisa and the slab were the same temperature as the cold room.

Dibbs pulled the sheet from her. Having already seen her wounds, I braced myself, yet still darted my sight away once the sheet was gone. Dibbs' T-incision over her chest and down her abdomen was actually welcome—something familiar to focus on. A cut that meant to find answers. Then I looked down and saw her left wrist.

"She was tied?" I said.

"Yes," said Dibbs. "By her wrists and ankles."

The area around her nipples: the cuts were not as circular as I had first thought. Rather, they were more oblong, like the shadows of eggs. The oblongs each pointed toward her shoulders.

Nancy saw this as well. "They tied her up first." Nancy turned away, then looked at Dibbs. "But the cuts, they're fairly clean, like she didn't put up a fight. Was she drugged?"

"Nothing came back from the blood tests. But I don't doubt she did fight. Those bruises, on her upper arm, and her thighs. Hand prints. They held her down, tied her very tight. Stretched her out. You'll see here, on the anterior compartment of the right leg, all this bruising just above the ligature mark. Internal tearing of the extensor hallucis longus. I don't doubt she ripped some of the ligaments around the ankle as well. She was fighting."

Fighting. While they cut away. At some point, she must have stopped. Her body may have shot her up with some numbing adrenalin to alleviate the pain. I wanted to believe that.

Dibbs scratched the back of his head, then brought us all down to the largest mutilation. "The wounds to the pelvic region: he began cutting low. He penetrated, with his blade, just above the anus, and cut under both the labium majus and minus. Both are gone. As is the clitoris and half the vaginal canal. Then the cut becomes more shallow. He left the bladder intact, no doubt because the frontal compartment of the pelvis was getting in his way. Shock set in after that. She had two heart attacks from the trauma. And he kept cutting and didn't stop. It looks . . . it looks like he lifted out her entire organ, in one piece."

This body might be a changing point in Dr. Dibbs' career, when he might consider hanging it up, becoming a house painter instead. Or he would go on in this world, but become numb so as to do his job, objectively, while deadening himself at home, later, with a bottle.

At least, I knew those were my plans before sleep.

Nancy had the file open in her palm. She looked at it, looked at the body, then asked Dibbs, "It says something about burn marks on her back?"

"Yes. You can see from the photos. Here on her back, and on the soles of her feet."

Dull red marks on her buttocks, around her shoulder blades, the backs of her arms. Rounded areas of baked skin, rounded except for on her shoulders, and along her upper arms. "So she was tied to something hot," said Nancy, staring at the photos.

In those blotches, there were lines. Distinct burn lines on her arms. Perfect, straight. But I couldn't see which arm was which, not in the photos.

"Could you turn her over please, Dr. Dibbs?"

He complied. Adroitly, Dibbs lifted and turned until the entire back of her body showed. Her hands were tucked to her sides, against her waist. But I didn't want them like that. "Could you move her arms, please, like this?" I put my arms out in crucifix form.

He did, allowing the arms to rest momentarily on the high edge of the autopsy table. This allowed us to see the pattern clearly: on the back of her left arm, just below the shoulder, were two short, parallel lines of burn, looking more deep than the splotchy burn marks across her buttocks and back. But on her right, the two parallel lines ran long, from her shoulder, almost touching her elbow.

I said, "They tied her to the hood of a car." Then I pointed to the sets of parallel lines. "Those are the windshield wipers."

Nancy and Dibbs stared at Marisa; then the image set in, enough to make Nancy blink, open her mouth slightly and look at me.

"During the day," I said. "And in the desert. Those burn marks are from the hood of a car." My voice twittered, and then the anger followed. For I could see it too clearly, thick ropes pulled through the closed doors, other ropes tied from ankles to a front fender. More than one man involved, pulling tight the ropes. I could see it, then my mind let me see one lone man, without clear features, lean over the hood toward her pelvis with a blade and that's as far as my mind would go.

Nancy said, "I take it, the cutting, that's what killed her."

"No. No he didn't cut any of her main arteries. The internal iliac was just nicked, but not enough to kill her. And he missed the external iliac and the femoral. Which makes me think he knew what he was doing."

Or he had done it before, I thought.

"She bled," said Dibbs, "but that didn't kill her." He moved toward her head, where I saw what had been on the edge of my attention: a large blotch of blood in her thick hair. "She was struck with a blunt, solid object. I'm sure it was a rock, I found some bits of stone around the laceration. It broke the skin, but once I open her skull, I'm sure I'll find internal bleeding, epidural hematoma, which causes death by displacement of the brain, compression of the brain stem . . ."

"What, they mutilated her, then beat her over the head?"

Dibbs nodded.

That disrupted the flow of my imagination. "Maybe they slammed her head against the windshield," I said, more a mutter.

"No. It's not a smooth hit, and there's that stone fragment I pulled from the laceration."

"Could have fallen from the car," said Nancy, "when they untied her."

I looked at the body one more time, then turned away. "We can take the file?" I said, pointing to the file in Nancy's hand.

"Yeah. That's yours," said Dibbs.

I thanked him. Nancy and I left.

"Where to?" said Nancy.

There was young Robert, back at the Bureau office, getting shaken down by Randall and Shrieber. They knew what questions to ask him, better than I, given their obsession with internet viruses. Then there was Mexico. I chose Mexico.

Chapter 16

Karen knew how utterly wrong it was, watching her adopted big sister go down like that, right in the middle of the handprints at Grauman's Chinese Theatre. Still, she couldn't help but cringe at the scene, not in horror, but in a spark of delight, of laughter. Courtney had tripped Romilia and, in the split second before running off, looked Karen's way, gave a thumb's up sign, then sprinted toward the Kodak Theatre stairs.

Karen couldn't see if Robert had gotten away, as the crowd of tourists was so thick, all those people standing around the cement plaza, staring down and reading the signatures written half a century ago. A hundred people thick, but Karen still pushed her way through and out of it, then crossed the sidewalk to the dark blue car that waited for her. The driver of the car, a woman, motioned to her with a frantic hand to get in. The front passenger door was already open. Karen slipped in and closed it. The driver took off.

"Hi. I'm Ingrid," she said, and laughed, which made Karen laugh. They shook hands.

"I'm Karen." She looked down, as if gathering strength around her joy. "God, it's so great to meet you finally."

"Yeah. After all that email, I feel like I already know you. Though, I got to say, you write a lot better than me."

"Oh, that's not true," said Karen. "I mean, you write from your gut. That's one of the reasons we liked your group." Karen laughed to hide her lie, one that she considered small. For Ingrid did have trouble with writing. All the misspellings, the fragmented sentences, revealed a grade school education, hardly that. But Ingrid could express herself. She spoke about life on the border for women with a passion that Karen wished to have. And she was poor. You could tell it from her speech, the fact that she was either Mexican American or Mexican or at least a Latina, but she spoke between the two languages, as if unconsciously unsure which language would express her ideas better.

Ingrid was once pretty. Karen guessed they were about the same age, but Ingrid wore a bit more makeup, especially around her eyes, which looked hardened from the work. She was heavier than Karen, stout; her legs stretched the jeans and her chest pulled taut the black T-shirt.

"Sorry about the smell," said Ingrid. "The cigarettes. This is my boss' car. He must burn a pack a day."

"Oh, so your group, you have a boss? I thought you all were, you know, only women."

"Yeah, well, he's the one who handles the finances. Oh, there's some colas in an icebox in the back. And I thought we'd stop at a Taco Bell or something. We got a long drive ahead."

"Thanks," said Karen, and reached back to the box. The half dozen colas were cold and packed in tiny cubes of ice. "You want one?"

"Yeah, I'll take a Mountain Dew."

They drove out of Hollywood, then took Sunset toward the 405 Freeway. In Beverly Hills, somewhere near Beverly Glen Boulevard, Ingrid asked, "So, is this the area you live in?" She smiled. Not in judgment, but that strange admiration, the awe, that Karen had seen in others' eyes before, in the eyes of what her mother's friends called civilians—the people who gazed at the screen.

"No. We live in, in Brentwood."

"That's nice too, huh?"

"Yeah, nice. Well, it's embarrassing!"

She said that too loudly; she suddenly felt terribly young, immature, before this woman. A woman who had seen more of the world and its suffering than had any of the people in Brentwood. A woman who had chosen to give her life to helping others, fuck.

"It ain't embarrassing. Shit, you're lucky. Gotta enjoy it when you got it. And your mom, jeez. My brother and I were big fans of hers growing up. I bet we saw all her movies."

They ordered from Taco Bell, ate in the car. Ingrid was dexterous behind the wheel, driving around cars while chewing on the burrito. "It's great using the carpool lane," she said, "I never have someone else with me."

"Yeah. I don't think you're supposed to weave in and out of it though. They might uh, might stop you for that."

"Really?" Ingrid pulled the Camry into the carpool lane one more time and stayed there.

Once past LAX the traffic loosened up and Ingrid could keep it at sixty-five. They talked. Karen picked up the conversation as if lifting it out of all those emails that they had exchanged, emails that, once they had begun a few weeks ago, Karen looked forward to with anticipation, with a certain glee. It had been Courtney who had found the site, and who had shown it to Karen. A woman's organization, one run by women, to the complete exclusion of men. Only women can stop the horrors happening along the border. Only women can show the world the atrocities of little girls from Mexico, from Armenia, being sold into sex slavery in the United States. Every time a man got involved, said one of the hyperlinks on the site, the cause was ruined. It did not apologize for its exclusivity.

Nor did Ingrid's group hesitate in its infiltration of the dirty world of the sex trade. Karen's group had only been able to go so far, taking pictures out in the desert. It was time to take the next step, and expose the sex cartels from the inside.

Words and phrases that Karen and Courtney and, with some hesitation, Robert had used. This was their developing vision, their new beliefs.

Karen began with the light questions. "So did you grow up in San Diego?"

"Me? No. I was born in Mexico. But I lived most of my life in the Valley."

"San Fernando?"

"Uh huh."

"Wow. I thought you were from the border area."

"Nope. I'm a Valley girl."

Karen laughed.

"I've got so much to ask you," said Karen, "I'm not sure where to start."

"Start anywhere. Hey, you never made it to that apartment on Barrington, did you?"

"No, I didn't. But a friend of mine did."

"Really? Who's that?"

"Well, she's a good friend, but she's with the FBI."

"Oh. You've got a friend in the FBI?" Ingrid smiled. She shifted in her seat.

"Yeah, she's more like a big sister, really. Which means sometimes she's a pain in the ass."

"So what'd she do when she got there?"

"She saved a little girl." Karen said it with pride.

"Oh. That's good."

"Yeah, we could say it's our first save working together." Karen smiled, and Ingrid finally turned and smiled back.

"The girl was with a woman, can you believe that?" Karen said. "She was driving a van. God, I hate to think what happens in a van, with these kids."

"They go through a lot," said Ingrid. She shifted in her seat again, as if uncomfortable, perhaps due to a day of driving. She was larger than Karen, more portly; she smelled of strong cologne, one that tried to mask her own cigarette odor. Karen didn't mind the cigarette smell, as her mother lit up from time to time, and Karen had come to associate the smoke with calmness, a certain quietude.

"How do they survive it?" said Karen.

"You can survive anything, if you put your mind to it. Except a bullet of course, or a knife." Ingrid chuckled.

"Yeah but what do they do to the girls to make them into sex slaves? Do they just rape them, or let the Johns rape them, or . . ."

"No no no, it's not like that," said Ingrid. "I mean, yeah, that happens, they get raped. But they got to be trained you see. They got places on the border where they train them. Warehouses."

"But, how do they get them?"

"Well they grab them off the street, you know, girls walking around, they get grabbed."

"But there are a number of girls from Eastern Europe, Armenia. How do they end up down in a warehouse?"

"Oh that's different. That's a whole other setup. They tell the girls over in Armenia that they're gonna go be models in Hollywood. You know, the old American Dream shit. Life is fucked up over there, no money, no jobs, so they get on the plane with these nice men who smile at them. Before you know it, they're being shuffled off the plane in the international airport in Mexico City and making their way to the border."

Karen was shaking her head. "That's sick."

Ingrid, now on a role, said, "Once they get to the warehouse, it's where they go to school."

"How's that?"

"They get broken in, like they say."

"Shit. What do they do?"

"Well, this guy Ritchie? We've been following him for a long time now. He likes to use honey."

"Honey. What's that mean, use honey?"

Ingrid looked at Karen; and Karen wondered if Ingrid were unsure about soiling the rich girl's thoughts with the image. "You starve the girl. Five or six days without food. Then you walk into her room, with a jar of honey in your hand. Well, it's gotta be a guy, because he pours the honey all over his dick."

Karen covered her mouth with her cupped hand. "Sick," she said, over and again, "that's sick . . ." And then, as if already having received permission to curse, due to Ingrid's rough tongue, Karen said, "These sick fucking bastards, they should all rot in jail, God; on this one, I'd consider being pro-death penalty."

Ingrid stared down the highway as they passed San Juan Capistrano. "We'll be there soon," she said.

⇜✦⇝

It was close to dusk when they pulled into San Diego. Then they found a highway that ran by a dirt road, which Ingrid took. "This guy, Ritchie," said Karen, "does anybody know where he lives?"

"No, not really. He's more of a ghost than anything. Some people say he's the head of the *Pezoneros*."

"What's that?"

"You've not heard of them?"

"No. What's that mean?"

Ingrid looked down the road. "That's another ghost story. Some people say the *Pezoneros* are ghost bandits who wear pieces of their victims' bodies around their necks."

"Jesus. What is that, an old Mexican legend or something?"

"No. They say it's real. Men who do it, who wear the necklaces? They're committed to Ritchie, for life."

"So what do the authorities do about all this?"

"Authorities, you mean like the cops?"

"Yeah."

"Cops are in on it."

"They're in the business?"

"A lot of them are. They're on the take. You know, just like with the drug dealers. The girl dealers pay the cops off to look the other way. Only this Ritchie, he pushes it. He gets the cops involved. Training the girls, transporting the girls, killing some of them who run off. The cops are involved. They work directly for Ritchie."

"So this Ritchie bastard, he's not the only one in the business down here, is he?"

"Oh shit no!" Ingrid said. "One man couldn't get three thousand putas across the border in one year. That takes the work of a whole bunch of people. But Ritchie's a special case. He's different."

Karen knew the word *puta*. It sounded impure coming out of Ingrid's mouth. "How is he different?"

"He hates it when they bleed."

". . . When, who bleeds?"

"The girls. He hates it when they got their period. It drives him crazy. I mean, really crazy. He gets nuts. That's why he gets his girls so young. So they don't be bleeders."

Was her English getting worse the more they drove down the road? "So he kills them? Out in the desert?"

Ingrid just nodded, then kept driving. The dirt road had some gravel on it, but not much. And though this was supposedly San Diego, it wasn't, really. It was a desert of hills, brush, large stones and one house. Not a house that a radical feminist group would care to use. A broken house, collapsing in itself, as no one ever bothered with its upkeep.

"Hey listen, that FBI agent you were talking about, when she was at the apartment on Barrington, she get a good look at the woman driving the van?"

Karen did not answer. She stared at Ingrid, who was waiting kindly for her to say something.

A door slammed. A man stepped out on the raw wood porch. A thin man, tall, his hair slicked back. He smoked a cigarette.

"Oh, there's Ritchie," said Ingrid.

She got out of the car and walked slowly to the man. Karen got out too and did not shut the door. She bolted down the road that was so dark, a darkness that stood thick between her and the city's edge. She tripped. Gravel tore open her palms. Someone whistled, hard and piercing, then yelled *Conejo Suelto!* That was Ritchie. But he didn't track her down. Two boys from inside the house did. They were young, maybe sixteen, maybe not. They walked over to a four wheel drive truck and drove out across the desert, ignoring the rules of the one road. In the cab they laughed and talked in Spanish about how a loose rabbit was something new to break up a day.

Karen slipped on loose stones, fell and rolled. She choked. She breathed with a rattle. They corralled her one way, then another. She fell. They hopped out of the truck and snatched her up easily by her arms and legs. She screamed. She screamed a second time. The desert swallowed both.

Chapter 17

This time Nancy and I crossed the border legally. We showed our credentials at the gate. The border guard punched the badge numbers into a computer at his stand, then waved us on.

The irony of us being here, together, I'm sure was not lost on Nancy. The last time she and I had crossed the border from San Diego into Tijuana, she drove while I lay in the trunk. Bound and gagged. Now neither of us said anything about that day, like two good, dysfunctional siblings who both recognized a familial abuse, but remained silent about it.

A half mile south of the border, however, I asked her, "How long are you going to keep this up?"

She sighed. "You just can't accept the fact that I am truly FBI."

"You were a mole. For Tekún."

"And now that's over." I could hear, in her voice, a sadness. The slight revival of mourning. And a slip: usually she spoke about the matter as if there were always a microphone in the room or planted on me. But now she actually had affirmed my statement. Which showed, once again, how much she had cared for the man. "He was a father to me, shit, that sounds so trite, saying it like that. He was a dad. My Dad. I don't—I didn't want to lose him like that. He took care of me all my life, and asked very little in return." She looked to the east side of Mexico to keep me from seeing her eyes.

After a few moments I asked, "You keep in touch with your mother?"

"What? Oh yeah. Called her just the other day, after I dropped you off at your house."

"How is she?"

"Doing well. Moved to Oaxaca. She's opened a second clothing store there." She looked around, then ahead again, at the city of Tijuana. "It was hard, right after his death. I wasn't sure how she'd do. But then she got the business going in Oaxaca. I figured she was forcing herself to move on."

"Was your mother one of his lovers?"

Nancy laughed. "No. Though not for lack of interest on Mom's part. I grew up hearing her talk about how hot he was."

"But he never dated her."

Nancy looked at me. She recognized my fishing expedition of questions. "No. They were not a couple."

"But did he call her *mi amor,* or *mi corazón,* like he did with you, or with that woman in that small town on the border, the one who helped smuggle us back into the States?"

"You mean Ricarda? Lord no. Ricarda was like a sister to him."

"But I heard him call her *mi amor.*"

"He called every woman he knew something like that. For me it was *mi corazón.* My mother, either *mi amor* or *mi alma.* He could be like that. Whenever he wanted to woo some girl into helping him with something, like a pick-up place or a drop-off, he'd haul off and call her *la reyna de mi alma.* He could put the Latino on thick."

"Yeah, he could," I said. "Like calling some women *mi vida.*"

Nancy paused before she responded, as if considering the weight of that. "No. No I never heard him call any woman *mi vida.*"

And that ended my fishing expedition. I turned to the passenger window and looked out at Tijuana and saw none of it. I rubbed my index finger underneath both eyes, a trick my mother taught me, to keep the liner from smearing.

⋘ ✦ ⋙

I've never cared for Tijuana. That may have to do with being forced to visit it last year. The streets and their Cholos, the legion of kiosks selling everything from tiny guitars to miniature guayaberas for your boy's first communion to incense, and all the coke and heroin and grass hiding behind God knows how many of those kiosks, along with the meth and the Ecstasy shoved into the glove compartments of souped up low-rider Hondas and Cadillacs and Camrys, from which spilled out the latest narco-corrido from the accordions of *Los Tigres del Norte*—none of it's for me.

I had never been in a Tijuana police precinct before. Our federal badges got the fellow at the front desk to sit up with a bit more attention. "We're looking for an officer named Saenz," I said.

"That's a pretty common name," said the corpulent fellow at the front desk. He smoked a cigarette. Why are you looking for him?"

"He was helping us with a border case."

He glanced at me, then at Nancy. "Which case is that?"

"It happened near Tecate," said Nancy, in Spanish.

A blonde gringa, speaking perfect Spanish. It always throws these guys. "Lots of things happen near Tecate," he said, still staring at her.

"Really? And who would answer those calls?" Nancy smiled at him. I saw the first movement of an ensuing cockfight. This always seemed to happen so quickly in Tijuana. Another reason I didn't care for the place.

"The precinct over on the east end of town, number seven. It's the closest to Tecate."

I asked for the address. He wrote it down, then explained to me how to get there. Nancy half-listened to him, no doubt because she already knew where Precinct Seven was. She was busy fishing something out of her purse.

"Thanks very much, Officer . . . Mendez." She read his nameplate. She also stared at his badge, memorizing the number. She shook his hand, slipped him a U.S. bill. "By the way, no need to call ahead to tell them we're coming." She smiled, and for good measure, stared once more at his badge number.

"*Vaya. Vaya,*" he said. A Tijuana way of saying either Okay okay or Kiss my ass you güera bitch.

⚜

At Precinct Seven the guy at the front desk was just as guarded. "He's off duty now," he said.

"So let's have his address," said Nancy. She had worked with Mexican cops before and knew when to finesse them and when to be more blunt. She flashed another folded U.S. bill.

The cop pursed his lips, turned and looked through a dusty Rolodex. He gave us the number of the apartment on Avenida 15 de septiembre. "He's either at home or in the bar next to his building."

It was the bar. Saenz was shooting pool with friends. He drank Lite Beer and smoked a filtered cigarette. No uniform now—he wore jeans, boots, and a tight, off-white T-shirt. He saw us coming through the door.

This dance, as always, was difficult. I had to speak with him. I had to get him to, if not want, then at least feel obligated to talk with me. If we talked in Spanish, everybody else in the busted-down bar would hear us and understand. If we spoke English, some would understand but most would not, and they would be suspicious and he would be put on the spot. He was, however, a cop. Whether or not he was on somebody's payroll other than the low wage of the State, he did have official obligations. Still, with all those men and women's eyes on us, two decently dressed gringas who were obviously not here for a drink or a game of pool, I was sure Saenz would not cooperate so easily.

He surprised me. "Agents. How are you? Memo, these are the two federal investigators I was telling you about, the ones I met up near La Cruz."

Memo, the bartender, raised his head, smiled at us in greeting, and asked Saenz, "You mean the murder of that girl?"

"Yes. Get them something, will you?"

Memo offered beer, whiskey, wine, on Saenz's tab, "He will pay it, someday," said Memo in very broken English. Nancy said she'd be happy with a Pepsi, in Spanish, to which Memo grinned and said to Saenz, "You weren't kidding! Talks like a Chilanga," and they all had a good laugh over that. I asked for a diet Pepsi.

Saenz invited us to a table. "How is your investigation?"

I was still a bit puzzled over all this cantina good will. "There's a possible child prostitution ring involved," I said.

We spoke in English, only because Saenz took us that way. It was better to follow his lead. He lit a cigarette and offered us the pack. Nancy declined. I pulled one out and put it to my lips and Saenz lit it. It felt good, that first nicotine hit in this bar with this good-looking man. For a moment I believed in judicial camaraderie, and also imagined this man beyond official business. He was gorgeous and fit. He made time for the things he loved, such as working out his thighs on Tuesdays, his chest and shoulders on Mondays and Thursdays, swimming on the other days. He was that good-looking, and with that smile, and now, with these nicer manners, well, I wondered if Nancy were feeling the same warm sensation that I was feeling within.

She could flirt, that was for sure. "Thank you so much for your help the other day on the border," she said. She smiled that pretty, slightly innocent yet knowing smile which made my stomach feel razors of jealousy. Blonde, blue-eyed Nancy had all that the billboards taught us was beauty, that the media teaches us is alluring, and right now, in front of Saenz, I was buying it all. She was gorgeous, and I was just another brown-skinned girl that Saenz would have no interest in.

Especially with this scar on my neck.

He had glanced at it, surreptitiously, twice since we sat down. Something he had not seen very well in the early morning hours out in the desert. His glances were furtive whenever he placed the cigarette to his lips; but all the years that I've had this damn scar, I've seen how the eyes of others move over me.

There was a time when I once believed that I was okay, in fact, better than okay. I had felt pretty good about myself. I felt like I was once a hot item. Back when I was in my twenties and I was thinner and didn't have this scar. Back when I didn't drink every single night and I didn't measure out what I drank and I didn't measure out a little more, just a half inch more, to get me to bed. Back when I didn't think about every single thing that I ate, the bread and the tortillas and the beans, and then the ice cream that I'd scrape into, at night, before sleep, as if the ice cream and the peanut butter, together, calmed me. Foods that I would eat only after drinking, and right before bed. No wonder those jeans Mamá bought me didn't fit anymore. No wonder Sergio looked at me the same way I looked at my father when I was Sergio's age: with a loving, frightened weariness. With the question, Is she going to be all right? How's she going to be when she comes home?

I had to pull back on the drinking.

"You want to fill Officer Saenz in on the apartment? Romilia?"

"Yes." I looked at the table, swept the previous notions from my head, and told him about the apartment house in Santa Monica, the girl Prissy, and Mr. ATM.

"That is horrible," he said. "But what does that have to do with the girl in the desert?"

"One of the members of that activist group told us about the apartment," I said.

He nodded, long and slow. "You mean those computer-hippie kids," he said, "with that website, lasmujeresdeldesierto.com?"

"It's in Spanish too?" said Nancy.

"Yes. They are trying to propagandize the Mexican population as well. Against the police."

"Do they have reason to?" I asked.

Saenz looked at me. He smiled. "We have our issues. But as you say, how is it said, 'One bad apple' . . ."

"Officer Saenz, you said to me that there was something else happening on the border. A third country. What did you mean by that?"

He raised his hand, the one without the cigarette, and just slightly moved his fingers in the air as if to wave my question away. He glanced around the bar.

"Look," I said, "the girl was killed in Mexico. She was thrown into the United States. I still believe that's some kind of statement."

"Or just a way of throwing you off," he said. "Throwing us all off. We always think in terms of the border. But maybe the ones who killed your little girl threw her like that just to confuse you."

Our little girl. I wasn't sure what to make of that. "Do you have any ideas, Officer Saenz, about who killed Marisa Jackson?"

"No. I do not."

"Do you know anything about prostitution rings involving children?" asked Nancy.

"What, do you mean here in Tijuana?" He shook his head slowly. "No. We have drugs, yes, and we have prostitutes. But children? That is not inherent to our culture, to have sex with our kids."

An all-out bullshit line, and he delivered it with such sincerity and such a grave tone that I almost laughed. Either he believed what he had just said, or he was one hell of a bravado actor.

"But as for the United States," he said, "that is another matter."

"Yes? How so?" I felt my cockles go up, something in me standing on the defense.

"Have you read that website? All those theories on child prostitution making its way from Mexico into the United States. Los Angeles, New York, Chicago, Atlanta. Supposedly, according to those hippie activists, *and* the *New York Times*, there are up to thirty-five thousand child sex slaves in the United States at any given time."

"You should be careful about what you read on the internet," said Nancy. A defensive tone had crept into her voice. "Besides, we caught a suspect in that cyber-crime."

"Oh yes. Karen Allende."

I didn't like it, hearing Karen's name coming out of this guy's mouth. Yet he had probably read about her in the papers. It was big news, the daughter of an international star involved in computer guerrilla warfare.

Nancy's cell phone buzzed. She checked the number, excused herself and walked out of the bar for a clearer signal. Saenz and I kept talking, moving toward an argument.

"Don't you find that strange?" he said. "That Karen Allende was taking pictures of dead little girls? What kind of person does that?"

I was about to say, Someone who gives a damn. Someone who was willing to risk her life and her freedom to stop the killings. But I didn't react, I didn't have the chance to say anything, for Saenz said, "And did you hear, she jumped bail?"

"How'd you know—where did you hear that?"

"Internet," he said. "*LA Times* site, and *La Opinión*. Both reported on it just a couple of hours ago. I'm sorry, I'm an internet junkie. I love reading the papers on the web. Are you all right?"

"Yeah, listen," but I had nothing to ask. Karen was getting in the way. I was staring at a section of the floor just behind Saenz. Nothing else to do but leap at an image I remembered about the other day at dawn when all of those Mexican cops had been staring at Saenz and me. "Why did your fellow officers look at you and me like they did?"

He smiled. "The sun was coming up. They saw I was talking with a beautiful woman."

Right.

Nancy walked back in and sat down. I said, "While your men were out there, did they find anything?"

"No," he said, "nothing worth noting."

"Were they looking for something in particular?" said Nancy.

"No," he said. He raised his eyebrows as if the question seemed strange; but he also crossed his arms over his chest. "Why do you ask?"

"Oh, they looked like little boys on a playground," said Nancy, "and they had lost a ball." She smiled.

He smiled back, then just shook his head, No.

I had no more questions. And Nancy had run out as well. She pulled a card out of her pocket and gave it to Saenz. "Let's keep in touch," she said. "I think this kind of cooperation will ultimately get us somewhere. Thanks much, Officer Saenz."

"My pleasure." He shook each of our hands. But he looked at Nancy with the slightest gesture of concern.

In the car I found out why. "Who called?"

"Dibbs. The second blood sample? It wasn't Marisa's. Completely different blood type and DNA."

I recalled the stain of blood on the flat rock and the amount of blood that had coagulated in the sand. At the time, I had figured it to be Marisa's draining out of her as she wandered about. "Another person," I muttered.

"Yep," said Nancy. "Double homicide."

Now Saenz's look of worry made sense. "The cops. They were looking for the other body."

"That's what I thought," said Nancy. "But why would they be doing that, and how would they know?"

"Why and how will be answered when we find out who."

Chapter 18

In the car we tossed data to see what pieces were missing, what scenarios made sense. After twenty minutes we came up with little.

I broke the silence. "So, what did he ask you to do?"

"Who?"

"Tekún Umán. Come on."

"Jeez, you're worse than a teenager asking about a boyfriend."

"Was he your boyfriend?"

"Romi quit being so goddamn jealous."

"I'm not jealous."

"Yes you are, you're jealous and you wear it like bad perfume." She laughed at me.

"Well *you're* the one he hung around with all the time. Both of you living in that house outside of Tijuana." I was probing, with a little tease here and there; but whenever I teased, it opened up something that pissed me off. "And you, I mean shit, Nancy. A *mole*. You actually keep doing it, you're still working for the Bureau, acting like nothing ever happened. Every time you walk into the office you're lying. And I have to go along with the lie. Here you were, working for an international drug runner, reporting to him whenever the Feds got close to his ass. Why don't you just leave the Bureau, quit living this lie—?"

She braked, swerved, and pulled over on the side of a very desolate road. I lurched in my seat.

She unbuckled her belt in order to lean in that much closer to me.

"Now listen to me, you whining . . . It was a mistake, what I said earlier, about Tekún asking me to do very little in return for all he had done for me. He was like a father to me, he never asked for anything, until four years ago. Then he asked if I would like to do one, single thing. Become a Federal Agent. Get to the Los Angeles Field Office—"

"And be a narc." Oh, I was mad.

"No. To protect you."

It's quiet out in the desert, especially with the motor turned off. Already the heat was making its way through the roof.

"What?"

"He asked me to be your bodyguard, Romi. Live with it."

"Bullshit. Don't tell me you didn't call him every time we had a lead on his whereabouts."

"Ah, shit." She turned the motor over, shoved the car into gear. "You are the most pigheaded *guanaca* I've ever met."

She sprayed two large fans of gravel behind us.

❦

Ten minutes later.

I began it. "Well?"

"Well what?"

"Did you ever narc out? Did you tell Tekún whenever the Feds were getting close?"

Nancy laughed. "It never happened. The Feds never figured out where he was. There was no need to call."

That stung. But it was true.

"Did you want us to get him, Romi?"

"We've got a job to do."

"That's not an answer."

"*Dejáme vos en paz, carajo.*"

But she wasn't about to leave me in peace. "He just wanted to make sure you were okay, especially when he couldn't be around."

I stared out my window at the desert. "So when did he come up with this brilliant plan?"

"Once he heard, back in Nashville, that the Feds wanted to hire you. He made arrangements. I was at Quantico the year after you were there. I got to L.A. as soon as I could."

"So all this time you've had my back." I said it with a thick dollop of sarcasm.

"Since the moment I met you, amiga."

I held my forehead as if a huge migraine had invaded. "Is that what you are?" I said.

"Like I said before. Your best friend."

"And what was Tekún?" I looked at her.

"A man who loved you, more than I've seen any man love anybody. God knows why." Half kidding, half serious. "I know you find it hard to believe, but he would die for you, Romilia."

"Die for me. If he were alive." I turned away, because the eyes, again, started to steam over. When was I going to get over him?

"Right," said Nancy.

Chapter 19

It was mid afternoon. We still had time to make it to the crime scene before nightfall. Then we could either get a hotel for the night in Tijuana, or drive late into LA.

I preferred the latter; I was missing Sergio and looked forward to more time with him. And with my mother. I was hoping to sit with her tonight and not drink and show her that I was not having a drink. This was one of those afternoons when you find yourself making decisions, to drink or not, to have a cigarette or no. Those inside struggles that others never see, difficult choices that you hope no one realizes you're making.

Then you have a conversation with your partner, who tells you that a man loved you so much, he set you up with your own bodyguard. That's why I was crying, because bottom line, I didn't believe it: I didn't believe I was worth it. Which made me crave a shot of whiskey now.

Sometimes I wondered, was I simply hot-wired for drinking? For smoking? My father had been an alcoholic. We had all known that. Some blamed it on the hard life back in El Salvador and his involvement in the quiet, hidden movements of the revolution. Others said it was because the military had fingered him as a subversive and had put him on the death squad list. But Mamá always said it had to do with coming to America. "He was never much himself after we crossed the border," she'd say. "Oh, he drank as a young man, but back in the old country he had a purpose. Here? He washed cars. He worried about health insurance for his family. He felt guilty for being here, becoming one of the bourgeoisie, as he put it, while the war was still going on back home and his comrades were getting slaughtered." Even after the war ended Papá drank. He probably drank more, having lost any chance of being in El Salvador in those last days of rebellion.

As a kid I promised I'd never be like him. With the drink. I loved Papá; but it was frightening to see that long, silent face on him after three, four, then six shots of Wild Turkey. He never hit Catalina or me, never raised a finger against us. But he'd stare at me, and I couldn't tell if it was a look of longing, rage, or loss. Or was it regret? That instead of sticking it out in the streets of his hometown Usulután, he had sold out, followed his woman to Los Eunited Estates, had kids. Girls. While his comrades were getting their testicles shoved down their throats back home.

More than promising myself I'd never be like that, I believed I *couldn't* be like that. It was a macho thing. A man thing.

And here I was, attempting to choose not to drink tonight. And remembering the look on Sergio's face the other night when I had stumbled into him. Throw a tiny wig on him, he could have been me, twenty-one years ago.

I was about to say something to Nancy about all of this. Just about ready to tell her, "I think I need help," or some stumbling phrase like that. Throw a tether to her, have her catch it and help pull me out. Considering what she had just told me about Tekún Umán, I now believed that yes, she was my friend, *mi cuate,* the most intimate amigo you can have, a Salvadoran word that struck at the soul of friendship. I could tell her anything.

"There's the site," she said. She pulled the car to one side. She pointed toward the north. There was the cross in the bright light of day. Below it was the small corral of yellow Police tape flapping in the wind.

I'd talk to Nancy later.

We stepped into the closed mouth of one of the hottest days I'd ever felt. The sunlight hit as if to burn all shadows away. Sweat burst over my forehead and under my armpits. I shucked off my suit jacket, tossed it onto the seat, put on my sunglasses. Pulled at my cotton shirt, already staining with sweat as if the air were sucking the water from my skin. I adjusted my shoulder holster and worked with my bra strap to let some air in and keep a rash away.

"Where was the stain, the rock?" Nancy said. She wiped sweat from underneath her sunglasses. "Damn, should've brought sunblock."

I looked over toward the empty space where Marisa Jackson's body had been, looked at the cross, gauged where the border was, then turned to my right at a four o'clock position. "Over there," I said. "And the Mexican cops, they were ambling around behind in that scrub."

"Let's figure out what they were looking for. I bet you a box of Krispy Kremes they knew about the second vic."

"That I don't doubt," I said.

The flat rock was gone, sitting in Dibbs' forensics lab in Los Angeles. But there was blood still in the sand, coagulated, desiccated and making its way into dust. Not Marisa Jackson's blood.

Nancy bent down, crouched over the stained sand. "You think the vic died here?"

"I'd bet that," I said. "Look at the way the blood's patterned. Looks like it puddles here from the wound. And it made a puddle, not a spray. Bullet wound, or knife. The vic apparently dropped right here, after being wounded. Then they carried her away."

"Think it was a woman? Another girl?" said Nancy.

"I don't know. Maybe. But then, why leave one girl out here and make the other one disappear?" I looked up at Marisa's flapping yellow tape. "And why throw one into California? Unless the other victim got thrown over there too, and we just didn't find her."

"I don't know. San Diego boys crawled all over those hills, even behind the cross. Nothing."

"Okay." I turned and looked into the scrub, where the Mexican cops had walked. "They were looking for something. Maybe it wasn't a body. They may have been doing one last clean up."

I took a careful step into the scrub, more concerned about meeting up with a sleeping snake than I was disturbing a crime scene. The sun fell blatantly into the areas between the scrub bushes, the cacti and the stones. There were no shadows. Without the sunglasses, I would have been white-light blind.

Nancy walked into the scrub to my right toward the west. She bent over in a position similar to mine. She looked from section to section, examining each area for any anomaly, any shape or form or object that was trying to blend in but that most definitely stood out. That's how it works: you see the desert or the bathroom floor or the library walls or the messy kitchen, with specific sight. You look, not for the one strange thing, but the ordinary. You study the ordinary, a quick study in which you hope to find the one thing, as they so wisely say on Sesame Street, that is not like the other.

I thought of Sergio again. He didn't watch Sesame Street anymore. He'd grown up. He hated Barney. He and his friends had composed a new Barney song, with the purple dinosaur meeting some horrific end.

Such a cutey.

I wouldn't drink tonight. Though now, suddenly, a shot of whiskey sounded so good. I wondered, that desire, how could it rouse itself out here in this desert?

This heat and this desert where there is little to no trash. For no one lived out here. Those who passed through here, illegal immigrants trying to find their way North at night, doing their best to avoid helicopters and SUVs driven by bored and stressed-out Border Patrol Agents, were not ones to waste anything. My mother has said before, the poor do not leave much trash behind. Which was why that tiny, thin strand of red rope stood out.

Though it was more like thick thread. I bent lower, crouching now, and lifted my sunglasses. The thread was thick enough that I could see the curves of its twist. Like the thread used to hold canvas sacks together. Twine used to bale hay. A small piece of thin leather flicked low in the string's curve. A second shred of leather was hooked in the brush on the opposite loop of the twine. I first thought it was a religious artifact: my mother had worn something like this, no wait—she had talked about having to wear something like this as a kid. I examined the leather up close, crouching deeper into the desert, feeling the heat as if it were sixty blankets heaped up on my shoulders. Later I would remember my first thought of this thing as a holy object. Someone's holy object.

The leather pieces were completely desiccated. Mummified. I looked at one: it still retained some of the shape it had had when it had been alive. The tiny round nub in its center. But the string passed above the nub and into the spread of skin, where the skin turned from a dark brown to a lighter shade.

Oh. No. Son of a bitch—

"Romi get down."

Nancy stood over me. She squatted and grabbed my waist from behind and shoved me to the ground. Then came a crack through the heated air, like the distant snap of a large, dry tree limb. Nancy dropped on top of me. She knocked us both flat onto the ground.

The sound of sand, the thwup of bullets missing a target and slamming into a hill of desert, just a few feet to my left. I couldn't move, with Nancy's body laying on top of me.

That thread in my fingers now. When Nancy knocked me down, I had it in my grip. I felt the shrub brush try to keep its hold on the thread and on the skin. The bush's tiny, brittle limb snapped. The shots popped into sand around me. They came from the north, from the border. But at a distance, for the small hills must have hidden me. He was shooting with guesses. One shooter, according to the pauses between shots, the time to shove another shell into the barrel. He could get lucky. His next shot could penetrate one of the small hills and hit me and I thought of Sergio and promises about whiskey and my partner on top of me and the gush of Nancy's blood on my shoulder.

Another shot fired, then a pause, as if the shooter were gauging. Then one more. Rifle shots. Long distance. Then a pause. Then no more. A belief, a hope, that I had been hit as well.

Which meant either he would depart or he would be here standing over me. Soon.

I could hear little except my own breathing, which I tried to regulate, tried to keep low so he couldn't hear me. Nancy's body, though thin, kept my face in the dirt. I had to risk a pushup to roll her off.

No more shots. They must be gone.

Nancy fell onto her back. Her face turned into a grimace. Her legs straightened out, as if she knew she had to hide, which was a good sign, a very good sign.

A red, wet bloom had spread over her chest. The desert air already sucked at the edges of the stain. She breathed against the two holes. I flipped her onto one arm, held her sideways, put my right hand over the entrance wound in her lower back, my left on the exit, just below her collar bone and I cursed her back toward me, back toward the living Come on Nancy come on *mi compa*, shit, motherfuck come on girl you're with me you stay with me.

Closing the holes to save her made for a moment of air pressure. "Phone," she said.

Her phone. The Bureau phones. I let go of her back and wrestled with the cell phone holster on her belt, unsnapped it, pulled out the phone. I did not waste time trying to get a regular signal. Out here there were no good signals, no time or chance for a phone conversation with Leticia Fisher. I pushed the GPS switch on the side of the phone then hit our code, fourteen-twelve, sent it into space to the FBI satellite somewhere above the earth. Distress signal, sent to D.C., which would bounce to Los Angeles. I left the phone open as a tether to the Bureau on Wilshire.

But she was dying. I knew this. I knew it the moment she fell on me.

Were there thirty seconds left? Were there ten?

I drew my pistol and flopped in front of her face. With my gun on my thigh I could hold her wounds like this, my right arm circling her waist to press my hand on her back; my left palm pressed over her breast. And then, for no practical reason, my forehead pressed against hers.

Her eyes were not lost yet. She still saw me. I pulled closer to her, hugged her as if to use my entire body as a staunch.

Her breath rattled.

Then the litany, always the litany: Nancy, Nancy listen Nancy it's gonna be fine, keep breathing, got you, I got you, they'll be here soon. I jerked my head to the north, gun on my thigh and cocked, waiting for the shooter to walk up, find us here like two lovers and finish us.

Nothing.

My forehead again on hers, I whispered to her, my lips moving an inch in front of hers, Nancy. Nancy you'll be fine, just breath *mi amiga, eres mi compañera, verdád? Vas a llegar a casa, sí,* come on honey just breathe.

She looked at me. Though the sun beat on her, her eyes were wide open, and yet it looked as if they were shut.

"He's—"

And that was all.

The gunman never came. I can't remember how long we lay there before two choppers made their way into the territory, circling, one surveying the perimeter while the other made its descent. Finding two women there, two partners in a snuggle. One woman weeping, the other silent. They had to pry me from her. One set of fingers clutched to her tricep, the other clutching her thin waist. I can remember the smell of her neck, pungent in the desert heat, a nice perfume that I could never afford, and the curve of her light pink skin, just under her jaw.

Chapter 20

Karen wished she were still asleep. For this was worse, much worse. This was what it must have been like when she was asleep all those hours, several years ago, when Minos had her bound and gagged. Minos had used a drug on her and on his other victims that made them forget everything. She remembered nothing of the abduction, nor the night spent in a storage warehouse, certainly not the next night, tied to a tree in a national park. Through the years her mind worked at retrieving those memories, as if needing them for some reason that she could not fathom. Yet it never succeeded.

Whatever Ingrid gave her now did not wipe out memory. Just a rag over her face, smelling of something wet and alcoholic. She remembered the chase in the desert, the two men grabbing her, carrying her to the house, she screaming all the way. In the house they shoved her against the mattresses of an old, dusty couch, and she still screamed. The Latino teenage boys did not hit her, they just held her arms and legs down and laughed, almost embarrassedly, while looking to the open front door at Ingrid and Ritchie, who chatted with each other on the front porch while Karen screamed. Ritchie handed Ingrid a pack of cigarettes. They smoked. Karen's yelps softened out of exhaustion, but after a minute's rest she started again. "Could you shut her up?" said Ritchie, blowing out smoke.

Ingrid walked in, put the cigarette to one side away from the glass bottle. She poured some of the bottle's contents onto a rag and pressed the rag against Karen's face. She saw the boy at her feet release her. He flicked his wrist and smiled at Ingrid, said "Thanks Ingrid," and that was all Karen saw.

Now she awoke to the same place, the same old house, the smell of the decrepit couch. But the doors were all closed, as were the windows. No one was around.

She was bound. Her wrists behind her, pressed against her lower back, not only by the cuffs, but by a rope that circled her abdomen, that held her wrists tight against her back. Her feet locked together as well, duct tape wrapped around her ankles. The same tape, no doubt, over her mouth—and her tongue, it did not move, due to a wad of cloth inside, pressed tight against her palate. She was naked.

Someone in another room. A pot clanged against a stove. A radio played—no, a television. Spanish news. Univisión. Smells came from under the door, toasted tortillas, beans.

Karen turned onto one side. She pulled her hands away from her back. Hardly an inch of movement.

The television in the kitchen went dead. The door opened. Ingrid walked out. She sat in a chair next to the sofa, found a remote and turned on the television on the other side of the room. She tore the tortilla in half, rolled each half into a scoop and dipped a piece into the beans.

Karen heard the pop of a cola can being opened. The spray of bubbles, the first gulp—if Karen turned her head, arched it back on the couch, she could see Ingrid holding the can to her lips and drinking. It made the cloth in her mouth feel harder, dry with evaporated saliva. She moaned; did Ingrid not hear it, due to the wad of cloth and the tape? Or did Ingrid just ignore her?

A cell phone rang on a table to Ingrid's right. "Yeah?" she answered. "Yeah, she just woke up, I heard her. Yeah she's fine. No she ain't started yet. I checked. This morning. Yeah. Listen, when can I get out a here? I'm tired of this shit, being in this house all alone. Why don't you take her, watch her yourself? I know you're busy, but what about me huh? Got that fucking funeral to go to. Yeah. I don't know, and they ain't said anything in the news, the Feds are keeping quiet. No, it's all right. Better than staying in this shit hole with your latest girlfriend. You know you really gotta get over this thing, it's slowing down business."

The man on the other end talked loudly.

"Look, I'll go to the funeral, then I'll drop her off. What? No she won't make no noise. I'll knock her out. Yeah. Yeah, then I'll bring her to the school, okay? Okay. Yeah. Bye."

She clicked the phone closed, put her back knuckles on her hips, looked down at Karen, addressed her as if talking to an unwanted housecat, "Time to go. Shit."

Ingrid took Karen from behind, hooking her hands into the space below Karen's armpits. She was strong. She picked Karen up without dropping her to the floor, then dragged Karen backwards to the door.

Chapter 21

I couldn't see much. Not because of my sunglasses—most everyone there wore sunglasses. It was a hot day when we buried Nancy. The Presbyterian Church in Santa Monica had been air conditioned. The moment all of us got in our cars, we had to flip the air on high to escape the bake of the afternoon. But now, in the cemetery, no escape. No water bottles, something I could use, something that may have cut the wave of nausea beating through me.

No one's fault but my own. The drinks from last night, then the two shots this morning to take the sting off the hangover. Before the funeral, while Mamá got dressed and we waited for the babysitter, I walked into the kitchen for another shot. Just one more, to take me through the afternoon. These had been days that made a swallow of whiskey early in the day seem normal, seem to be the only thing right. But now with the heat and my black suit, and the lack of water, if I looked at the coffin for too long, I was in danger of retching. Right here, next to Nancy's mother, who I had just met yesterday, before the minister and in front of all those neighbors of Nancy's, and in front of my boss to my right, and all those agents in the crowd, I'd puke up the remnants of a twenty four hour binge. That couldn't happen. Not here, at an FBI funeral, where the primary emotion is not sadness or mourning but rage. I knew that, after the ceremony, my colleagues would leave, gathering in groups of two and three, light up cigarettes in the parking lot and talk of vengeance. Where to go for lunch. Some favorite diner where they could talk more about my partner, Nancy Pearl, fine agent, damn fine human being. They'd remember the moments in the hallways of the Bureau when Nancy was nice to them, and then they'd talk again about vengeance. I'd no doubt they would want to give me some leeway, and that some of them, after their own drink and a loosening of their tie, would say Let Romilia find the fucker on some off-duty night, go out and sniff the streets and shoot the prick in both knees, one at a time, then the elbows. Watch him flop around on the pavement like some fucking Pinocchio with his strings cut then put the barrel right at the top of the nose where the nerves pop if you just touch there with your finger, then say to the dickless fucker some words you want him to hear before you gut out his skull with one unmarked bullet of an untraceable pistol.

Their thoughts. My thoughts.

There was too much going on here. Too much for me to keep up with. The preacher was the only one doing anything, reading from his little black book and speaking out to us all and to Nancy, sending her off to some wondrous place where people don't aim an MP9 semi automatic at your back and shred your insides with a bullet meant to kill a horse. Only he spoke; but there were things around that I could not understand. Those two agents, for instance, out in the middle of the crowd, whispering to each other. They were having a full conversation together. I knew them, only in the hallways of the Bureau. One was Lenny, the guy who made a crack about me drinking whiskey. I didn't know the woman. Lenny was doing most of the talking. The woman was responding with short phrases, as if asking for more info. I stared at the preacher, which put the whispering couple to my left at forty five degrees. With my sunglasses on, I could watch them without them knowing. Yes, they were talking about me, shit—for Lenny made the quick mime of a shot glass movement, and the woman made an O with her mouth.

Fuck.

But that wasn't all. Just, those things you notice in a crowd, things that are a wee bit off, and maybe more off when you're battling the whiskey in your head. Or maybe you're using those anomalies in the crowd as ballasts, something to focus on, something to keep you from stumbling. The woman who cut through the mourners, for instance. She was casual about it, but she was definitely moving forward. She kept her face turned away. Then, abruptly, she headed back to the rear of the crowd, passing a tall man with a Panama hat.

Did I know her? The whiskey was not helping at all. Not the whiskey, but the sickness—my stomach, my head. Even the Panama hat guy seemed familiar, but now I was doubting everything. Of course I was doubting everything. My job. My life. The losses of these past years. What was it about this line of work? You try to make things right, you try to do the good, the just, and it just keeps getting fucked up and the people closest to you end up getting hurt or getting buried like Nancy. Nancy, she lay there on me, she held me down with her dying body to keep me covered, to have my back, to do the one thing that a dead man had asked her to do years ago. And why, as I stood over her grave, watching as the undertakers pulled the latches that lowered her into the ground, why did I first believe that for some reason she did it out of love, and in the next moment I doubted that belief?

Because I couldn't believe anybody wanting to do that.

"Romilia. It's okay, está bien está bien." Not my mother, but my boss. Lettie Fisher bent over and put her hand on my back. And I poured tears toward Nancy Pearl. I believed they would reach her, how hard I cried.

Then came a sober thought: I shouldn't do this. Break down like this. Not in front of my boss, and all those agents out there, and the press, waiting outside the gate—the hungry pack of television reporters who had been on us since the afternoon she died. I had to be strong, which meant no crying. In a Bureau dominated by men, with its military shade of training, there was no taste for the weakness of mourning.

Something with which I agreed. I didn't want to be sad. Let the rage come forth and make the decisions for the next few days.

I stood up quickly, shook my shoulders. A guttural sound came out of my lungs. I looked out at the crowd, who were now dispersing. I stared hard at anyone who cared to look my way as if to say *I will find you.*

Nancy's mother, dignified to the end—a tall woman like Nancy, lovely in her late fifties, wearing a dress from a village in Oaxaca, walked toward the preacher to thank him. She was weeping; but she was calm. Beyond her the guy in the hat stepped into my view. Ms. Pearl turned to me. "Romilia, could you escort me out, dear?" She took my arm. I gladly walked with her. My mother and Lettie Fisher followed, speaking to each other in Spanish.

The crowd dispersed. At the gate, I turned to look one last time. Ms. Pearl held my arm tighter, as if to say, Do not linger. The two undertakers finished their jobs, one calling on his cell phone, perhaps to the migrant workers who would do the shoveling. Then there was the man with the Panama hat who, I now saw, leaned on a cane. An old man, though I could not see his face. He wore a fine suit, well pressed. He stared at the hole. He rubbed his forehead with his free hand, then leaned more on the cane, needing more support.

"Wait a minute," I said, "Who is that guy?" I made to walk his way.

He turned and walked toward a hill of graves. He could walk quickly, even with the cane.

"Romilia. Romilia."

With the second call, Ms. Pearl choked. Then she wept, hard, a sorrowful yawp of mourning from the empty, meaningless loss that only mothers know. I turned back to her.

"Romilia *hija*, I need to go. I need to leave her now."

I obeyed. When we walked through the gate I glanced back, but the guy in the hat was gone.

Chapter 22

"She's still alive. The Latina bitch. Yeah. She was there. I got the white one. No, no it was the Latina puta who saw me on Barrington. I know. What, you wanted me to do it at a fucking funeral? Look I got to take care of your new love, then I got to find out what the cops are doing, I mean the fucking Feds, shit Ritchie it's the Feds! Nobody's listening to this call, because up until now we never fucked up. But now we have. So I'm dropping off your girl and then I'm hiding at home for a while. And you better stop this shit with this one, no more after that. That's why we're in this fucking mess—don't blame everybody else for your fuck-ups, you and your goddamn weirdo turn ons— oh well FUCK YOU back you don't scare me I'll put a jodida bullet up your ass like I did the blonde. What? Yeah, yeah I'll be there, at the school. Yeah, save me a couple of pieces. Pepperoni, yeah. No onions or peppers."

This was all Karen could hear, from the stove-heat of the trunk and the muffle of the back seat. Though awake, her body could not move, not after the injection of whatever it was Ingrid had put in her. During the funeral, Karen's entire body had gotten slick with her own sweat. Now it was dry, with deposits of salt all over in white patches. Still, she had tried to get someone's attention: she kicked the side panel of the car, breaking through the cardboard that housed the jack and tire iron, slamming her bare feet against the folded iron jack. The iron had bit into her soles; she knew she was bleeding. It was enough to make her stop and drift toward passing out.

There was no one in the parking lot. Everyone was in the cemetery. No one heard her.

Then Ingrid came back. She rushed into the car, drove off quickly, called Ritchie. Very little of the air conditioning penetrated the back seat. Karen finally fell under the heat, seemingly the only safe place for her now—exhaustion. Yet she still did math, as she had been doing all these hours, more in a panic, now out of habit: what was today's date? How many weeks had it been? She tried to trick the math, to make the dates come out different, but they never did. She knew her body. Her cycle was clockwork. Two days, three at the most. A thought that, before losing consciousness, made her cry one more time, squeezing out the last of the water in her.

Chapter 23

I awoke with a hangover two days after the funeral and one day after the mandatory visit with one of our federally funded psychologists, a young fellow by the name of Larry who insisted I call him Larry so that we could be friends. Larry tried really hard. He ended up doing most of the talking, which obviously made him nervous, or at least frustrated. He ended the session with, "Okay, Agent Chacón, just remember, we're here, all right? Our services, they're part of your package. Got that?"

I got it. Then I went home and drank.

And cried. I sat in our living room with Mamá while Sergio pretended to watch television. Mamá and I talked; or rather, I ranted while she sat there. She listened, hoping I would calm down, yet not wanting to say that, as if trying with all her might to respect what had happened to me the past few days. On her face I saw the look of two losses: a mother who had nearly lost her daughter to a killer's bullet and a mother who was losing her daughter, right now, one more time. She barely glanced at the bottle of Wild Turkey that I had oh so ostentatiously placed on the coffee table next to the couch. I had set the bottle on her copy of García Márquez's *El amor en los tiempos del cólera,* which seemed an abomination and which somehow pleased me. Had I placed the bottle there as a way of being somehow spiritually close to Gabo? Or was it an act of disdain, and if so, for whom? Certainly not Gabo—my mother perhaps? Her sobriety? Her continuing rituals that we had both followed together once, that of reading books throughout the nights, waking up in the mornings and snatching a few pages before I went to work or she made breakfast for Sergio. Was I rebelling against that? I didn't know; and I knew I didn't know. While saying something about

Nancy and how she took that bullet for me—no other way to say it—I saw Mamá's casual glance at the bottle. Then her eyes scraped over the cigarette in its ashtray. So I swiped at it. The cigarette and the tray went flying. A flick of ash flipped up between us. The tray thunked against the far wall, just under a primitive painting of a Salvadoran landscape. The lit cigarette's coal landed somewhere to Mamá's side.

"*Ya, basta,*" she said. She walked to Sergio, who had turned around and who looked at me in the way I never wanted him to look. She shuffled him to his room and closed the door and stayed in there the rest of the night, leaving the *borracha* in the larger section of the house. Leaving me to pace about, mumbling, then yelling in Spanish and English about how fucked up this all was and how can you expect me to sober up and be such a *jodida* perfect *madre* when I've got people shooting at me and taking away my partner who always lied to me and who ended up being my only goddamn friend? And then I cried; and then I slumped against the couch and that's all I remember.

The next morning I awoke at five. Alcohol tended to trick me that way, making me think hey, not so bad. I'm awake. Okay, woozy, but still functioning, which at the time I told myself was only a half-lie.

An hour later I knew none of it was true. I could hardly stand up. It felt like a good quart of alcohol was still in my stomach, siphoning its way into my system, an image I could have believed once I saw what was left in the bottle. Two inches, an inch. Only enough to assure myself that I hadn't finished it off.

Mamá took Sergio to school. She came home. She said nothing, but I could hear her sighs in the kitchen while she cooked us breakfast. Not forced sighs, not at all. Real sighs, real exhalations of weariness, fear.

I ate what she made me. It actually looked good: eggs, rice, a small plop of refrieds, fresh tortillas. This did not surprise me, her going out of the way to make all this. But her taking my pack of cigarettes and lighting up did.

It looked familiar. I recalled a moment from childhood. The remnants of the alcohol let me feel that child again, Romilia, age eight. Watching my mother light up with my father. A pleasant image, as they were always resting, letting their breakfast settle while drinking coffee and smoking. An image of my father, sober and kind toward Mamá.

She had quit smoking after his death from a heart attack. To stay alive, she once told Catalina and me. Caty was a teenager, I was still a kid. "You've got one parent now. I need to stick out this life, make sure you two get raised."

And now, after twenty-plus years, she lit up. That certain joy: she closed her eyes slightly at the first hit of nicotine. I suppose she didn't have to worry about sticking around so much now. Or maybe she didn't want to stick around.

I took a cigarette from the pack. She handed me the lighter. I took that as a sign of camaraderie, a mother and a daughter lighting up together. Which should have been a warning.

"I'm worried, hija."

"I doubt they know where we live, Mamá." But then I mumbled out an idea, about her and Sergio going over to Uncle Chepe's house until we sorted this case out and caught the shooter.

"You know that's not what I'm talking about."

I slumped toward the table. And to the table I muttered, *"Ay no me empiece por favor, déjeme tranquila, carajo."*

She let me mumble into the tabletop a minute. After that, she said nothing about last night, how I scared Sergio, how I needed to think about my son. Rather she said, "Chepe and I have been talking."

I couldn't believe what came after that. What they had talked about. What they were trying to decide. Oh I heard it, all right; but I shut that shit down right then and there. Not by arguing with her, or even by trying to reason with her. I stood, grabbed the smokes and my keys and left. In the car I tried to light up again, but the fucking flame on the lighter danced around too much.

Chapter 24

Lettie Fisher had given me time off, as much as I needed. She had handed the entire case over to Randall and Shrieber. One of the many reasons I got so drunk.

I didn't go to the office. I drove straight to Ballys Gym off Victory Boulevard in North Hollywood. Spent half an hour on the Stairmaster, twenty minutes lifting dumbbells, and another twenty doing laps in the pool, dodging the older folks who swam slower but much longer. A new day, someone might have said, a new start. But I knew better. After all of the sweating and a steam shower topped off with a blast of freezing water to close off the pores, no one would smell me.

While on the Stairmaster I had the choice of programs on three different television monitors: Judge Judy, The Price is Right, and the news. I watched the news. There was a follow-up to Nancy's death, ambiguous news about the ongoing investigation. Once again they played the tape of the funeral. There I was, with Nancy's mother Rita, and my mother. There was the priest. All in fairly close-up angles.

And there she was, little Ms. Whole Foods Salad Lady, smiling at the camera and giving us the latest updates in southern California. Slow day for her—not even a car chase to follow live from a chopper.

I'd give Maggie Contreras something to work with.

After the workout I called KSAL 9 and asked for Contreras. I got a secretary who kept me at bay. "Just tell her Special Agent Romilia Chacón called," then gave her my number.

I wasn't two steps into the Coffee Bean & Tea Leaf when the cell phone rang. "Hi this is Maggie Contreras, KSAL 9 News, is this Agent Chacón?"

As much as she tried to be professional, I could hear in her voice the happy growl of a carnivore who has just smelled meat.

~✦~

Maggie Contreras had made decisions in her young career. She had not gotten tit-replacement. Other news babes in southern Cal had made themselves into model material: Channel 12 had some blonde spilling out of her tight Macy's T-shirt every evening, giving us a meteorological report that no one cared about since we lived in southern California where the weather rarely changes. And, of course, due to all that breastwork, guys on Stairmasters next to me watched the weather report with slack jaws.

Maggie hadn't done that. She was a slim lady, very slim, high cheekbones, perky little pear-like breasts, a not-too-short Santa Fe colored skirt that showed off just enough of her legginess.

I had kept her at bay during the Minos case. I couldn't stand her. Some of it may have been jealousy—those emerald eyes in a Latina woman's head, were they colored contacts? That perpetual six-hundred-dollar-laser-whitened smile. That overall look of confidence.

Yes. Some of it was jealousy. Especially when she once asked me, during a curt interview, "Detective Chacón (as I was then), do you feel hardened by the work you've chosen?"

Hardened. Mamá has used that word before when describing me. "You'd be more bella, hija, if your face wasn't so, well, maciza."

Maciza. Hard. Firm. Like a cinderblock.

Maggie found me at the coffee shop. She smiled. I tried not to look so hard. Being soft might make her feel more comfortable, let her guard come down, so I could trap her.

Because at the funeral, yes, I had been mourning. It was painful, watching Nancy's neighbors carry her gray steel coffin from the hearse to the hole. It had been a terrible day. But I had not been blind.

"How *are* you?" said Maggie. She sat down after shaking my hand. She might have tried to hug me had I given her any leeway. Such is the way in LA. Our ability to feign empathy is enormous, to the point that we believe it.

I asked if she wanted coffee. She hesitated; having made it to my table and so close to me, she didn't want to lose leverage, afraid I'd change my mind and skip out of the coffee shop while she was ordering. "I need a refill anyway," I said.

"Oh let me get it," and she took my cup. I barely protested. "KSAL can surely afford a refill," she said, then gave me that on-screen smile. A smile, I was sure, she wanted to carry all the way from regional news to New York or Atlanta, sitting in a CNN chair.

We sat and talked about the bracelet on her wrist, given to her by a really cute gentleman who was no longer her boyfriend. That done, we both cut to the chase. "I suppose you're wondering why I called you."

Oh how she lit up.

I dashed her first hopes. "I'm not giving an interview."

"Oh."

"Not yet, at least."

"Oh?" Again, a slight brightening. "I can understand, so soon after the, the attack, you might not be in the right frame of mind?"

"That, and I can't speak. It's an ongoing investigation."

"Can you give me a little idea of what happened out there?" The thrill was getting to her. "I mean, all we know is that a Federal Agent was killed in the line of duty out in the desert. They couldn't keep the funeral from us, since she was local. Several sources verify you were with her. It can be off the record for now. Did you see anything?"

I said nothing. Just stared at her.

"Sorry," she said.

"I actually asked to see you because I thought you could help me out."

"Oh? Of course, Romilia. How?"

"I saw your coverage on the funeral. Were you there? Because I didn't see you in the crowd of reporters."

"Oh, no. I wasn't there that day."

"But you narrated the piece."

"Yes. Randy, he asked me to step in and narrate."

"I see. Who's Randy?"

"Randy Patikin. He's one of our cameramen."

"Oh, okay." I wrote his name down in my little notepad, conveniently placed to the left of my coffee.

"Do you need to talk with Randy?"

"Yes. What's his phone number? I'd like to meet with him."

"Really? Why?" She played with her bracelet.

"Because his footage was really good. He got some great close-ups of the family. Of me and Nancy's mother. And Nancy's coffin."

"Oh yeah. Yeah our cameramen, they're terrific. And the technology today, whew, those telephoto lenses, they're amazing."

But she knew that I knew. She abandoned the bracelet; now she was twiddling her left gold earring with her thumb and finger.

"You were close to the grave, weren't you? Taking pictures. That was you I saw cutting through the crowd."

It looked like she wasn't breathing. Her fingers froze on the earring.

A man came up. Middle aged, white. He smiled at her. "Excuse me, you're Maggie Contreras aren't you? I watch you every night." He led straight into a request for an autograph.

She smiled. She signed a napkin, handed it to him, barely glancing at him, then turned and looked back at me.

"My understanding of the law, Maggie, is that cemeteries are considered private areas. And I called the funeral home just to verify. That cemetery in particular is very strict about the policy of not taking photos inside the grounds for public use."

She had returned to earring-twiddling. Now she released it and put both hands on the table, palms down.

"And I'm sure," I continued, "that you knew about this, considering the stink that Kappela-Price Cemetery made, bringing on a lawsuit against that reality television show, what was it called, *Second Wave?* You know, the show that got canceled after the trial and after the network paid, what, three million to Kappela-Price?"

"So what do you need, Agent Chacón?"

"The mini-cam you used."

"Why?"

"I want to study it, see who else was in the crowd."

A pause before she said, "And if I don't?"

I tapped Randy's name three times with my index finger. Randy, who no doubt knew nothing about her hidden camera, and who would not want to sink with her.

She paused. She was thinking. "Why are we here?" she asked.

"What?"

"Here, at a coffee shop. Why didn't you just go to the station and demand the footage?"

She was smelling me out. "I haven't reported back in yet. Since Nancy's . . . Agent Pearl's death."

"I see. Post-trauma debriefing?"

I didn't want to go there with her. But she was on a hunt now, as much to defend herself as to get a story. I had to be careful; my last conversation with Mamá came to mind, about decisions being made. About my drinking. Conversations I didn't want Maggie to know about.

"Can I get anything out of this?" She stared at me, her arms crossed over that perky chest. She had cojones, I had to give her that.

"Okay," I said, "after all this, after the case is closed, I'll give you an interview."

"Really." She didn't believe it.

"Yes, really. As much as my superior will allow."

"Which will be shit, with Leticia Fisher." She drank coffee, glanced at her purse. Did she have a tape recorder running in it? Or maybe she thought about her pack of cigarettes. "I know the rules of the Bureau, Romilia. They pack you in silence until you retire. Or die. I'd get the same info from you as some little NPR segment."

She huffed, because she knew I had her. She had to give me her digital camera because she had broken the law. And unlike some grocery store rag that had no sense of ethics, she worked for a respectable news program, one that could give her a strong ladder to the top, or could hack that ladder in half and send her tumbling down. I had her. But I had no need to be cold. And I didn't want her as an enemy.

"Okay," I said, "try again."

She hadn't expected this. But suddenly she looked prepared. "A book," she said.

"A book?" Oh but then I knew. Shit.

"The Minos case."

"Jesus," I said, turning away a moment, looking at the two women across from us who were obviously on a first date, the way they flirted. "There are already books published on that son of a bitch."

"All unauthorized studies. Boring books on Dante and the Inferno and Minos' psychosis in the serial killer section of Barnes & Noble. And the shit they play over and again on Court TV, don't you ever get tired of that, Romilia? Your picture, along with your sister's photo, framed alongside that killer on some show narrated by Morgan Freeman?"

"I don't watch TV."

"How about it? Your own story, with me writing it."

"So you're a writer?"

"Yes." She said it as if she herself believed it. But then a certain reality-check shot into her head. "And if not a book, at least a one-hour special that we could pitch to Primetime, or 60 Minutes."

My turn to sigh.

"We'll see," I said.

"Is that a yes?"

"Careful," I said. I thought of my boss. Fisher could really do nothing about such a deal, as Minos was a case that had occurred before I had joined the Bureau. But she could give me grief for actually volunteering myself to go into the media spotlight. One thing the Bureau doesn't like, it's celebrity agents. "I said we'll see."

She grinned. "You know where the station is? Or you can just follow me. You know, I think a tv special about Minos would be better. I mean, who reads books anymore?" and she laughed.

"I do."

Chapter 25

Each time I believe I've caught up with digital technology, another surprise comes along. A lens in a pendant. A microphone in an earring. James Bond stuff, bought at Circuit City.

"It's fairly sharp, for a micro-cam," said Maggie. We were in her office at KSAL. She had closed the blinds so I could see the laptop screen better. Or maybe so no one out on the street or in the hallway would see what she was doing. "We only used a few seconds from my footage. But it was very effective."

I recognized the footage from the news report. It was a quick shot of the coffin, the family, neighbors and me. Then a shot of Nancy, alive, smiling at the camera, a photo of her taken when she first joined the Bureau. That shook through me while I had stood on the Stairmaster, seeing Nancy's calm, smiling face on the screen. Still, I had noticed that the angle of the camera in the cemetery was not from long distance, nor from a telephoto lens, but obviously from within the crowd of mourners.

Specifically, from where Maggie had been standing.

According to the angle of her shots, Maggie had wandered around as much as one can while standing near a grave of mourners. A couple of times individuals looked toward her, as if wondering why she was maneuvering herself around like that. They may have mistaken her for a friend of the family who just wanted to get closer to the mother or the neighbors. Much is forgiven, I suppose, at a funeral. As long as they didn't discover she was from the media, she was safe.

There was that guy in a Panama hat, tall, who stood in the distance. The shape of his body . . . but he had a limp, which made him look older, and made me realize how bad off I was, having such wishful thinking.

Sometimes I wonder if, even when you're sober, alcohol can play tricks in your head.

It didn't take long, maybe four minutes of watching the film, to tell Maggie, "Whoa, wait a sec, wind it back there, just a little." Maggie did. The camera panned backward over the priest at the hole, me, Nancy's mother, reversing and putting a handkerchief to her nose once more. She hit pause. People froze. Then she played it forward. Still, the camera was too fast. "Can you slow that down a little?" I said.

"Sure."

"Still may be too blurry for me to see . . ."

"Not with this camera."

She slowed the movement. It wasn't like old film or even video: the people moved in digitized blocks. With it slowed the few whispers in the crowd. The microphone picked up the priest's prayers in the distance. But someone else was talking, two people whispering to each other, holding one of those surreptitious conversations in a venue that asks for silence. Now the voices were mottled with the slow motion. That didn't matter; I saw the face that I had just barely caught.

Caught, both in the first viewing of this recording. And almost caught on Barrington. In the van. The woman who had slammed the driver's side door into me. That was she, no doubt about it. She was wearing sunglasses and a small, black mourner's hat with no veil. She dressed like a young, humble housemaid out of some movie. She was the one.

But she wasn't the one talking. Someone around her was. That guy next to her I recognized as Lenny, the fellow agent who had made a cut about me drinking a man's drink and who, at the funeral, did a mime of a shot glass. There was the woman agent next to him. They were whispering. "Can you somehow make the sound go on naturally, in regular speed, but keep the frame frozen?" I asked.

"Sure. The sound can be played through a separate track." Maggie did some push-button magic on her little computer. The voices were mottled, but still clear enough to hear. The screen remained the same, keeping the young Mexican woman frozen and held.

Young. But toughened. Solidified. There was something frightening about her.

And then the voices, talking over her. *Would you? Sleep. Shit. I'd be awake all the time, looking for the prick. Take him out before Fisher and the*

brass got to him. Yeah. Shit yeah . . . you know, Chacón, it's not just lack of
sleep making her look like hell. . . . What? . . . She's, you know. . . . No shit. . . .

I didn't move. Maggie had heard it. No doubt it wasn't her first time
hearing it. She had watched these tapes over and again, looking for something
juicy to show on the airwaves. I suppose I could count my blessings, that she
didn't depict me as a lush on the six o'clock news.

She was good enough to say, "Sorry about that."

I stumbled back to something relevant. "I need this film, along with all
the other film that your cameramen shot outside the cemetery walls. But
first I need a print of that woman's face. Can you do that?"

"You got it." She turned to her color laser printer. "You think this woman
is somehow connected to Agent Pearl's death?"

"I can't say anything right now."

She made the print. It was clear enough; but no doubt Randall and
Shrieber would make an even clearer one from the digital file, and they'd
have it disseminated throughout the national Bureau by late afternoon. I'd
hang onto this copy.

Chapter 26

Elaine Madson returns to her home in Encino after visiting her husband Bill in the Van Nuys jail. It's the only time she's ever gone to Van Nuys—to visit her husband in jail. Her husband, who was moved from a precinct cell in Santa Monica to the Federal building in the Valley. Van Nuys. Before today there had been no reason in her life to visit that burg, though it's not very far away. She's thirty-seven years old and married fifteen years to a man who hadn't been the hottest pick in the college bunch but who was nice to her and never raised his voice in the house. It's why she never followed up on that possibility of an affair with Roberto, her personal trainer at the gym. Rather Elaine comes home every day to this house that she now unlocks and enters, hitting the code on the alarm system automatically, not noticing the beeper has not gone off. She's still thinking of her husband in a jail cell for crimes she never wanted to believe possible. But now she will believe them. She calls out, I'm home honey, but Jessica doesn't answer. Elaine wonders if Jessica's running a little late from soccer practice, if the other mom doing the driving today was running behind, but Elaine knows immediately that that is not so, for she is a mother whose logic is quick and who knows the patterns of her family's life. And Jessica has been home, for over an hour, in the upstairs bedroom. Elaine knows she's home before she sees her. She knows something is wrong because she recalls now that the alarm did not go off, which should mean Jessica's home, but if she's home she would have answered Hi Mom like she always does because she's a good girl who has not yet cultivated the impatience of her pre-teen friends. Which is why Elaine runs up the stairs and looks in Jessica's room and finds in there nothing and no one. She goes to her own bedroom where she once thought she made love to her husband which is now a lie it wasn't love it hardly was sex and finds the message written large over the wall with the girl's blood. *Conejo Suelto.* And there's Jessica naked, from the waist down, her bloodied soccer jersey still on her shoulders and covering her chest but pulled up from her navel and little hips. There are no clothes on her spread legs nor nothing to hide the fact that what once made Jessica Jessica is no longer there.

Chapter 27

"What are you doing here?"

Sometimes when Special Agent in Charge Leticia Fisher stands in front of you and addresses you like that, she looks eight feet tall. Bigger than Shaq. Especially when you've just turned the corner and there she is, signing another agent's papers about some other case.

"Just handing over some digital videos to Agents Randall and Schreiber." I filled in the details, that the videos could lead us to the people behind Marisa Jackson's murder. I showed Fisher the photo of the woman at the funeral.

She looked at it, but then looked at me. "Regulations say you need at least ten days down from duty."

"Yes ma'am."

She sighed. "So how you doing?"

"I'm pretty tired."

"I'm sure. What's better for you, rest? Or following up on this?" She motioned her head toward the photo. Then, instead of waiting for my answer, she touched me on the shoulder and walked toward the elevator. "I'm going out for a smoke. Want to join me?"

Outside we smoked and talked about the new-wave fascism of California, of no smoking in bars, public places, or, lately, the Santa Monica Beach. "They're squeezing us out, Romilia. Nowadays the only safe place to smoke is at home."

"Hardly there," I said. "The school has my kid indoctrinated. Whenever Sergio sees me light up, he thinks I'm cooking heroin."

Fisher laughed. "How's he doing?"

She asked that in light of and in reference to his kidnapping, along with Mamá, last year. "He's okay."

"Your mother?"

I blew smoke out of my nostrils. "Nothing breaks her. But Sergio just doesn't talk about it."

"Think he should?"

"Maybe. I don't know." Why is it, whenever I get with my boss I become inarticulate? I say little. And yet I enjoy her presence in some way, like she's taking the place of fatherhood in my life. "That was good of you, to have one of our psyche-boys meet with Sergio."

"Well. One of those unspoken perks." Fisher looked around. We were the only two in the pit, which was a corner of the second floor balcony. We looked out over Wilshire and the 405 Freeway just beyond. "You've been through a lot in your life, Romilia."

That should have been a warning shot. But it was said with such empathy. Or perhaps I was just so grateful for the words that, at their heart, were nothing but caring. And still I waited for the next phrase to be *It's come to my attention* or *Rumor has it that* or just plain old *I need to talk to you about your drinking.*

But it was none of those. Rather, "You know what my favorite label is?"

Label. That sounded so reasonably soothing. A connoisseur's word. I didn't say anything.

"Maker's Mark. I love that bourbon. Pure Kentucky, straight and singular. I love its smell, and the way it looks in the glass when you hold it up to a candle. That light amber color, beautiful, like looking at Will Smith poured into a glass. And the taste. That first burn that smoothes itself out into an oily river, nothing like it. I love it from the moment I pull the candle-wax top off the bottle until that final sip two or three or five hours later."

Lettie Fisher is African American and Latina, her mother from Chiapas, her father from Birmingham. The way she spoke about the whiskey, I couldn't tell which culture sang more: the warm sibilance of a southern afternoon, or the sensuality of deep Mexico.

"I love whiskey, Romilia. Just like my father liked it. Too much. Daddy died with a liver this big," she held up her cigarette butt. "So you know when I had my last sip?"

I shook my head, no, and I was afraid of the answer, as if I would be saying goodbye to my last sip soon. By mandate.

"You know what happened to Chip Pierce, right? Six years ago now. How he walked with a team into the Smokey Mountains, looking for Bitan, the anti-gay terrorist? Bitan had set a trap for them. The shrapnel's what took Chip's leg, part of his hand, his eye." She stood closer to me now, but not in a threatening way. More the way two friends share something dark between them. "He was under my command. I was the regional SAC out of Nashville. After I visited him in the hospital, I went home and got soundly drunk. Next day I went to see him. He knew me, Chip. We'd worked together for five years. There he was with pieces of him gone, and he says to me, he asks me, to stop."

A pause, a silence. Then me, "Did you?"

"Hell no! That night I went home and tied one on again, took the sting out of the hangover." Fisher turned, looked at the floor of other agents' cigarette butts, as if recollecting the past there. "It took me another two months. I remember my last drink. A Tuesday night. Knoxville, Tennessee. Around eight thirty.

"I almost drank last year, when Chip was killed. That morning, after I met with you at the crime scene, at Chip's house? I stopped at a liquor store on Venice Boulevard before going back to the office. Walked in, looked at the whiskey rack. Then turned and bought some really ugly sunglasses and walked out. Then last week, Nancy. I slowed down after the cemetery, there's an Albertsons near my house. There's been a thousand times at least since my last drink that I've wanted to break. But losing your agents, that just about snaps you in half. Maybe it does snap you in half, no way it can't. Then the fucking media, breathing questions down your neck on whether or not the Feds have their act together, losing agents. I should drink. I really should."

She was looking away. Then she turned and looked straight at me. Perhaps she thought she had said too much, had confessed too much to one of her subordinates. She looked angry. But something wrestled inside of her. Compassion, for lack of better word.

Then both her heritages broke protocol. She turned and walked right up to me. She grabbed the back of my head, like a mother grabs a daughter. She leaned in, right next to my ear, whispered to me words that I will never forget. I didn't want her to let go. I wanted those words to be said, over and again.

She pulled away and headed toward the balcony's sliding door. Before she walked through, I stopped her. "Wild Turkey," I said. My throat closed up.

She looked back at me.

"My father. It was his favorite booze. Mine now."

Her fingers thrummed once against the glass of the sliding door. "Ancestors. Gotta love them. Even with the fucked up habits they leave us." She walked inside.

Chapter 28

There was a phone message at my desk from the Medical Examiner's office. "You were right," Dibbs said.

I called. He explained. "The object you found in the desert, the two pieces of leathery material are human flesh, apparently skin from around and including the areolas. DNA has yet to come back. But I eyeballed both pieces, compared them to the wounds in Marisa Jackson's chest. They're a close match."

"Okay. Okay what about the string?"

"Nothing out of the ordinary. A thick twine. It has a purplish dye in its weave. And no prints to lift, from it or from the desiccated skin."

I thanked him. We both hung up, making no editorial comments, at all.

I thought about the pendant. For that's what it was. How could it be anything else? Two cut nipples pierced through with twine. The twine looped and knotted together, long and open enough to encircle a neck. *Religious,* I had said to myself out in the desert, right before the shooting. A holy, or spiritual concept—what did they call those things that old women wore? My mother would remember, but I wasn't about to call her. Some pendant, worn by people who share the same ideas, the same beliefs.

An afternoon in the desert. A little girl brutalized on the hood of a car. Mutilated. Smashed in the head and thrown over the border. Her skin, dangling from a string, which hung on the limb of a desert bush. Hanging from a tiny limb instead of dangling from someone's neck. Whose neck had it been intended for?

That was the scratch in the record, the glitch in the imagined film of my mind.

For I could see that afternoon, could picture it. I could see the car, and the girl's ankles tied to the front fender, her wrists pulled back by a rope that ran through the two front side windows. I saw not one man, but two or three, because of those footprints in the desert.

My imagination had to skip in order to make the rest of the story work: Marisa stumbles about naked and barefoot, within a circle of men. She bleeds. No longer tied to the car. Then one of the men smashes the back of her skull with a rock.

Then the final image: the necklace dangles on a bush in the wind.

How did the necklace get there? And how, and why, did Marisa go from bound onto a car to stumbling through the desert?

Did someone arrive? The authorities, cops or Border Patrol, which scared the killers, so they untied her and killed her quickly and lost their new pendant? Then why toss her like they did into California?

My little film had skips and glitches. The other blood, for instance. A large puddle of it. Someone else was killed out there that day. Yet we found no other body. Which meant it was either taken away, carried out of the area, or maybe buried somewhere. But our agents found no burial site.

The mind-film skipped again, into real images of my own memory: Mexican cops walking along the southern section of the crime scene. Saenz, whispering to me about a third country. Saenz then talking with us in oh so slippery fashion in the cantina in Tijuana. Then Nancy, killed less than two hours later.

I called Randall and Shrieber. They were still working with the digital footage. "This will take most of the afternoon," said Shrieber, a little impatient.

I considered Mexico and the cop named Saenz. Lettie Fisher popped her head into my cubicle. I smiled, still feeling the gutsy warm fuzzies of our smoke together. "You'll want to head out to Encino," she said, then told me about Mr. ATM's daughter. "It's going to be a territorial cat fight. LAPD's got Homicide on it. Santa Monica's sending over that fellow, Blaze, who questioned Madson. You need to wrestle it from both."

Chapter 29

The killer had laid Jessica out as if on a cutting board.

Why I thought of that image, I don't know. Did anyone else in the room, Detective Blaze from Santa Monica, the detective from the San Fernando district, and all of those Valley cops, did they think what I thought, gutted on a cutting board? Or did they simply see what perhaps I should have seen, a little girl hurt until she died?

Still, the cutting board analogy was apt. It helped me know something about the killer. He hated females.

"*Conejo suelto,*" said Blaze. He stared at the blood writing on the wall. "And our Mr. ATM was all so worried about himself getting killed." Blaze looked down at the girl as he said that. His voice almost became a growl.

"A message," I said, "but just to his family?"

"No. It's a warning to other clients. All the other men in the city who like their sex young, and who buy from this guy." Blaze had his hands on his hips. He studied the message again, as if giving it a handwriting analysis. He turned, looked at me, and answered my puzzled look. "I was in Special Victims for three years," he said. "Sex crimes. After a while, you learn more than you care to."

"You've not seen this before?"

"No. Not this over-the-top. But the pedophile community, it's a tight little family. Word will get out. Whoever was selling to Bill Madson is telling the other clients to stay clean, don't get caught."

Or else he'll come for your family. But there was more to this. I had never thought of pedophiles as being in a community; I always thought of them as loners, people who drifted in and out of neighborhoods, people we never knew about until one of our own kids became a victim. But what Blaze was saying made sense: like drugs, the sex trade had to rely on word of mouth. Maybe it began with the billboards for the men's clubs all over the Valley.

"Blaze, how would a guy who likes child sex make contact with our killer?" We both turned away from Jessica on the bed, walked into the hallway. "How would he get into the loop?"

Blaze had his hands in his pockets. "It'd start simple. With his kiddie porn contact."

"Okay. How does he make the kiddie porn contact?"

Blaze grinned. "Agent Chacón, men who want something bad? They find ways to get to it. Maybe he starts light, by visiting his friendly neighborhood video store. Hang out in the porn section. He'd start to notice who shops there, and become acquainted with the other guys. They begin with casual conversation about some of their favorite flicks. They smell each other out, like dogs. Soon one guy says he knows a fellow on Vanowen and Woodman who sells some nice, slick magazines out of his apartment. Photos of ten year olds sixty-nining. You've got a child, don't you?"

I looked at him. I was already looking at him, but his question had shaken me from a sudden bad image. "Yeah. I do."

He smiled. "Thought so. The look on your face, I've seen it a thousand times."

"What look's that?"

"Of a mother who hears about this shit and then imagines her own child in such a magazine and tries to chase the image from her head. The horror, the horror."

He was literate. I liked him, even with his quick honesty. Maybe because of it.

"Yeah. Sergio's ten."

He nodded. "So you can follow the trail. Guy buys kiddie porn from some slug in North Hollywood who happens to have contacts with the distributor of the man who prints the magazines. That guy has access to children who, by force or by coercion, are in the pictures. So he might just have contacts to someone who has kids for sale. Like Marisa, or Prissy."

"Where is Prissy, by the way?"

"In a juvie home for now. Santa Monica. Tried to get away three times so far. Hasn't said a word about the woman in the van."

I told him about my photo of the woman, and that I'd have one sent to him right away.

We walked back toward the bedroom. "By the way," he said, "Sergeant Powers over there, down the hall? She's the detective who got the call. I've already talked with her, explained the situation. She knows this is a Fed case."

"That was easy."

"Well. So now I owe her one." He grinned, like a boy.

"And I owe you one. Thanks."

We walked through the house, where women and men bent over or reached up high and dusted doorknobs and table edges and cups, spraying ninhydrin all over the place, making the rooms smell like overripe bananas. I'd have to leave soon: the anyl acetate in the spray always gave me a headache. One guy worked on the obvious trail of bloody footprints, which were not prints of feet at all, but oval steps: the killer had worn some generic boot, maybe rubbers for the rain. I doubted even the young woman plucking a fiber off the bedspread would find much to work with. The killer no doubt wore a bathing cap as well. And I imagined him clean shaven. He had come fully prepared to write that note to us all.

Chapter 30

There are moments in a cop's life, or a detective's or an agent's, that make you feel you are not worthy of the job. When you doubt everything you do. The gutting sensation of knowing that you are inept, impotent before the great charge of energy and power that is murder. Nothing rouses this sense of nihilism quite like meeting up with the mother of the victim.

Sasha Jackson stood at the opening of the Bureau's parking ramp. She was looking at cars as they came and left the building. She stared at the cars and their drivers, hoping to find the one person she was looking for. That someone was a Latina agent. And I was one of the few in the Field Office.

I wouldn't say she lit up when she saw me. There was no more lighting up for her.

I barely waved at her while driving into the building. A way of acknowledging her, that I'd be with her soon, after I parked, after I got my head together to take on whatever it was she was going to ask of me.

Her daughter was dead. She knew that. I was sure she had already seen Marisa's body, though hopefully Dibbs had only lifted the sheet from Marisa's face and stopped at the neck.

How had Dibbs been with a mourning woman? I couldn't imagine him putting his arms around anybody, much less a stranger, and certainly not a mother.

Had anybody put their arms around this woman? From the look on her face, no. She stood in the opening of the parking garage, waiting for me. She was alone; she had two other kids, according to Karen. Perhaps they were with neighbors, in an apartment, down the decrepit peeling hall from where Sasha Jackson lived.

Karen. I hadn't thought much about her. Actually I had, but in a pissed-off manner. Here I was, taking on a case that was getting much bigger than I had been prepared for, and Karen had run off to do some more righteous guerrilla work. God knows what she was doing now. Where do you go from cyber-criminal? What's left after making the world stare at images of little girls left torn in the desert?

Yeah. I was pissed at Karen. And worried. She simply looked for trouble.

Sasha and I spoke in Spanish. She was Mexican, maybe a few years older than me, though not much. She was pretty; and she was tired. I walked up the entrance ramp to her, moving from the shadow of the parking structure to the light of day, where she stood, all the while trying to guess what she wanted. For she had lost most everything; what would be her desire, except to find the killer?

We barely shook hands as she muttered her name to me with a quick, protocol *Mucho gusto*, hardly even that. "Is it true?" she said. "What they say about my daughter? What they did to her?"

"Señora Jackson, I'm not at liberty to say anything about a case that's—"

"No one's at liberty, God dammit."

It seemed strange at first, hearing such a curse as *al carajo* coming out of the mouth of someone I had considered *humilde*. It slipped from her mouth as something more than natural; such language she obviously used every day. Not spoken in a high tone, no crescendo of anger with the curse. But her voice rattled with demands that have never been met.

She asked, "Is it Los Pezoneros?"

"Excuse me?" That was a word I did not know. This had happened before, especially among northern Mexicans, who speak a Spanish distinct from Salvadoran. Sometimes they used words that confused me, and I had to catch up with their sentences while trying to figure out what they had just said. They made up words. I suppose we all do that, but the Mexicans I knew had their own way of playing with the language. Taking a word we all knew, for instance, and either stripping it down to something barely recognizable, or adding on to it, to make it bigger than it was, which was the case here. For I heard, within Pezoneros, the word peson, which sounded like a derivation of *peso,* or "weight." Until I moved the accent over the second syllable, which of course was *pezón.* Nipple.

She saw in my face that I had figured something out.

At first it all sounded like myth. Stories about a band of ghostly men who hunted women in the desert. "Do you listen to the *narcocorridos*?" she said.

I thought about my collection of CDs at home: Bach. Miles and Coltrane. Cecilia Bartoli. My pick in Latin music began with Mercedes Sosa. No Tigres del Norte, no norteños whatsoever, which were so popular among the Mexican Americans who dominated southern California. Though I knew about the narcocorridos, the love romance ballads sung either in honor or at least remembrance of the drug cartels. I had little use for drug dealers, and even less use for those who celebrated them in song.

We were on the outside patio of a nearby Starbucks. I picked this so I could smoke. She had her own pack and lit up before I did. She leaned into the table, not to speak in private but from exhaustion: the table held her up by her elbows. "I have to get back before three," she said, and muttered an explanation about the woman down the hall who was watching her two surviving kids. That woman had to get to work at three. She also referred to the fucking bus route, how lousy LA's transit system was.

"I'll give you a ride," I said.

She glanced at me. That tiny piece of kindness sunk somewhere into her world.

"They've written a song, for the Pezoneros," she said.

"Who?" I said. "Who's written a song?"

"I don't know. One of those groups." She paused, looked around. Behind us some guy was pitching a screenplay to someone who kept saying I'm an Indie type of comedy director, I like wacko. Give me wacko.

"They say the bands are politicized," she said, "that they're singing to the world about the struggle, the life on the streets. But they're making money off their songs. And the drug traffickers look like heroes, and now the Pezoneros, shit."

She might have cried, had she not been so exhausted. And enraged.

She smoked. "So. Is it true?"

There was no bullshitting this woman. "We don't know who did it," I said. "But yes, they did that to her."

There was silence between us for a while. She shook, a dry-weep. Still, even the Indie man who liked wacko turned to our table to look at the shaking Mexican woman.

"Look, Sasha," I said, "I'm on this case. We've got some leads. We'll find out who did this to Marisa."

"What do you know so far?" she actually smiled at that. "What are your 'leads?'"

I made general references to the sex business, the porn and the prostitution. I hesitated at first, not wanting to give her the wrong impression. And yet I knew she wanted me to be blunt. "But I don't think Marisa was involved in any of that," I said. "She was purely a victim."

Again, Sasha half-smiled. But there was no happiness there. "Yes. She was innocent. But she did get tainted."

"What's that mean?"

"You were born here, weren't you?"

"Yes," I said. "I was."

"It shows. How you carry yourself. You're what, Honduran, Salvadoran?"

"Salvadoran."

"I thought so. Your accent. But you're also gringa."

The few times I've had this conversation with other Latinos, I've hated it. Yet it's all true, and we all know it. I had Salvadoran blood, and I had Georgia as my birthplace. Not only gringa, but Southern gringa. Which, in many Latins' eyes—Latinos from the mother countries—made me less than one of them.

"My daughter was a gringa," said Sasha. "I'd thought that would have protected her from a lot of things. A lot of things. Her dad was a gringo, but he was Black, which made her more morena. If I'd had a white man to make her, things might not have happened." She smoked, blew it out the side of her mouth. "Well, maybe not so true. They're bringing girls from all over the world now. Even white ones. But of course, if your mother turns tricks, well, you're not high on the social ladder. Who cares about a puta's dead daughter?"

I wasn't sure what to say to this. So I kept quiet. But then she didn't say anything. So finally I muttered, "I'm sorry."

She shrugged. As if to say *Not your fault* or *Shit happens* or *Thanks for all that compassion, gringa.*

Still, it gave her passage. She began to talk about things that I didn't doubt she had never told the boys in blue at her local precinct. "It's money, you know? You got three kids, you need the cash. I made more in one afternoon in some pendejo's apartment than I could in four days sweating in a maquiladora, sewing jeans for Levi."

Her words and her body did not go together. Her words were that of a hardened soul who was tired of wearing hip-hugging miniskirts and bikini tops and glittering make-up with a wad of condoms in her purse. All that, coming out of the mouth of a mother of three-now-two, who dressed as if ready to spend the entire day ironing.

"So one day Pico gets pissed off at us all, and he says—"

"Wait, sorry. Who's Pico?"

She looked me straight in the eye, as if suddenly sorry for my loss of understanding, my, for lack of better word, innocence. And then I knew who Pico was.

"He was, high, Pico," she said. "He'd get that way. Crazy, after an afternoon of crack. One day we're all sitting down in Yolanda's living room watching television, waiting for instructions, you know? He gets going on how little we were bringing him. We just kept quiet. Then he says 'I'm gonna get Los Pezoneros onto your asses, then we'll see how hard you work.' One of the girls laughed. Called him a pinche brat, for using old wives' tales on us. 'No,' he said, 'no, they're real.' Then he gets into this story-telling way, and there we are, ignoring the television and listening to him. I mean, it's like he's the only family you got here, right? And you know families, they can be messed up anyway. So it's like you're sitting there with your screwed-in-the-head cousin who also does a good job of telling a story. He's talking about Los Pezoneros, how they're on the border, how they haunt the desert, shit like that. Then he says 'And they're coming this way ladies. That's right. Coming to L.A., Los Pezoneros, just like the Killer Bees man, making their way up the coast.' Well we just laughed at that. Which was our mistake. Maybe. I'm not sure. But maybe it was the coke, you know? Makes your personality switch like that. He got all pissed again. He slapped Yolanda, I guess because he thought she was laughing the loudest. We told him to calm down *cabrón*, get his head on straight, we were just enjoying his story. But he gets up and walks out. Yells at us from the door to get our pinche asses back out on the street and that if we didn't make enough that week he'd send the Pezoneros to hunt down our children.

"Which we wanted to blow off as his bullshit. But we all have kids. And he sounded, I don't know. He sounded real."

I waited to make sure she was done. Then I said, "Have you reported this to anyone? Have you told the police about Pico?"

"Right. They come after him, then Pico's boss, whoever that is, comes down on us. Or we're the ones who get arrested. And maybe you haven't figured this out yet, Agent Chacón, but I don't have papers."

"What part did Karen Allende play in this?"

Though you can smoke outside in California, there was no ashtray on our table, no doubt a way to give evil smokers a harder time. Sasha dropped the butt onto the cement sidewalk and crushed it with her heel. "Karen. One of the nicest people I've ever met. Very naïve. But a good heart."

"Did she, know about you?"

"No. No. All she knows is that my daughter disappeared."

"How did you come to know her?"

"One of them showed up, two days after Marisa disappeared. She interviewed me, asked me all sorts of questions about what had happened, and how the police were doing so little about it."

"Karen came to you?"

"No. Courtney."

Courtney. The shit who tripped me at the theatre. We still didn't know where she was. Though we still had her cohort, Robert, in custody.

"I think they heard it from the police band. I'm not sure. But Karen and her friends tried to help me find her. I haven't heard from them, though. Not since, not since they found Marisa."

And now it was my turn to think, how gullible *you* are, Sasha Jackson. I wanted to ask if she had seen the news lately, about Karen jumping bail, but obviously she hadn't, and thus knew nothing about how Karen had taken pictures of her dead child, that Courtney had helped Karen break bail, and that Robert was being held for cyber crimes. Gullible, to believe that the guerrilla team of Desertwomentruth.com actually was there to help her find her daughter, when really all they had done was follow a lead to yet another victim of the great conspiracy on the border. High intentions. Political intentions, for the good of all. While Sasha Jackson mourned her child.

Oh how Karen could piss me off. Her heart was in the right place. But her ass needed a thorough kicking.

"I'd like to know where Pico lives," I said.

"I don't know," she said. "We always meet in one of our places. All I've got is his cell phone."

"Let's give him a call."

Chapter 31

"What have you said to the cops, you bitch?"

Pico didn't speak fluent Spanish. He was a *pocho*, a Latino in the States who struggles with the mother language. And he lived up to the name: 'Pocho' is an insult. It's Spanish for "hollow log." Nothing inside. When he got mad, he didn't say puta, but bitch.

"I didn't tell them anything," said Sasha. She did a good job of ignoring all the technicians around her: the woman who kept her eye on a monitor, the fellow behind Sasha who was watching the screen of his laptop.

"He uses Verizon," said the guy at the computer. "I've hooked onto their satellite and locked into their ubication system. We should have a location within a minute."

"Hurry," I said, "it's not going well."

I was sure the technician did not understand Spanish. Yet he heard what I heard, for we all wore headphones. Pico was frantic and angry. Sasha was doing her best to keep him on the phone. "I just want to know what the hell happened to my daughter."

"You should have done better, girl."

"Done better what?"

"Better business!" Shit.

At least that's what I thought he was saying, his Spanish was so bad. But I understood. And my mind started to play with what I was going to do with this guy once I caught him.

Sasha shook. Was part of it embarrassment? Even though the shield of language stood between her conversation with Pico and my two fellow agents, it didn't matter; shame rattled through her.

"Why did they take Marisa?" Sasha broke and cried.

"Why? Why you think? You didn't work hard enough."

But his voice had faltered, we all heard it. That wasn't the reason Marisa died.

And Sasha recognized it. "What did you do, Pico?"

He stuttered about, as if just maybe he had a conscience. "Shit. You know, sometimes he asks for things."

"Who?"

"The jefe, man."

"What? What does he ask for?"

Good Sasha, I thought. Good.

"He wants pictures. He wants to see the kids."

There was a silence, in which all we heard was the slight crackle of Pico's cell phone.

"What pictures? What pictures, Pico?"

"No, shit, not those kind of pictures. Just some shots, you know, when we're together, in the apartments. Photos of you and your kids, eating lunch or something, no selling photos. I don't do that. I gave him shots from that birthday party last month for Yolanda's boy." He spoke like a man who had the remnant of a need to come clean. Or to escape both the authorities and the gnawing voice in his head that told him he was little more than a walking bag of scum.

"You show him photos. You show him photos of our kids, you *hijo de la gran chingada*!—"

"We've got a connect. He's not in L.A., he's in a car, heading south. He's just around the exit to San Juan Capistrano, on the 5 Freeway. He's passing Ortega Highway."

And not going there to see the swallows. "I'd bet he's heading for the border," I said. "Tijuana."

Which meant I had a lot to do. Ask for clearance to go to San Diego; inform San Diego of Pico's arrival and tell them to let him pass through; and request a chopper and pilot. All from Fisher. Still, I touched Sasha on her shoulder. "You can let the *pendejo* go now," I said.

She looked at me, through tears. She covered the phone piece and asked me in Spanish, "What do I say?"

"Tell him how you really feel."

She did. The computer technician and her assistant looked at Sasha and her sudden eruption of Spanish. The guy shifted in his seat at the way Sasha spoke. There was no need to translate.

Chapter 32

Sasha hadn't blown it. She didn't tip off Pico that we were coming after him. As far as he was concerned, he simply had a heated conversation with a pissed-off, mourning, laborer.

Sasha had given us the make of his car, a three year old Lexus, dark brown with gold trim. "He shines it like a new pair of shoes," she had said.

San Diego soon found him making his way down the Five. They kept behind Pico and radioed all nearby San Diego Police to let the speeding Lexus keep on speeding. Give Pico a break today. The guards at the posts on the border let him through easily, with just a quick glance at his passport. Such were some of the advantages of being with the Bureau: our reach could extend so quickly into the other agencies.

The San Diego Field Office gave us a fellow named Bruce to be our escort. Once I had flown into the city, Bruce had a car waiting for me. He drove. We talked little beyond my filling him in on the highlights of the case.

In Tijuana, Pico knew where he was going. He drove south only so far, then started taking streets whose names I did not know, but which were familiar to me. Sadly familiar. Streets I had taken with Nancy only recently. Pico found a parking place just a block away from Precinct Seven and walked in.

Officer Saenz walked out of the precinct doors with Pico by the arm, almost tossing him out into the street. Pico turned to the cop, obviously pleading. Saenz said something back, made hand movements, all of which appeared to be the basic Don't ever come to my job, idiot. I did manage to catch Pico saying something about a daughter. He knew that word, *hija*. *Su hija*. Was he talking about Marisa, Sasha's girl? Is that why he ran down here?

Saenz looked up and down the street. I bent my head and hoped to God he didn't notice us. It seemed he didn't. Saenz spat, then turned and walked back into the cops' offices.

"That cop," I said to Bruce, "is dirty."

"Mexican cop. Isn't that the definition of dirt?"

I wasn't sure what to say to that. I didn't like the prejudicial edge to it, but also agreed with it. I told Bruce about my encounter with Saenz on the border.

"So," said Bruce, "your next move?"

I rubbed my forehead, rested my head in my hand. "I'm not sure. We talk with Saenz now, we won't get anything out of him." Though I wanted to talk with him. I wanted to put my barrel in his face and make him confess to Nancy's murder, and his role in Marisa's killing.

Instead I said, "Let's pick up Pico."

"Here? We're not stateside. Isn't Pico Mexican?"

"No. Hell no." Acid in my words. And prejudice: the attitudes sown in us early, in childhood. "He's a damn *pocho*. No country wants to claim his ass."

～◆～

That was not fair. Even my mother might have pointed that out to me, though she was the one, when Catalina and I were kids, who drilled into us the importance of knowing Spanish. But she would not have cared for my attitude toward Pico, even though Pico evoked every single attitude about pochos that I had ever heard: that the ones who had not dealt with their pocho-ness ended up hating their own kind. It probably didn't help that Spanish speaking Latinos made fun of them while growing up. Having fun with tongue-twisters like Pinche-pocho and pocho hasta lo' hueso. Maybe that's what made some pochos so bitter. Maybe that's what had made Pico who he was.

But I still hated him.

He panicked when Bruce tossed him into the back of our car. He must have thought we were Mexican Mafia, or the Gringo Mafia, until he saw me. I let him see the scar on my neck. That's always a great way of freaking out somebody on a first impression. "Jesus what you want man, híjole I ain't done nothing *malo*, I ain't ratted, no narc here man, me entiendes?"

I showed him my badge, credentials, and said the letters.

"Ah shit."

Then, as a last thought, he looked back at his brown Lexus with the gold trim.

"Don't worry," said Bruce, "it'll be there when you get back." Then Bruce did something cruel. He glanced about at the world of Tijuana and said, "Well, then again . . ."

"What are you doing with Officer Saenz?" I asked. I refrained from referring to Saenz as the *jefe*, for I had my doubts about that.

"He's my cousin's boyfriend. He's, he's gonna let me stay in his place in Ensenada next weekend."

"Okay, Bruce. Let's go home."

Bruce took the roads back to California. Pico, his hands cuffed behind him, jerked around and looked back through the rear windshield at a Lexus whose time on the street was limited.

He rattled around in the back seat for a good four minutes before blurting, "What? What do you want to know?"

We were near a park. Bruce found a nice jacaranda tree to park under, which gave us shade. Still, he left the car and air conditioning running.

"What does Saenz have to do with your pimping in LA?" I said.

"I, I really don't know what you're talking about."

I just leaned on the back of my seat and looked at him.

"Nothing man . . . nothing."

"Los Pezoneros," I said, "you're involved with them."

"No, no, I don't know what that is."

But he did. Because he shivered. I said, "Marisa Jackson," and he looked ready to bolt. So I said, "Jessica Madson," and the choking, pre-vomiting sounds told me he knew about the newest killing, the killing I had just learned about myself. A murder that the media had yet to learn about. We stood in that fleeting moment when only the cops and the killers knew about a dead girl in her mother's bedroom.

"Pico, your involvement with both killings will put you away for a long long time. In a prison system that's loaded with pedophile victims turned murderers who don't take kindly to your type. Tell me, how big is your asshole now? How much you think it can stretch before it tears?"

Pico started to cry. And out of the corner of my eye I saw Bruce, who didn't care too much for my technique, one I had learned before joining the Bureau, when I was a cop. For there is a difference between pure agents and cops-turned-agents, and sometimes, such as now, the difference shows itself.

I got what I needed. No, Saenz was not the *jefe*. He just delivered the photos.

Chapter 33

Bruce called for another car to meet us near the border. We handed Pico over to the two agents, who would take him to the San Diego field office. Then Bruce and I returned to the neighborhood of Precinct Seven and waited for Saenz to get off work.

I figured Saenz would head home, change clothes and spend the evening either in a gym or at his pool hall bar, nursing one beer all night long. But he did neither. He did go home and change, but not into workout clothes or a tight T-shirt with a gold collar around his neck. He walked out of his apartment in a pair of black dress pants, dress shoes and a pure white guayabera. The two stripes of embroidery down the front of the shirt, running over the four pockets, looked freshly ironed. The pockets were empty, save the bottom left one, in which something, maybe a bunch of coins weighed down the cloth.

He met a small, older woman who wore a veil over her head. She touched him on his arm, just above his elbow. They walked down the street and met another woman. Then a man joined them; he also was older and had a thick moustache and wore his own guayabera, cream colored. The older gentleman greeted Saenz with a handshake. He and the women, and another woman who stepped out of an apartment building and joined the group, all seemed deeply pleased that Saenz was with them, that he was walking with them down the dusty street to the cemetery.

A larger group had already formed there, women and men from the neighborhood. Most came from walking distance, so few cars were parked nearby. They greeted one another. A number of them went out of their way to say hello to Saenz. Yet it was not fear, as if he were some *patrón* who had stepped into their midst. Rather, it was pure *cariño*, the way they patted him on his broad shoulders, like he was one of the neighborhood boys they had seen grow up. A neighborhood boy who had turned out all right.

And yet I couldn't help but think that Saenz, as he stumbled in his response to their warmth, their open arms, was uncomfortable with the interpretation of his outcome. That perhaps he could not agree with them.

Bruce and I sat in the car and watched the service to its end. No priest showed up and I knew why: this was not a mass, nor a burial. It was a day in a *novena*, in which women gather as many of their barrio as possible and lead them all through a rosary. Men and women and maybe a few kids stand around the fresh grave and finish off the five decades, bless themselves, then go home to tamales and coffee.

A novena is a nine-day ritual. I was betting these folks were in day six. For that's how many days had passed since Marisa Jackson's death. Though of course that was not Marisa Jackson in the grave.

Once they started praying, they all got into the groove of the *Ave Marías* and the *Padre Nuestros*. I sensed, even in this distance, a certain unquietness rustle through the gathering. They looked about, and each time someone new came to the grave, they smiled, as if there were safety in their numbers.

Something then occurred to me: novenas are usually held in the home of the deceased. Yet these folks had chosen the gravesite itself. Had the dead person been without a home? Hardly likely. That was a decent looking tombstone standing there, pink marble, which had taken some real money to buy. No. These folks had gathered here, in a cemetery, as if to make their prayer public.

As if to make a statement.

"How long's this going to take?" said Bruce.

"Twenty minutes for the decades. Another ten for the litany."

"You religious?"

"Not at all."

"How come you know all that?"

"As a kid, I went to funerals. Most of our neighbors in Atlanta were Mexicans. The adults would do the rosary for the dead. We'd wait around for the tamales to get served."

Which was another thing that didn't seem right here. In my childhood there were always other kids around. Mexicans, and my own folk, didn't shy from showing children the fact that we're all going to die. But in this crowd there was not one child among them. Not even a mother holding her baby. Only adults.

As if this ritual were some sort of risk. Too big a risk to get their kids involved in.

It ended. They did what I figured they would do. They scattered quickly. They moved like people getting away from a target. Respectfully, as they walked among the dead. But fast. I wasn't surprised, though I wasn't exactly sure why. And I wasn't surprised either when Saenz turned, spotted our car, slipped his rosary back into that pocket and waved slowly at me.

I waved back.

"Wait here," I said to Bruce. I got out of the car and walked toward Saenz.

Now Saenz and I were the only two standing near the grave. Flowers lay upon the freshly dug dirt, roses and bougainvilleas placed there by the folks. We did not shake hands. We kept a space between us and spoke in English. Perhaps he assumed I preferred it, as I was American. I assumed he preferred it as a way of protection from anyone listening. "How long have you known I've been following you?" I asked.

"Since Pico paid me a visit this afternoon."

"Pico a friend of yours?"

"He is *mierda*."

I smiled in agreement. "You stage this for my benefit?" I said, gesturing to the already ended novena.

"No. Not at all. I've been coming every day."

This I believed.

"I am very sorry about your partner," he said. "She seemed to me an upstanding person. And, may I say, very lovely."

I didn't say anything to that. I swallowed. My throat felt tight. I read the stone. The man's name, Alfredo Ortiz García. Born fifty five years ago. A prayer to St. Joseph, the saint of lost causes and cops, underneath his name. Below that his dates, nothing more.

I said, "He died out in the desert that day. Didn't he?"

Saenz said nothing.

"Who was he?" I said.

"A cop." Then he said, slowly, saying each word with the clarity of a larger anger, "A good Mexican cop."

"I see."

"There are such things, you know."

I looked up from the grave to him.

"Such people as good cops in Mexico. There is such a thing."

"Are you a good cop, Officer Saenz?"

He didn't answer that.

"Why did he die?"

No answer to that either.

"What you all were looking for that night," I said, "I found it. A necklace."

His hands were in his pants pockets now, the botto seam of his guayabera bunched up just above his wrists. An endeavor to look casual; or perhaps some acquiescence to the way things were going.

"You know about Los Pezoneros, right?" I said.

The name disgusted him. Visceral response. I thought he'd lose his stomach contents. But he regained a quick composure.

"You with them?"

He stared hard at me. "I have nothing to do with them." Then he added, as if it were necessary for him to say it, not for my benefit, but for his own sense of order, "I did not believe they really existed, until recently."

"Who are they?"

"I don't know."

"Don't bullshit me. Are they the ones behind the sex trade? Who are they?"

He started to walk away. I followed. He turned, and this time we were just a few inches away from each other. Just like we had been in the desert, when he was coming on to Nancy and me; now he wanted to whisper to me.

"Ritchie. That's what they call him. I don't know a last name."

"Where can I find him?"

"That is impossible to say. He just shows up, when he wants something."

"Like pictures of little girls."

Saenz looked down.

"Did he kill your friend here? Alfredo García?"

"I wasn't there."

"But somebody else was, right? All those footprints in the desert, there were other men there when Marisa got killed, when Alfredo was killed. Who, other cops?"

He was walking now, repeating what I had just said, Other cops other cops.

"Who's this Ritchie, he Mexican or American? Where's he from? Come on Saenz, you're the one who whispered to me about a third country. So who runs this third country? Who's in control?"

He turned to me and smiled, as if that was the last thing his fear was going to let him do. "Neither of the first two countries. That I assure you."

In the car Bruce said, "Get anything?"

I was pissed and tired and hot from the Tijuana afternoon. "Ritchie. We're looking for some guy named Ritchie."

Chapter 34

Randall and Shrieber had the video all ready for me. "I think you will be very pleased," said Randall. He turned to his partner. "Got it all set up, Klack?"

So. Not only had they heard about their nicknames, they had embraced them.

Shrieber took a DVD, smaller than the ones we rented at a movie store, placed it inside his laptop and slid the cartridge in. He clicked around with the built-in mouse. "What we've done here is taken your friend Maggie Contrera's illegally shot footage within the cemetery and 'spliced' it with the footage that her cameraman shot outside the cemetery gate. This way we're able to take the people who were inside at the funeral and follow them out to the parking lot, to their individual cars. We're lucky. Your female perp? Contreras caught her enough for us to get a make on her. On the outside cameras the perp never shows her face; in fact, she goes out of her way to keep her face opposite the lens. But we could make her, through her clothes, and her hair and height and body form. There she is."

The footage began near the grave. There were all the people that I had seen before, those who gathered for the final rites. Me, my mother, Nancy's mother. The neighbors, whom we had all interviewed in the days after Nancy's death. And her. The woman who stood between Lenny and the young female agent.

The camera angle then switched. We were now looking from outside, through the raw footage of the regular cameraman. All of the people making their way through the gate. All of the agents looking around the area, as if too well trained not to look. Most everyone wore sunglasses. Shrieber hit a few buttons on the laptop. The computer had its own internal lens: it pulled back, wide, then pushed back in. The screen filled with the image of one person. The woman. The bitch who dropped Prissy off at the apartment on Barrington, then popped the van door against me and drove off.

"Now she moves to the edge of the crowd. Then she looks back, see? Like she's changing her mind. Then she turns around and heads off. Look how she turns her head. Yeah, she knows to keep away from the newsmen. She's the one." Shrieber smiled, and fiddled more with his buttons.

"You're good," I said.

"You ain't seen nothing yet." He pulled the mouse over the screen, and with it drew a perfect square into one section. The rest of the shot around that square froze. There was only movement in the frame that he had created. He pulled the frame out until it took over the screen. "Look at her. Heading toward her car, a blue Camry. And check it out." He made another frame, right in the back end of the car, then drew it out and displayed, as clear as a day on Zuma Beach in Malibu, a California license plate. "How about that, Romilia?" he said. "We're already on it, tracking down the plate as I speak." He crossed his arms over his chest.

How I wished I could have crowed with him and praised him for his stellar work. For it was incredible work. But I had seen something right at the instant he pulled up the license plate. "Could you go back to the car, please? The whole car."

"Yeah. Sure." He pulled the screen out again and showed the woman opening the door to her car and ducking in. Shiny blue Camry. And as if to make it easy for me, the camera had caught the car in the same exact angle I had seen it at Grauman's Chinese Theatre. Only now, there was a tiny dent in the side, pushed out, obviously made from the inside of the trunk.

Karen.

Chapter 35

Nobody saw what I saw. And I didn't want to see it.

Fisher tried to be rational. "Lots of blue Camrys in the world," she said. "And the dent, that may mean it's clearly another vehicle." But then she added, "You really think it could be the same car?"

"Yes."

Fisher studied. "I don't get it. She gets in the car of a woman who's involved with the child sex trade. Like she's involved with her?"

I had thought that. But it made no sense. Karen now dedicated her life to exposing this world of sex slavery. To climb into a car with that woman, a young woman whose face had hardened into stone, seemed beyond contradiction. And that dink on the side of the car, the more I looked at it, the more it bothered me.

"She's not involved," I said. "It's a kidnapping. I'm sure."

Fisher looked at me.

"You shouldn't be doing this one, Romilia."

"You can't pull me off this."

But I heard it too. The tremble in my voice. As if I had just heard news about my own son or my mother. I was too close. We all knew it.

"Please," I said.

She sighed, looked away. "Stay with Klick and Klack on this," she said. "All three of you, together on the entire thing. Joined at the hips." She walked toward her office. She had just taken on another burden: keeping an agent who was personally involved with a case on the case.

I needed to follow up the new lead on a guy named Ritchie. But that lead felt tepid now; and now, Karen flooded my mind.

Shrieber joined me downstairs in the catacombs of our holding cells. "The boy you brought in from Grauman's Theatre? His name is Robert Johnson."

Even with my new worry about Karen, this did not escape me. "You're kidding."

"Nope. No relation I don't believe. Though he is singing the blues now." Shrieber smiled. "He's twenty-three, his family lives in Connecticut, he's been in L.A. for a couple of years. Dropped out of college and started his own internet engine website, he's done fairly well for himself. And on the side of course he was breaking federal cyber laws."

"What's he said about the group?"

"He alleges to be low man on the pole. Maybe the only man on the pole."

Robert was asleep on the cot in his cell. I didn't wait for the clank of the door to wake him up. I yelled his name. He jumped. "Come on out here," I said.

We sat at the table in the middle of the main room. There were no other people around, just Shrieber, Robert and me. Out of all the approaches to pick from, I chose direct. "Tell me where Karen is, Robert, and don't bullshit me."

"I told him earlier, I have no idea." He glanced at Shrieber.

"You know she's in a lot of trouble."

He nodded. His eyes didn't know where to go.

"But she might be in more trouble than any of you."

"What? Why?"

He was a good kid, you could tell that. He had little deceit to him, at least, none that showed itself. He looked worried for Karen's well being.

I said, "I think she may have gotten into the wrong car."

"Wrong car, what's that mean?"

"At Grauman's, in Hollywood. When you tripped me, when she got into—"

"Hold on ma'am. I didn't trip you. I told you that was Courtney."

"Okay when Courtney tripped me. Karen got in a car and was driven away. I need to know whose car that was."

"I don't know."

"What do you know?"

"Only what they told me."

"They? Who?"

"Courtney and Karen. They were in charge. I just did the plumbing."

"How'd you get involved in all this? How did you come to know Karen and Courtney?"

He blew a breath, as if he had told all this before to Randall and Shrieber. "UCLA. At a rally."

"What kind of rally?"

"Some political rally, sponsored by one of those justice groups on campus."

"So you're involved in politics?"

"No, I hate politics. Just a bunch of noise. No, I was in a class with Karen, poli sci, it's a requirement. They didn't offer the class in the summer at her college, so she took it at UCLA. She asked me if I was interested in going to the rally."

"And you were."

"No. No I was interested in seeing her." He smiled, a shy smile.

"I see. So you went."

"Yeah. And it was more interesting than I thought. It was about human rights. This guy from the *New York Times Magazine,* he was giving a lecture on the sex slave market. Not the one like in the Philippines, but here in the States."

His voice lifted. Robert Johnson did believe in this cause. But he had come about it for love, through a crush on Karen.

"So, that's how we got started."

"Wait a minute. That fast? How do you go from attending a lecture to doing what you were doing? Was this part of a bigger group you joined?"

"No. This was all Karen's gig. And Courtney's. Courtney more than anybody."

"What do you mean?"

"Courtney was the real head of it all. She's great at, well, at getting her way." Robert barely chuckled. "That's okay I guess. All for good intentions. You know, noble stuff. This whole thing was Courtney's brainchild. Karen, she had the bucks to pay for it. And me, well, you know what I did."

Another reason for me to hate Courtney, besides what she did to my leg at the Chinese Theatre. She also had roped Karen into this childish, dangerous act of protest. Or warfare. Or whatever it was they wanted to call it.

"Where is Courtney?" I said.

"I have no idea. They didn't tell me their plans."

"Plans, for what?"

"For whatever happened after, if you ever shut us down."

"So they had a plan."

"Oh yeah." Again, he laughed. "Courtney, she always had a plan."

"And you weren't part of the plan?"

"No, I guess not." He stared at the table, then back up at me. "I guess, they went beyond what a computer geek could do. But Courtney did tell me to meet them at the theatre, to help them in case something bad happened."

He seemed more calm than what I had expected him to be. Perhaps it was due to having been in this holding cell for two, three days. But no, it was more than that. It may have been, simply, the act of confession. He had gotten caught, and had told Randall and Shrieber all that he had done.

Which was a lot. Which could send him to federal prison for a long time. That's why his calmness didn't make sense.

"I need to find Courtney," I said.

He leaned into the table. "I've thought about that. I don't know if she'll be online anytime soon. I bet she saw you take me away."

"So do you know where she ran?" My voice raised. I didn't like the way Robert leaned into the table, as if he were suddenly my colleague. As if he were working this case as well. Behind him stood Shrieber, who moved his hand slightly in front of him and looked at me. Shrieber was trying to mouth something toward me.

I leaned back in the chair and crossed my arms. That didn't feel right, to cross my arms in front of someone I was interrogating. But to drop my arms may have been too quick, showing my own discomfort. I tried to speak casually, as casual as my worry and my anger would allow. "Any chance she'll get online?" I said.

"Maybe. I don't doubt she'd be trying to get a hold of Karen, to keep up with whatever plan they had. Hey, what did you mean, about Karen getting in the wrong car? It was the car they had set up the meet with."

The meet. This kid had watched way too much CSI. "We have reason to suspect Karen's been kidnapped."

"What?"

I said nothing.

"Shit. By who?"

"That we're not sure of."

"Nah. It can't be." He laughed. "They had a plan."

"Well, until we know what that plan was, we need to find out where Karen is."

"Okay," he said. He was nervous. "Okay. What do you want me to do?"

"Contact Courtney."

"All right. I'll need a computer. A good one."

"You've got it."

"And I'll need to . . . I'll have to get off the beaten path, if you know what I mean."

"Meaning break a few net laws?" I said.

He just barely grinned, like a little boy, ready to play.

"Kla—Agent Shrieber here will get you a computer. You can drive it. But Agent Shrieber will be in the passenger seat."

In the hallway I asked Shrieber, "What the hell's going on?"

Shrieber answered in a roundabout way. "You know the DVD, of the funeral?"

"Yeah."

"Well, you know the interface telescopic retrieval lens?"

". . . No."

"The . . . when I made a square with the mouse, and zoomed into the license plate." He mimed that with his hands.

"Yeah. Okay yeah what about it?"

Shrieber pointed back to the holding cell.

"What, you're saying Johnson did that?"

"Well, he showed me how to reconfigure the program so I could utilize the mouse to create a portal to—"

"Hold on hold on. What are you telling me?"

"The boy. He's good. Really good." Shrieber's chuckle sounded more like a cluck. "I mean, I should be jealous. But instead I'm, well, you could learn a heck of a lot from someone like him."

I crossed my arms. Stood upright, before him in the hall. "Did you cut some deal with him, Agent Shrieber?"

He stuttered out several sentence fragments, about talking to Fisher, and about how adroit the kid was with pointillistic graphics and digital-something-or-other. I may have cursed. But I walked away, knowing that Robert Johnson, after serving some menial term for federal crimes, would be on the Bureau's payroll. "Just get him a computer, okay?"

Chapter 36

Agent Randall and I stood outside the room at the open door, drinking coffee. Shrieber sat next to Robert at the laptop. Shrieber was giddy. Robert was pleased to have an older guy sitting next to him, both of them hunched before the screen. Sometimes I picked up phrases they said, but they may as well have been speaking Yemeni.

"He could be a real asset," said Shrieber. "The cyber world is huge. And getting larger. Lots of areas to hide in."

"Oh come on. It's a computer. How does anybody hide in the internet world?"

"You'd be surprised. It's all sleight of hand, when you think about it. When you think they're in one place, they can be in another. Courtney could be in Jamaica, but she could send Robert an email from some internet network of doctors in, say, Mississippi. So we think she's in Mississippi, that maybe she's broken into the doctor's office in Meridian and is using their computer to contact her friend. But really she's just used a program to enter the Mississippi computer from Jamaica. She could be anywhere. Which means she's nowhere. Instead of chasing her, you've got to have ways of pulling her out in the open. And the only way to do that is through the web. And you need guys like young Robert here to do that."

He was enthralled with his own interpretation of both the real and the virtual worlds. I was beginning to wonder if he could distinguish the two.

"I just want to find the little bitch," I said.

I was nervous, but didn't want to show this to either of my new partners. It could get back to Fisher, and she'd feel compelled to take me off the case. But in my head two images were colliding: that of dead girls who had been carved in horrible fashions, and Karen, getting into a blue car. A car that looked too much like the blue car in the cemetery. A car that, at the cemetery, had a dink, made from the inside.

"You got anything on that license plate?" I said.

"Still waiting for the DMV to call."

"I'll call them if you want."

"No. That's all right. I can do it. You're right, they probably need a nudge."

I needed a smoke. I needed a drink.

I needed a drink. Badly.

The sun was setting in the Pacific. This I saw from the western windows of our offices on the seventeenth floor. The sun was setting on Los Angeles and I had yet to call home to tell them I'd be running late because not only had Karen run off but now we had to consider her missing as well. Had anyone called Rigoberta?

"Agent Shrieber," I said, in a low voice, so Robert didn't hear, "how long will this take?"

"I don't know. Could be a while."

"What's he doing?" I spoke as if Robert were not sitting there in front of the laptop in a Zen state, at one with the mouse and the clicker and the screen.

But he was there. "She's not going to use just any email address to communicate," he said. "So I'm surfing throughout all the websites that had contact or hyperlinks with desertwomentruth.com. It's the blogs that I'm checking now. She may be in one of them."

"How could you tell if she were?" I asked.

"By the sound of her voice," said Robert. He smiled. "By the sound of her . . . authority."

He feared her. Was that in our favor?"

"I'm going to have a smoke," I said. Shrieber nodded. I turned toward the door.

"You smoke?" said Robert. That actually got him to look up from the screen. He looked at me like a disappointed boy looking at something old and, I don't know . . . awful.

⚔

I wasn't three breaths into my cigarette when Randall came looking for me. "DMV had the plate. Registered to one Mr. Richard Tanner. His address is in the Valley, in Van Nuys." Randall grinned as if to say silently that the name Van Nuys, my home burg, conveyed it all.

But all I heard was the name. Richard Tanner. Richard. Ritchie.

We drove to the Valley. I checked my gun twice while Randall drove. Just patted it, to make sure.

⋙✦⋘

The address was on the edge of Van Nuys, on the border with Balboa Heights, a new neighborhood that had until recently been Van Nuys, but had changed its name for one reason: not to be Van Nuys. Balboa, White Oak, I rarely came out this way, for I lived on the east side of the Valley. This area was a little more expensive, from what I remembered of real estate properties. But not by much.

I expected to find a porn shop. Not a martial arts studio.

A very clean martial arts studio. Full of kids taking a class from the Asian man up front. I guessed Vietnamese. Just a bit shorter than me. A couple of decades older. He no doubt was both the sensei and the owner. He had decorated his establishment with all things positive: posters in Spanish, English and an Asian language, advocating self-worth. Push yourself. Discipline as the key to success. Inner power. And all those photos of proud graduates from his school.

He may have seen us, but he did not react. He took his students, mostly girls who all looked around nine years old, through a complex set of movements that ended with a thrust into an invisible abdomen.

The young fellow at the desk, a Latino kid, maybe fourteen, greeted us. "May I help you?"

We introduced ourselves. He raised his eyebrows, hopped like an acrobat from his stool and walked into the dojo. He wore a black belt. He spoke to the sensei. The elder man gave him instructions. The boy led the class while the man approached us.

"I help you, officers?" He smiled. He too had a black belt, but it was turning white and frayed on the edges from the years.

We exchanged names and credentials. His name was Ngakpa. I asked him if he knew a Richard Tanner. "No," he said. "What again?" I repeated the name. No, he had never heard of the man.

"Mr. Ngakpa, how long have you been here?"

"Two years," he said. "We first were in Sherman Oaks. But the rent, too much."

"So the rent's better here? Who's the landlord?"

"Oh, no landlord. I buy this." He was happy with this, though not proud.

"Oh. So you own it."

'Oh yes. It is mine. Better to own. Landlords, they are difficult." I was about to ask other questions, but he helped us all get to the point. "I buy this after they kick sex man out of here."

"Excuse me, the sex man?"

"Yes. How do you say, the pornographic? My English, forgive."

"It's fine," said Randall. "So this was a pornography shop?"

"Yes. A very bad one. Pornographic is very bad for people. It makes desires take over."

"Yes, okay," said Randall. Obviously he didn't want someone preaching to him. I didn't doubt both Randall and Shrieber, with all that time they spent on computers, had a nice collection of virtual sex flicks. "So, the guy got kicked out. Why?"

"His pictures. The children."

Before we could get to the next question, Mr. Ngakpa motioned us to follow him.

We walked through the dojo. The girls paid little attention to us. They kept their eyes on the young Latino teacher. One girl glanced our way, curious, but then refocused on her crescent moon kick.

Mr. Ngakpa opened a door and motioned for us to follow. The room had a large window that faced the dojo, like an open market store front. Behind the cabinet were his tools of trade: punching bags, punching gloves, blue padded bats with the logo of his studio on them. "Here, this way," he said. He opened a door. We walked into a small room where nothing but a fairly large Buddha stood, right in the middle of the floor, about knee high. Before it was a thin pad, no doubt where Ngakpa sat in lotus every day.

Mr. Ngakpa grabbed the Buddha and lifted it from the floor and moved it to one side. "This is where he did it," he said. He pointed out through the open door, to the dojo, to where the girls were practicing a high kick. "Out there, he sell the adult books. And the movies, the videos. But here, he keep the children."

It frightened me, the way he said that. He reached to the area on the floor where the Buddha had sat, touched the wood, searching for something: a nail. A nail that looked like all the nails in the wooden floor, flush with the floor itself. He dug his fingernail underneath the nail's head and lifted it easily. There was a whispered sound, air released from a tight chamber. The floor opened. A small opening, hardly as big as the top of an end table.

The light above fell into the hole. It was not a chamber for humans. Just a storage hole, well hidden.

"Here," he said. "He hide them here. The magazines of the children. Place raided two, three times before they caught him. Never find anything, only adult sex pictures. Then, the police send in what do you call him, an undercover? Yes. He pretends to buy. He buys and buys until man trusts him and then they talk about business, so bad man, he shows the hidden policeman this," Mr. Ngakpa gestured to the hole, to the well-built, now empty wood separators that once acted as shelves to keep the magazines from getting dog-eared. "They arrest him. They close down sex store. I buy it."

He stood up. He was very agile, as several black belts and a life of praying to Buddha would make him. He closed the door. The seam disappeared into the floor again. He placed the Buddha back in its place.

"So," said Randall. "What do you use it for now?"

"Oh. Nothing," he said.

"What, you don't hide stuff in it?" said Randall. I wondered too; it was a perfect safe for one's valuables.

"No no," he said. "It must be empty. Forever."

Then he looked at us with a quick study. He appeared slightly sorry for us, as if we were yet another two poor westerners who just didn't get it. "The children in the pictures, in the magazines. They hurt. They hurt still. Hole must stay empty forever. I pray for their emptiness. Best thing. Only thing to do."

Chapter 37

"Oh yeah," said Detective Blaze. "The porn shop off White Oak? I remember it. One of those times the local harping from the neighborhood paid off."

"How's that?" I said. Randall drove back to the offices while I talked with Blaze on the cell.

"That's the Balboa Lake area. They were cleaning up the neighborhood, trying to be more respectable. Did it too. Two things they wanted to do: separate from Van Nuys, and shut down that porn shop. The first they could do through legislation, just draw up some new borders for themselves and change their name. But getting rid of a porn shop is more difficult."

"Why's that?"

"Because it's legal."

"Yeah but they were selling child porn there."

"We didn't know that at the beginning. But then we were following the trail of kiddie porn rags, and there were arrows pointing to that shop. We sent in an undercover, got the guy."

Exactly what Mr. Ngakpa told us. "Was his name Richard Tanner?"

Blaze paused. "No. That name doesn't ring a bell. I thought the guy had some Irish name, Mac-something."

"But no Richard Tanner."

"No. I can run the name through our system, if you'd like. You think this Tanner is the killer?"

"Could be. He's still driving around. Or at least his woman is, the one who was at Barrington."

It was mid afternoon. Traffic on the 405, going South, moved at a fair clip. But this was Friday. The clog on the north side looked like it would never clear. We'd be at the Bureau office in just a few minutes. After work I'd be in traffic, heading back into the Valley, for an hour. An hour in which I'd sit, going twenty, ten miles an hour, listening to NPR over and again until I heard the news three times, then switching over to AM talk radio just to hear something ludicrous, something that would keep me awake.

I dreaded home. I had managed, since Wednesday morning, to avoid any in-depth conversation with Mamá. Since her final statement, that she and Uncle Chepe had been talking, I knew to be careful. Which I hated. I hated having to be careful in my own home. It was my house, god dammit, and okay, though Chepe had helped us with the down payment when we first moved to Los Angeles, I had been paying off that down payment to him, little by little, sixty-five dollars every month. Just like a bill, I sent Uncle Chepe a check for the sixty-five. And though I never got the checks back with all the other cancelled checks from my bank, and knew that Chepe had not cashed one of them, I sent them. And he knew I sent them. I did not want to be beholden to him; I hate feeling dependent upon anybody.

Now that monthly check was some of the little leverage I had. They had been talking about me. There, in my own house, where I paid the bills and the mortgage, they had been making decisions. About me. About my problem and my drinking habits and no doubt they'd start up soon enough about my smoking and I knew if I heard even once the word rehab I'd lose it. To think the word, it was like considering a Hell that you never asked for. A specific Hell that your dear relatives were building just for you.

I had managed to avoid my mother on both Wednesday night, after the Madson crime scene in Encino, and Thursday night, after the sudden trip to Tijuana. Each night I had drunk from the bottle in the bottom drawer of my dresser, along with a tumbler, which I kept there so as not to disturb the house in those late nights when sleep just would not come. Not much; I was actually too tired to drink. Just a couple of glasses. Each night I had told them both, Mamá and Sergio, that I was really, really tired, that this case was going nowhere, and since Nancy's death . . . I had done most of the talking, as little talking as there was. They both just looked at me, though Sergio had said, "Yeah Mamá, that's fine," as if giving me permission to go to bed early, to not be in the kitchen or the living room or anywhere else they were. So I had. I took my plate of supper to my bedroom, closed the door, drank and slept and woke up, each morning, to a plate half empty of food.

I was tired of this. I wanted my fucking house back, I didn't want to walk on eggshells any more around them. I would offer the promise to my mother to watch my drinking. But I'd make it clear to her to call off the dogs of worry, tell Chepe to back off, don't be planning to send me somewhere to dry out, I'd be fine, once I handled this case and found the *pendejo* who killed my partner and who might have Karen.

Which made me think of Rigoberta and if she had been notified. I doubted she had, as there was no verification of what had happened to her daughter yet. As far as we knew, Karen had simply skipped bail.

Rigoberta. I had not heard from her. Which meant she had cut herself off, for the sake of trying to keep this private. It had been in the papers enough, about her daughter being arrested last week. She had done what was necessary for an Oscar winner to do: close down the lines of communication in order to salvage some crumbs of a private life. Which meant she was inside, closed off, waiting for word. Living her own private hell.

I knew what would happen tonight. I would go home and wait to hear from Shrieber and Robert, once they established any contact with dear Courtney. Which meant I'd drink in my room. I longed for it.

Then Blaze called and changed the entire night of events. "Your Mr. Richard Tanner's name showed up. In Missing Persons."

"What? When?"

"Seems he disappeared just a little over two years ago."

My thoughts stumbled. I had a slew of questions fighting one another to go first. "Who, what happened, where was he?"

Blaze laid it out. "Says here that one Candice Seaburt filed the report. A relative. We're trying to verify where she is now. She doesn't answer the phone number here. It's been disconnected. According to the detective who filed the report, Tanner was last seen two years ago at a bar in North Hollywood."

This made no sense. "DMV still has him driving around town," I said. "Or somebody's driving around in his Camry."

"Yeah, the system's not perfect, that's for sure," said Blaze. "DMV has to catch up."

"No. No they don't," I said. "Somebody's paying the registration on that car. We got the name from the DMV, and it's still registered. According to Motor Vehicles, he's not missing. He's still a good taxpayer. Who'd you say the woman was who filed the report?"

He gave me the name again, Candice Seaburt. For some reason that name sounded vaguely familiar. "Looks like she's moved a couple of times, according to the most recent records we have," said Blaze. "First address was in Brentwood, second was, let's see . . . Sherman Oaks. Then she moved . . . oh yeah. Falling star." He laughed.

"What?"

"That's what I call actors who fall off the big screen, who lose popularity. They start out big, living the rich life in Bel Aire. Then their show gets cancelled or they don't get another movie deal, and they can't afford that rich life. They move to the Valley, but try to stay south of Ventura Boulevard. To be north of the Boulevard, well, that's the Hollywood Siberia. Once they move north, they've lost all hope. This girl I bet you was a flash-pan star. But I don't remember the name. Maybe if I saw her face."

"Where are you now?" I said.

"Home precinct. Santa Monica."

"You busy tonight?"

I pictured him smiling on the other end. "No plans."

"If you get her most recent address, maybe we could see her face. Tonight."

He liked that idea. Randall was fine with it, once I told him about Blaze's experience in Special Victims. And the notion of getting it over with tonight suited me just fine. I wouldn't be able to sleep well, considering the case. And, bottom line, I didn't really care to go home.

Chapter 38

"She was a James Bond background babe," was the first thing Blaze said after he shook hands with Randall. We stood in our offices, around my cubicle. "And she played a sexy nurse sometimes on MASH."

"How'd you figure that out?" I said.

"Her name was familiar. Usually in this town, that means they're in the business. So I plugged her name into the IMDb and low and behold, there she was."

"Whoa, what's that?"

"What?"

"The, IM . . . whatever. Some legal network?" I was thinking VICAP.

"The Internet Movie Database," he said. He looked at me as if I were the only person in L.A. who didn't know that website. Which may have been near the truth.

He handed me a fresh file, thin, with his recent downloaded and printed pages. Cartoon rolls of movie film on top of the page, with an internet commercial for movies released on DVD below that. And there was Candice Seaburt, beautiful, in the head shot. Young, blonde, in a hair style of at least fifteen or twenty years ago.

"She's in her mid fifties now, I'd guess," said Blaze. "Started her TV career when she was just out of high school. A real looker. I remember her from one of the Bond episodes, in one of those tight spacesuits. She was hot. Excuse the excitement."

"Boyhood fantasy?"

"One of many," he said. He smiled. "But then she pretty much dropped out of the picture. She did some sitcoms in the nineties, not much, just walk-ons. Never really got a career going, I'm surprised she got her pic in the IMDB. Must be because of the popularity of MASH."

"You didn't get her address from that website?"

"No. I called the precinct she first filed the missing person's report in. They had more recent records in their database."

"So where to?" asked Randall.

"We follow the trajectory of the falling star," said Blaze, happy his own theory of throw-away actors had come true. "She moved to Pacoima."

Two neighborhoods north of Van Nuys. I knew that only because of the one time Mamá, Sergio and I had made a pilgrimage, in our first days of living here, to Ritchie Valens' gravesite. Again, I had no other reason to go there after that, for it was not a neighborhood I felt comfortable in. It looked a lot like my own neighborhood, but rougher. Pacoima felt more run down, with teenage boys hanging out on street corners, in small packs, no doubt selling their illegal wares: drugs, guns, whatever moved. A rough place, that's what I had heard from other agents and even a few of my own neighbors. The same words I had heard some agents use about Van Nuys. Rough.

I supposedly lived in a terrible area of Los Angeles. But I liked it there. Every place in L.A. had a sense about it, a feel, which the general population agreed upon. Encino, money. Sherman Oaks, money. Van Nuys, porn. Panorama City, poor. Pacoima, watch out. I didn't like these generalizations, yet the more time I lived here, the more readily I bought into them. But also, the more I felt at home here.

And now we were going to Pacoima. Where a TV actor's career shot out and fizzled.

Chapter 39

"Mom died two years ago," said the young woman who lived in Candice Seaburt's small house with the dry rot window frames and the chipped stucco. The house stood on Eustace Street, just a block away from Ritchie Valens Park and below the roar of the Ronald Reagan Freeway.

Her name was Patty. She lived alone. She had hints of her mother, when I compared her to the woman in the internet printouts. But Patty had done little to nothing with Hollywood makeup. She wore no rouge or lipstick. She smelled like a hundred cats, or at least the ten cats that sat perched on bookshelves or lay sprawled on the floor. After a few meows, some left the room. Others walked by, looked at us, walked on. She smelled like them and the three kitty litter boxes in the front room and no doubt four other boxes throughout the house, down the hallway, in a bathroom.

She let us in and offered us something to drink, coffee, maybe a soda? But I declined. I couldn't think of putting anything in my mouth, not in there. I wanted to smoke, just to smell my own cigarette.

Cats and Christianity: there were two crucifixes on the wall, one made out of wood with a bloody plastic Jesus hanging on it; the other was a ceramic piece, an off-colored white, with a creamy Jesus dangling. A bible, or some kind of prayer book, sat on a table, next to a television remote control. Several ribbons, blue, red, gold, and white, peeked out of its pages. Well-thumbed.

She might have been my age, maybe a little older or younger, it was hard to tell by the way she looked at us. She was just a stick, as if eating were something she did on rare occasions, and only when the urge became pain.

There were no pictures of people anywhere. No relatives or boyfriends, and nothing of her mother.

She shooed two cats away, a thick brown thing and a skinny hairless one, to give us room to sit on the couch. Randall had stayed outside, several feet beyond the door. He was allergic. "I'll just wait in the car," he had said, reaching for his nose to shield it.

Blaze and I sat down. "I'm sorry," I said. "What happened to your mother?"

"Drunk driver," said Patty. "She was crossing Sepulveda, just around, where was it, Saticoy? Yeah, Saticoy. The guy ran over her. He was weaving, that's what some fellow in the bar said. They didn't find him."

"My condolences," said Blaze. "That must have been really hard."

Patty said nothing. She sat there, as if waiting for a cue.

"Where were you when she died?" I said.

"Oh I was at the home. Yeah."

"Home. You mean, here at home?"

"No, at the home." She smiled. "Have you been to the home?" She was fairly excited, though still sounding tired.

"No. No I haven't. Where is it?"

"In Granada Hills," she said. She stood up from the chair and walked to the one bookshelf where there were no books, just cats and some old cola bottles and a ceramic planter with no plant. And an envelope, thick with pictures.

She sat in front of me on a footrest, frayed all around its brown and yellow edges. She shuffled through the pictures and found the ones she wanted to show me. She smiled. "There. That's the home."

Before I studied the photos, I already had ideas. Patty sat close to me now, and I could see, in her cheekbones, that she was not thin, but beyond thin. She was starving. Literally. She smelled like the cats and something more: the odor of waste. Her teeth were beyond yellow. When she smiled I saw the brown of scurvy in her gums. She looked like a homeless person who happened to be in a home.

So it did not surprise me to see, in one of the pictures she picked out, the face of a smiling woman in a nurse's white uniform. A boy in a wheelchair, smiling through the distortion of mental disorder. And Patty, standing to one side. Not quite smiling. Not emoting in any way.

"I see," I said. "Do you like the home, Patty?"

"Oh yes."

"Do you miss it?"

"Yes I do." But you would not have known it, except for the words.

"Patty," said Blaze, "does anyone live with you? Does anybody else take care of you, or the cats?"

"No I'm fine."

"You're fine," said Blaze.

"I have the money," she said.

"Money. What money is that, Patty?" I said.

"He always said to use the money when I needed it."

"He? Who? Who said to use the money?"

She didn't say anything.

"Is the money here?"

Again, nothing.

I smiled, and backed slowly away from my own question, afraid to lose her. I looked down at the picture again, of the home. "Who took the photo, Patty?"

"Mom did."

"I see. Was she visiting you?"

Patty nodded her head. A smile, ever so slight. So quiet, those eyes of hers, as if all that silence shielded her from a great deal of noise that rattled in her skull.

"Can I see the other photos?"

"Sure," she said. She handed the envelope to me. Which surprised me. I figured she either would have given each photo to me and explained who was in the picture, or she would have held on to them, prohibiting me from seeing any more. But she just gave me the envelope.

I looked through them. Other shots of the home, with other children who had different levels of mental conditions. Sometimes you couldn't tell, in the frozen moment, if some of the kids and teenagers had any problems. Other shots were of a baseball field, Dodgers Stadium. It may have been a field day for the patients; a school bus was parked in the background. Another shot, of this house, in the front yard during the day, in days when the house was in better shape, though not by much. Again, kids in the foreground. But there, on the porch, sitting on the steps, a man and a woman.

I showed Blaze the picture. He looked at the woman, then looked at me and nodded. That was Candice Seaburt. Sitting next to her was a large man, heavyset though also broad in the shoulders, like a weight lifter who has left the sport behind. He had thick silver hair and wore sunglasses. A cigarette dangled from his fingertips; his hand dangled over the shoulder of a little Mexican boy.

The boy was Mexican, no doubt about it. He was staring at the children in the front yard who were playing a game of croquet. His thick hair was worn in a style from over a decade ago. The man looming over the boy was looking away, staring down the street through his shades, as if waiting for someone to drive by.

I said, as lightly as possible, "Who's that gentleman, Patty?"

"Richard."

Her head began a slow weave. Just the slightest movement, but immediately apparent: she swiveled her head upon her neck in a prostrate-8 rotation, smoothly. It became a perfect movement of the symbol of infinity. It seemed like the echo of something that had woken in her, one of the noises, perhaps, of a time when Richard was around.

"Richard. Richard Tanner?" said Blaze.

The infinity movement enlarged. Her face swung to the high corner then the floor then a high corner then the floor.

There had been a slipping since we had come to the door. At first I, and I was sure, Blaze, thought this young woman was simply that: a young white woman living alone in a house full of cats in Pacoima. Nothing unusual about that. Depressing, but not unusual. But she had been slipping further and further away from us, from the world. The closer we got to something through our questions, the more she slipped.

Enough that I was afraid we would lose her. "Patty, who's the boy?"

The infinity symbol ceased.

"That's little Ritchie."

"I see. Is he Richard's son?"

"He said I would be fine," she said. "I could use the money."

"Who? Little Ritchie? He said you would be fine?"

"I have to pee."

She stood up and walked down the hall.

"We can't lose her," said Blaze.

"I know I know."

I stood, made a hand motion for Blaze to stay put, walked down the hall and past two thick cats who looked at me but did not move. The bathroom door was open. Patty sat on the toilet, placed her feet on either side of another litter box. The urine splashed the water. She stared ahead at the bathtub. No toilet paper. She stood and pulled up her jeans.

"Are you okay, honey?"

She faced me, but looked toward the floor.

"Patty, do you know where Ritchie is now?"

"He took Richard with him. He took Richard away."

"I see. Was Richard a problem?"

No answer.

"You know, I was looking for little Ritchie, and I was wondering if he's all grown up now. Do you know where he is? Or do you have some other pictures of him, you know, a little clearer? Or maybe when he's older?"

She looked at me.

"Ritchie doesn't get older," she said.

I hesitated, then smiled and said, "Really? He stays young?"

What made her walk around me, I'm not sure. Perhaps she was not the complete automaton that I was making her out to be. Maybe my probing hit something in her that led her to walk deeper down the hall through a door into the nicest room of the house. Dingy, and dusty, but there were no cats in it. No litter boxes. Just an old video camera sitting on a tall tripod, alongside a backlight whose bulb was blackened from use. The camera was aimed down at a bed. The bed, made up, was large enough for more than two people. But that's not what bothered me. It was the kitchen table to one side, with two bowls and spoons and three boxes of cereal set atop it, which got to me. A mini kitchen, right next to a massive bed. A baseball glove on one of the chairs. Beyond it was another set, a little boy's bedroom.

"Blaze," I called.

He walked in. I could hear the barely whispered curse from his lips. Patty didn't hear him; or maybe she did and knew his curse was to be expected. She was busy squatting to the floor and fiddling with a loose nail just like Mr. Ngakpa had done for us, then lifting a section of the floor and standing to one side. She did not move, as if she had come to a place in a road that she could travel upon no farther.

This small chamber was not empty.

She did not look down into it, like Blaze and I did. She stood above us, as we got on our knees to examine the contents. The large envelopes, closed and yet bulging with photographs, of what I had no doubt. Rows of videos.

And tucked away in the deepest part of the hole, the money that Patty had spoken of.

Her voice came from above us. "Please tell Ritchie and Ingrid that I miss them."

I looked up at her. "Ingrid, who is she?"

Patty's head turned slightly to one side, surprised at my obtuseness, as if I were the catatonic one. "Ritchie's little sister. Everybody knows that."

Chapter 40

Blaze put three black garbage bags of videos and photographs and cash in the back of the car. Randall was already sneezing. He drove with one hand and held a tissue to his nose with the other. But he didn't complain. "Where to?" he asked.

"Back to the Bureau," I said. I turned and looked at Blaze in the back seat. "You want to call it a night? Or do you feel like staying up?" That was more an invitation than a question. I could use his eyes on the television screen.

"I'm in," he said. He gave me the look of a man steeling up something inside. Getting ready to do something he had done before, in the Special Victims Unit. A job he had given up in order to live the more prosaic life of a homicide detective.

He made a call on his cell and spoke while waiting for someone to answer. "My precinct should have the number for a local social services office in the Valley."

"Thanks," I said.

For he and I both knew what would happen to Patty, now that we had taken the money as well as the videos and photos from the chamber. She would slip more quickly into the starvation that was already enveloping her, and she would lose her house. She would run out of money and food and become one of the thousands on the street, and one of the hundreds of the mentally disabled that walked amongst the homeless.

It bothered us both, to take the money out of the chamber. There was a temptation to leave it there; for obviously Patty had figured out survival strategies. She periodically had lifted a ten or a fifty from the chamber, just enough to walk down to the liquor store two blocks from her house to buy a candy bar or a cola. Just enough to keep alive. It was a surprise that no one had taken advantage of her, perhaps followed her home, broken in, and took whatever leftover bills she placed on a table or shelf. Or maybe they had. Two years she'd been alone.

Blaze had left two twenties on the shelf in the front room. Two twenties from his own wallet. All this money, now in the back seat of our car, would have to be checked for fingerprints, serial numbers, markings, just to see if they would give us further leads, something I doubted. For this was cash, simple cash collected from men who had purchased the videos. We had to take it all—procedure. But Blaze was not about to leave Patty in the house without money to get her through a day or two.

~*~

The movies were old. No digital videos here, no mini DVDs or camera sticks that held computerized photographs. These were all video tapes. The photos had been developed in a dark room. "Classics," said Blaze. He shuffled through a handful of pictures. He almost looked happy, or relieved. "All adults in this batch, mostly women," he said. "And a number with Candice Seaburt, see?"

He showed me Patty's mother, posing, her fingers held in an inverted V around her vagina. "Okay," I said.

Blaze flipped through a second batch. "None of them look like the woman from the cemetery, the one in the van who knocked you down. And no guy who looks like a grown up Ritchie. Mostly white people. I'd say mid to late eighties."

"Why's that?"

"Asian and Latino sex was just coming into the mainstream around that time, but hadn't caught on big yet. And these awful hairstyles, see? Mullets, Jeez."

His bravado seemed necessary to get him through the photos. But then something sliced the bravado in two, once he shuffled a bit further into the pile. "Here you go," he said. He handed me the pile of children.

A boy, sitting up, naked on the bed. Staring at the camera, confused. A dark skinned boy. Latino. But not Ritchie. In another photo another boy, white, maybe nine. Naked. Laughing. Covering his testicles with both his hands. An embarrassed laughter? Why does he laugh?

We found Ritchie nowhere in the pictures. So we turned to the films. Each video had a name taped onto its spine: Martha, Sarah, Renee, Jimmy, Pixie, Sam, Sparks, Ronnie.

No Ritchie.

Each tape had one child on it. Martha moving around for the camera on the large bed in Patty's back room. A man's voice giving orders, promising something to eat after moving this way, then that. Jimmy walks from the breakfast table and crawls onto the same bed. The cameraman instructs him how to shed clothes, then how to masturbate. "And make this noise, Jimmy, like this," the voice of the cameraman makes a grunting sound like a man would make, and Jimmy mimics it in a seven year old grunt.

I wondered if Blaze felt the same strange pressure in his throat that I was feeling. The desire to run out the door, pick up a trash can. Or did he study the videos for forensic evidence?

Ritchie did not appear in any of the marked videos. He was on a special one, so special that it had no name on it, and I didn't doubt was not for sale. It was for private use. It was a family movie. Blaze pushed it into the machine. The dialogue started immediately. "Patty, goddammit stand right here. Use the telephoto to get in close," said the same man's voice, "just like I showed you. Don't move the tripod. Right. Point it square, right there." We would not see Patty in the shot. She stood behind the camera, working the lens, necessary work because Richard Tanner had to step away and into the shot, where the actress, Candice Seaburt, naked, stood. In a shadowed corner sat, or knelt, a boy.

"Come on Richard, he doesn't need to do it, I'm a mess, look at me," and Candice gestured to herself. But all Richard said to that was, "He's hungry, right? So he'll eat."

I wonder if the separation from myself began to occur right then. Sometimes I believed that there was something in me, like a soul, that had gotten brittle. You can't see something like that without wanting to wash it away with whiskey or a bullet. Whiskey or a bullet. Why I thought of those two things, I'll never know. Those two things together, up against things to live for. I've got my son. Sergio, he's something, someone to live for. And my mother, the live-in pain in the ass that is mine and mine only. And that's about it really. Not the job, not any more. For the job is too limited, and the wrongs on the screen, too large. With Big Richard, a man so big, taking a small boy and making the boy do something he's already learned how to do, but not on a woman in this state, a woman who gestures to her heavy flow. She moves to clean the blood from her thighs but Richard says No, leave it there, let it drip. Which makes her laugh as if to blurt out, Jeez Richard, you sure as hell get boners looking at the strangest things! But she doesn't say that because the man is busy pushing the boy toward her. Do it, you little fuck, eat her out all of her, and to make the protest and the flaying eleven year old arms stop, Richard pulls a pistol from the back of his belt and shows the boy the barrel and then presses the barrel to the back of the boy's head. Now eat. Eat. Patty, get a close up. Patty, silent, obeys, and I wonder if Patty is Patty because of genetics or because of this boy pressed up into Patty's mother's thighs and the flow coating his face and him choking. Not even the gun can stop him from jerking away, coughing and spitting and then Oh you little shit stand up stand up, then Richard stomps toward the camera to us and the show ends.

Blaze saved me by saying the name. "Oh God," he said. No curse. Just the name.

Chapter 41

We found Shrieber and Robert hard at work, still in front of the laptop, with cola cans and empty Ding Dong and Pocket Lunch wrappers over the table.

"We've made contact," said Shrieber.

As if Courtney came from Mars. Along with all the trash on the table, there were printouts of long paragraphs. I picked up one, scanned it, picked up another. They felt heavy. Not the sheet, but the contents. All those words. Websites dedicated to eradicating pornography, child porn, the objectification of women. Agreed. But find me that shit Courtney. So I can find Karen.

"It's a chat room that he set up on endthedesertkillings.com," said Shrieber. "That was a website Robert had created before they got to work on the virus. Just a place where people could get information on the Desert Women cases."

"Which wasn't enough," said Robert. He didn't look away from the screen as he spoke. "Not enough hits. No one was interested. That's why we went for the in-your-face tactic." He didn't smile at that, but I could tell he was still very proud of his virus. "And we focused. The Desert Women, it's too big. No doubt the drug world is involved. But trafficking of children for sex slavery in the States, that's the issue that we got involved with."

I didn't want to hear about his guerrilla heroics. "So. You're writing to her now?"

"Yep."

"You sure it's Courtney?"

"Oh yeah," and he laughed. "It's Courtney all right. She's glad I'm okay, but she's afraid that I'll get caught using the internet." He laughed again, as if that thought, of him getting caught on the world wide web, were ludicrous. Then he looked at me and saw that I wasn't laughing.

His computer chirped. I looked over his shoulder. Courtney had just written, *What did they do to you?*

"She means you all. The FBI."

"What have you told her so far?"

"Not much. Just that I'm home now, looking for her. We've been spending time in these blogs, talking about the desert women."

"Did you tell her you were with us?"

"She knows you picked me up. She saw you grab me and take me away, right before she took off."

"Okay okay listen: tell her that you lied to us. You said to us that Karen had asked you to meet her at the theater, just to be with her, and that you showed up because you had a crush on her, and that's all you knew."

"But that's not all I knew."

"No. That's what you told us. And so we let you go."

"Oh. Okay yeah, I get it."

"But add that you think the Bureau is keeping an eye on your house. Or at least, you suspect that, since we let you go so easily."

"Yeah, that sounds good." He typed.

Blaze said, "If she thinks Robert's being surveilled, she won't come near him."

"Just give me a minute."

Blaze shrugged, as if he believed that I believed I knew what I was doing.

"Robert, how old is Courtney?" I asked.

"I think, nineteen. Twenty, maybe. Why?"

"Really? She's younger than you?"

"Yeah."

"But she's the boss of the outfit."

"Well, yeah." He added, "She can be, commanding."

"Okay. What's your relationship with her been like?"

"What do you mean?"

That gave something away. "Did you like her, or she like you? Did you fight a lot, or have disagreements?"

"No. Not at all. I never disagreed with her." He huffed a chuckle. "I wouldn't dare."

"Did she know you liked Karen?"

"I don't think so."

"Did she like Karen?"

"What, you mean was she gay? No. Sometimes, to be honest, well, it sounds kind of gnarly to say . . ."

"Say it."

"I think she liked me."

"Really? Why?"

"Well, because I did everything she told me to do." He stared for a moment across the room. "One day I was working on the virus, getting it ready for another launch. She wanted it done by two that morning and I said 'You got it.' So I'm working, and she comes behind me and puts her hands on my shoulders and kind of starts to rub them. And she says, 'You're one of the good men, Robert, you know that?' Which I thought was, you know, really nice. And then she bends down to kiss me, or I thought she was going to kiss me."

A long pause, in which we all were quite curious.

"But she takes her tongue around my ear."

"What, she licked you?"

"Well yeah. Kind of. Just around, you know, the rim, here." He vaguely traced the air around his ear with his index fingertip.

"And what happened after that?"

"Not much. We got busy, Karen had heard on the police band about Sasha Jackson, and her daughter."

"I see." I leaned over. "I think you need to tell Courtney that you need her. You need to hear her voice."

Chapter 42

It would take almost two hours to get her to a phone. In that time she and Robert turned to the more personal. Robert did a nice job of baiting her. He moved it along, starting with how insecure he was feeling, and that he was worried for her and for Karen. And then he focused just on her. He typed: *Courtney, you're so strong, I find that, I don't know, so amazing. So, attractive, really.*

Oh she liked that. And he inched toward that unforgettable ear-licking moment, but he didn't say anything about his ear, just that time when she said that he was one of the good men, how much that meant to him. Shrieber wanted to help out with some of the dialogue. "Tell her how hot she is. Girls like that. They want to know that you want—"

"Hang on Shrieber," I said.

He looked at me and backed away. Perhaps he mistook me for a woman from the likes of Courtney's camp—the take-control type. "Tell her," I said, "that out of all the many good women, she has set the bar even higher, for all people. And that there's something terribly attractive about that."

Robert looked up at me. Blaze and Randall and Shrieber looked at me.

"Come on just write it!" I said.

He obeyed. "Now," I said, "before she can write back, you write. Rush to her. Say 'I need to hear your voice.'"

He did it.

No answer. Then, after that hesitation, came her next line, *Hold on Robert, just a second.*

"Agent Randall, get a phone ready," I said.

"Why?"

"She's gone out to find her own phone. We need to trace the call the second she gives it. She won't chance using her cell."

Randall left the room. I knew where he was going: to the electronic surveillance station.

There was the phone number, starting with 310, our area code. She told Robert to use a pay phone, that his cell was no doubt tapped. Then she said what every other nineteen year old through the centuries has said in one form or another. *I'll be waiting.*

"Good," I said. "You just wait."

⚓

Randall didn't need the phone tap to find Courtney; she had given Robert her number. He sat at a computer in the surveillance station and clicked into a program that connected FBI with internal information from the southern California phone directories. "It's a booth on the Third Street Promenade, between Arizona and Wilshire."

"Get Santa Monica PD on it," I said, "but don't let them take her. Robert, call her. Agent Shrieber, stay with him and make sure he keeps up with the sweet nothings. I need a squad car, to cut us through the city."

"I've got a gumdrop," said Blaze.

Gumdrop. I hadn't heard that term in years, since Atlanta. "Let's do it," I said to him.

In three minutes we were in his car in the parking ramp. It was after seven at night, the sun was just setting. Traffic would still be thick. And the Promenade, I knew, would be full. We could lose her in the crowd of tourists, locals, the street performers and the homeless. I didn't want to leave it to the Blues. Not that they'd screw it up, in fact, I doubted they would. It just came down to me wanting to be there. To be the one to greet her.

Blaze had his gumdrop on the dashboard through most of West Los Angeles, with his siren blaring. All the good Angelenos pulled over to the side and gave us passage. But when we got to Sixth Street I said, "Okay, shut down the screamer."

"You were a cop once, right?" he asked that with a nice touch of veneration in his voice.

"Atlanta PD. Sentinels of the South."

He nodded at that. "I'll cut the light on Fourth. She won't see it."

At Fourth, Randall said to me over the radio, "It's the booth right at the corner of the movie theatre. Can't miss it, the only booth left in Santa Monica."

"Got it."

There she was, chatting away. The door was bent open; I could hear her. She actually had the steel cord of the phone in her hand, as if wanting to wrap it up in her fingers. She had her head down, blind to the entire Promenade. Blaze stopped the car and I got out. I walked up to the booth from behind and stared at her back. I stood there, long enough to hear her say, "Do you mean that? Really? I never knew . . ." And oh how she believed he meant that, right up to the point when she turned around and looked at me, our noses only six inches apart, with the booth's window between us.

I raised my arm and waved my fingers at her. And smiled.

She said nothing. The words coming through the line, so real, so Robert. And me, standing here with two, then three police officers working their way through the crowd and approaching the booth. So real.

I opened the door, pulled her out, handed her to a cop. Then her curses began, and man could she curse. But all grumbles, no shrieks. Robert hadn't heard her. That was obvious once I picked up the phone. "But that day, when you did what you did to me, your, you know, your tongue? You know, on my ear, and Courtney, please understand that in no way, when I say this, no way am I demeaning you, or belittling you as a woman because I'm not. It's just that, in all of your intelligence and jeez you're so sophisticated, you can make a man, well, feel like a man, you know? And I know that's wrong, those primal male impulses, but they're real and I just want to—"

"That'll do, Robert. That'll do."

Chapter 43

Courtney Singleton had a fine tattoo of a spiked dog collar completely around her neck. She had a belt of earrings all the way up to the top of her ear, a nose ring punched through the left nostril and an eyebrow ring, fairly new, according to the puffiness. Her hair was blonde and scarlet. Her skin was white as snow.

At first all she said was, "My dad teaches law at Princeton."

"Yeah and my mom taught me potty training in Atlanta. Let's talk about Karen Allende."

"She hasn't done anything wrong."

I looked across the table at the punk kid who dangled off Daddy's Ivy League. "Yes she has. And so have you. And so has Robert."

She cursed Robert's name. Then she sat up straight. "We used an unregulated venue in order to bring U.S. citizens, especially U.S. *men,* to the attention of spreading injustices against women all over the world."

"You broke federal decency laws."

She laughed at that. Then stopped, abruptly. "Decency," she said.

"Look," I said, "we need to find Karen. She might be in danger." That didn't move her. "We know about the virus, and what you were trying to do on the internet. But now Karen's disappeared. And to be frank, we're getting a little worried."

There was a shift. She looked over to a corner, before turning back my way.

"Of course it's dangerous," she said. "It was all a risk."

That was the beginning of a confession; it needed to be teased out of her. She had already been teased once today by Robert. I didn't want to lose her.

"Has something happened, Courtney?"

"She was supposed to call in."

"Yes? Call in to report on what, her progress?"

"Yeah."

"When?"

"Wednesday. In the morning."

Today was Friday night. Karen, and her absence, rattled inside me. "Courtney, what was she going to do?"

Courtney the revolutionary began to crumble. Courtney the girl, nineteen, who licked boys' ears and who wanted to call Daddy in Princeton, not for legal advice but for a hug, a big hug, started to appear.

"She was going to get on the inside. To take pictures. And to get reports. She was going to send us the pictures."

"The inside. You mean, inside where the kids are kept?"

Courtney nodded. Her chin quivered. She nodded harder.

"Okay. Okay Courtney, listen. How was she going to get on the inside?"

"We had a contact."

"Who?"

"It was through OWL."

"Owl? Who's Owl?"

"No no. O-W-L. 'Operation for Women's Liberation.'"

"Oh. Okay, a group. So where are they, this OWL organization?"

"Their main offices are in Washington, D.C. They're working on the Desert Women cases."

"Can you give me their address? Phone?"

"It's on their website."

"Okay, what's the website?" I was writing notes as she spoke. I wrote as if the pen scratched a path closer to Karen. She gave the site, owlsagainstthedesert.com. That seemed strange, the wording. Long and bulky, even for a web address. But Randall was on it. He took the name and walked to another room where there was a computer. In less than five minutes he was back.

"Here," he said, "but that's not a D.C. number. It's a San Diego area code. And their site, it's pretty lame."

Acid worked its way through my stomach. But I kept going; I pulled my cell phone from my bag, punched in the number. And I was not surprised, as the phone rang, that Courtney was muttering about the fact that Robert knew nothing about the OWL contact. Robert would have said the same thing Randall had said, that the site was lame, or simple, or too unprofessional. Set up quickly, by an amateur. All this verified by the answer on the other end of the call, "We're sorry, but the number you have dialed has been disconnected and is no longer in service." I was just about to report this to Randall and Blaze.

But Courtney spoke before I could. "Ask for Ingrid," she said.

Chapter 44

According to Rigoberta there had been no ransom note. No demands placed upon her for her daughter's return. Karen simply left the house on a Monday and had not been seen since. And when Rigoberta asked Randall, "Why? Why are you asking about a ransom?" Randall assured Rigoberta about the Bureau's need to be thorough.

Klick did a good job, talking with Rigoberta. I would not have held myself together like that in front of her. We were friends, close enough to know when the other was lying. Close enough to know one another's fears. She was a concerned mother who thought of her daughter as a loose cannon, some erratic child who meant either to save the world or save herself through rescuing the world. Did Rigoberta recognize in Karen the need, once, to die? A need that had morphed into something heroic, to help other people in dire situations? I had heard of this before, social workers who chose that line of work because of their alcoholic, sexually abusive fathers. My mother told me about missionaries in El Salvador who had come from the States supposedly to save the local souls, but what they really were doing was working out their own families' dysfunctions.

I couldn't help but think Karen fit in this somewhere. She had once been suicidal; she had almost been murdered. Did this somehow make her into a woman set out to save the world, even if it meant martyrdom?

A woman, now lost? I was lost. I did not know where to go. I was standing on an edge, and there was nothing in front of me but space. All that void, and I didn't know in which part of it to jump.

So I tossed things out. "The area code. San Diego. Can we follow that somehow?"

"Nothing much on it," said Shrieber. He was on his computer. Randall stood over him. "Its services were canceled on Monday." Blaze stood over to one side, his arms crossed, obviously thinking. For the moment he had nothing to say. This was my team, one that had formed organically, with our allowing an L.A. detective on the inside. And they all looked at me as the head, the primary, the one in charge.

I was in charge of nothing.

I took a sheet of paper and a pen and mapped out the information we had. "Okay. We've got Marisa Jackson, dead in the desert on the border. Just a few miles outside of San Diego. Jessica Madson murdered in Encino. A dead Mexican cop buried in Tijuana, who was apparently killed the night of Marisa Jackson's death. We have a sniper right on the border, who kills my—my partner. Who wanted to kill us both. Someone who has no problem taking down federal agents." I added that, just to keep moving with words, to keep from picturing for too long Nancy's face. "We've got a child sex slavery business being conducted in west Los Angeles in an apartment building off Barrington. A brother-sister team, Ritchie and Ingrid, who as children were being held or used by one Richard Tanner, who's been missing for over two, three years. And we've got an abduction in Hollywood, in which Karen, thinking she's going undercover to take pictures in some child sex training ground, gets into Ingrid's car, or rather Richard Tanner's car, driven by Ingrid. Ingrid, who also drives a van. And drops little girls off to their Johns. Shit."

It all fit together; but where it fit together was the issue.

"Tanner's the boss," said Blaze. His voice was hypothetical. "He's behind the scenes, pulling all the strings. He decided to go missing, so as not to be connected to any of this. He has his boy, Ritchie, and Ritchie's sister Ingrid do all the dirty work. He screwed Ritchie up enough as a kid, Ritchie probably does everything Tanner asks, without questioning."

"Maybe," I said. "But why? Candice Seaburt filed a missing person's report on him years before she was killed. Why would he just up and leave her like that?"

"Maybe he didn't," said Blaze. "Maybe she was part of the whole disappearing scam. She just followed orders, and had him filed as missing."

"Shit, nobody knows what the hell's going on here—" And then I corrected myself. "Prissy," I said. I turned to Blaze. "Prissy knows."

Shrieber spoke up. He had been on the computer for the past several minutes, clicking hard. "I've busted into that OWL website," he said. "It's home-built, very basic. Only has two pages on it. First page is information on the group. Second page is how to contact them, and it has three, no let's see . . . four hyperlinks to other websites. And one of the hyperlinks goes . . ." and he punched the link. The computer opened up to endthedesertkillings. com. Robert's first website that he had built for Karen and Courtney.

"I've weeded up through the OWL website, into the publishing engine that puts the site on the web," said Shrieber. "'Quarter-A-Day Web.' It's a small outfit in La Jolla, publishes web pages on the cheap. They've got the OWL email address, see? And if we reconfigure here, we can get into its trash. There. Look at that. All that mail, between someone at OWL named Ingrid, and Karen, at endthedesertkillings.com."

Friendly email that invited the other side toward a partnership, a working-for-the-same-cause friendship. Karen's first letters were sharp, intelligent, expressing the mission of their group. Ingrid's were more blunt, and hers had several spelling errors. Then Karen's letters became more simple. Still clear and articulate, but basic. As if welcoming Ingrid into their group, not wanting to overwhelm her with too much sophistication. Then Ingrid wrote, *We work hard here on the border, in California. To keep kids safe, you know. We lose so many to the coyotes.*

And thus bloomed the idea, between the two groups, to find out where the children went. To go inside. The pictures that Karen had taken and that Robert had sent to the world on the back of a virus, Ingrid had been very impressed by that. And Ingrid had something to offer: she knew some of the coyotes, the men who carried human cargo across the border. She had funds to pay off the coyotes to work for her, and no doubt the coyotes could get Karen on the inside of the business. *To get pictures from the inside, in the places where they hold the girls, that would be great, don't you think?*

Karen vehemently agreed.

What the hell had Karen been thinking? Going into the child sex industry to take pictures. And Courtney, Karen and Robert all believed they could get away with this.

They were young, I thought. Young people make bad decisions.

But Karen had been forced to grow older, quickly. Kidnapped by Minos. Almost killed. She knew how harsh the world can be. These other two, yes, I could chalk their actions up to childishness, a desire to be adults by doing something great and radical. But Karen, I believed, had known better.

Karen was gone, with a woman named Ingrid who was supposedly Mexican and poor but who could use a computer and sure as hell could put on an act. Ingrid, who dropped off little girls to the likes of Mr. ATM who now had no daughter because he was a loose rabbit.

"You okay?" said Blaze.

"What? Yeah. Yeah. Get me Prissy."

Chapter 45

"Child Protection Services will not let us get anywhere near the girl," said Lettie Fisher. "And if we do, they'll stink the media up like a mini-Waco, blaming the Bureau for psychologically traumatizing her even more."

Fisher explained how, after Blaze had initially interviewed Prissy, one of our own bilingual Bureau psychologists was brought in to talk with her, to no avail. The girl simply did not speak. She gave them nothing about her background, her family, where she had come from.

"I don't get it," said Fisher. "She's out, she's safe with the authorities. And yet according to our psychologist, Blanton, the girl acted as if we were the enemy holding her prisoner. Once Child Services steps in, they're lions. They do everything to protect the kids. Can't blame them."

No, I couldn't. But I couldn't leave this one alone.

Though Fisher told me to. "Just follow up on the website. That should give you something."

To protest, or offer any other idea, or try to argue with her in any way would mean I was too close. That I was worried, and not objective toward the case nor Karen. Karen who I could not find. Karen, who I felt was my duty to find. I would no longer find my partner Nancy. I had lost her. Forever. Here, in this moment, I didn't want to think upon it, no time for meditation or circumspection, but still, it invaded me. Loss. My sister Catalina, gone. My partner, murdered as well. Tekún Umán, dead. The people I loved, one at a time, taken from me, and Mamá wondered why I drank.

No . . . not now. This was not the time for introspection. And Karen was not Nancy, could never be. Nor was Karen my big sister. I was hers; that's what she told me once. I was her Catalina. She was my Romilia, still alive.

Still alive, still alive, be alive.

"Yes ma'am," I said, and walked out of Fisher's office.

~~✦~~

Blaze handed me a Styrofoam cup of coffee. I thanked him and asked him if he wanted a smoke. "I don't smoke, thanks," he said.

"I do. Sorry. Want to join me?"

He did. In the pit we talked about how screwed up this entire case was. Then he asked me about the Bureau life. I wasn't surprised; there's always some curiosity from local law enforcement, even one as large as LA's. I didn't doubt Blaze was interested in applying. Maybe he had.

"Do you like it?" he said.

"Yeah. Yeah I like it." An automatic response. I didn't know what I liked right now. All I wanted was the girl, Prissy. Grab her, shake truth out of her. But I waited, until he seemed satisfied with my answers regarding the training at Quantico, the government benefits, the fact that I made a bit more than he did. Then I asked, "Hey, where'd you say they were holding that girl?"

"Who, Prissy?"

"Yeah."

"It's a half-way house down in Santa Monica."

"Got a name?"

"Yeah. Iowa Day House, on Iowa Avenue. Why?"

"Just wondering. What the hell are they going to do with her?" But I was casually putting out my cigarette, with a quarter of an inch still in front of the filter. "What do you do with a kid like that?"

"I know what they'll do. Get her help. Shrinks. Doctors. Teachers. They'll put her in the system. And if she's lucky she'll be on crack in a couple of years and dead a couple of years after that."

That stopped me. "Why do you say that?"

He had his hands in his pockets. He rocked on the balls of his feet and grinned. Not a happy grin. "You ever work with sexually abused kids?" he said.

"No."

"Sartre got it right when he said 'Hell is other people.' Kids broken sexually early in life, they don't pull completely out of it. Kids who have been forced to do what Prissy has done?" He shook his head at the night beyond the balcony. "Suicide just might not be a bad option."

Karen shot into my mind. "I don't think suicide is ever a real option." It came out angry. But then I looked at him, at his face in the moonlight and in the glow of the city. I checked my anger, replaced it with something else. Not pity, but understanding.

"I . . . better get home to my own kid," I said. I made to move toward the door.

He pulled out of his own dark thoughts. "Listen, you okay?" he asked.

"What? Yeah. Why?"

"It just, I don't know. You seem a little edgy."

"You're not the first to say that."

"Yeah, but you're more rattled now. When Courtney mentioned Ingrid, I could tell you were upset."

"That bitch has Karen Allende. God knows what she's done to the girl." My voice trembled and he caught it.

"You're really close to her."

"Yeah," I said. Then I made curt references to the past that Karen and I shared.

"That's close," he said.

"Okay."

"Your boss know this?"

Watch it. "She knows."

He got quiet, looked out at the city, then looked back at me.

"All right," he said. "See you tomorrow."

Chapter 46

"I'm sorry, what group did you say you were with?"

"Children's Rights Division, FBI," I said.

The young man at the door of the halfway house was impressed by the credentials. And my badge, which said FBI but nothing about children.

His name was Peter. "Come in, please," he said, then called out for his house mate, a woman named Erica who was young like him but not as gullible.

"What do you need her for?" said Erica. She had solid eyes and was taller than either Peter or me.

"Just some follow-up questions."

"We were told not to let anyone speak with her," said Erica. "No one."

"Listen," I said, "we're on an active case, and the girl might be able to help us."

"That's fine," said Erica, and she crossed her arms over her chest. "But it will have to wait until tomorrow when Mrs. Samuelson comes in."

"Look, Erica? Erica, I can't wait. This has to be done tonight."

"Okay, just let me call Mrs. Samuelson to give you clearance." Erica's face slit into a professional smile. She turned to the phone. Peter was mute. He managed to grin sheepishly at me, though he was confused when I walked past him and down the hall.

"Where do you have her, Peter?"

"She's in room number four, one of the trauma watches, but wait, Ma'am? Agent? You can't go down there, uh—"

"Hey. You. Stop!"

That was Erica. She put the phone down and walked past Peter and toward me. Both of them must have been college students, maybe social work majors at UCLA, both doing this as an internship, and Erica was bound and determined to get an A. "You're breaking the law you know."

Peter would have been happy with a B–. "Come on Erica, just let her talk with Prissy."

"No! They gave us strict orders. Prissy's protected under Juvenile Code 87, she's been through way too much trauma to undergo questioning, that's what Mrs. Samuelson said and was very specific about it—"

She ranted on while I was saying to each door, *"Prissy, te manda saludos Ingrid. Prissy, te manda saludos Ingrid . . ."* until a doorknob to my left rattled. Just slightly. She was locked in. The name Ingrid was enough; and she did not know my voice. But I knew she knew my face. She knew I was some kind of cop, but what kind she wouldn't know: an agent, a detective, or just some *Chota* off the street. And she didn't know whether or not I was clean or dirty. For Prissy I'd have to be dirt.

The lock was a deadbolt, with a switch knob on the outside for quick, easy opening. This was one of only two doors that had such a knob. Two rooms for kids like Prissy who had to be held for their own protection, who were more than likely to run. She had tried to escape twice. That's why she was in here. A suicide watch room, padded.

I opened it. There stood Prissy. First she had a scant look of hope, that she was being released. Then she stared at me and made to shut the door. I grabbed her arm. "Hey!" yelled Erica from behind me, then quoted a juvenile code on the mishandling of minors. Prissy tried to pull away. So I painted a fast picture of trust for Prissy: I held hard to her arm and unholstered my gun and turned to the young college students. Which was more than enough to make Prissy believe I was a *chota sucia,* the dirtiest of cops.

⚜

In my car I handed her a package of gum. *"De Ingrid,"* I said. She took it, tore it open, unwrapped a piece and ate it. Chewed it three, maybe five chews, then swallowed it. She took another and did the same. I said nothing.

"¿Dónde está?" she asked.

"¿Quien?"

"Ingrid." She looked at me.

"Saber," I said, with a slight chilango lilt. *"Espero la llamada."*

"Tú eres chota," she said, using the Mexican slang for cop.

"Chota chingada," I said.

She laughed. She liked that. A fucked cop. Fucked up. On the take, more money in my pocket from drug runners and children salesmen. But fucked, all the more for that.

Erica and Peter were yelling now. No doubt about that. But that padded room would hold down some of their noises. The rooms of other juvie kids were upstairs. Erica and Peter were good white youths from nice upright middle class families that I was sure wouldn't have put up with too much yelling in the house. Still, Erica would put up a ruckus.

It would be twenty minutes maybe, before one of the kids in the house finally woke up and made her way downstairs and unlocked the door. A few more minutes for phone calls. The calls to the police. And of course to the Bureau. Fisher was home now, contemplating not having a cocktail. She would be called. She would return to the office. She had my cell phone number, which had the Bureau's GPS security tracer on it. Just like the tracer I had used in the desert with Nancy to call them in to save us. The same one that now would out me.

Maybe seventy minutes before they found me.

The phone rang.

I looked at the number. Not one I recognized. Not the Bureau or home, and not Nancy's number because Nancy would never call again. Not even Rigoberta, and not Karen who might have somehow miraculously escaped and was calling for me to pick her up, find her. No one I knew. "Yeah?"

"What are you doing?"

Blaze.

"Yeah?" I said. A vague word, for Prissy.

"I'm behind you," he said.

After having followed me. After having seen me at the half-way house. "What's going on, Romilia?"

"Todo está bien."

"No, everything's not okay. I know you've got her. Where are you taking her? Child Services will raise hell."

Child Services. Raise Hell. I should be scared of a social work office?

No: I should be scared of my boss, who would do more than reprimand.

Karen had warned me of this, how I had learned to follow rules.

What I wanted to tell Blaze: that they were going to kill Karen. If they hadn't already. They had hunted Karen down because Karen somehow was messing up their market or she was getting under the skin of one of their bosses or God knows what reason, but she was in their hands, the same hands that did what they did to Marisa and to Jessica.

Instead I said, *"Bueno pues, nos vemos allá."*

"Where? Where will we meet?"

"Adios." I hung up, tucked the phone in my purse after popping the battery off its back with my thumbnail.

She asked if that was Ingrid. "No," I said, *"fue Ritchie."*

She shuddered. And in that slight movement I saw a little girl once named Priscilla. But that was it. *"¿Se va a enojar conmigo pues?"* she said.

"No," I said, *"No les dijiste nada a la policía, ¿verdad?"*

"No. Nada."

"Bueno pues no te preocupes. Vas a estar bien."

So many lies. That since she had said nothing to the authorities, Ritchie would not harm her. She knew that Ritchie would not take it on her word that she had remained silent. She knew what it meant to report to Ritchie. *"Quiero ver a Ingrid,"* she said.

I faked balking, over her desire to see Ingrid. *"Bueno, no sé. Tengo mis órdenes. Ritchie quiere que yo—*

"Chinga a Ritchie, quiero ver a Ingrid.

Fuck Ritchie, I want to see Ingrid.

"Le diré que no dije nada a la chota, ella me cree, ella se lo va a decir a Ritchie, si no, pues, el desierto de él, donde te desmujera."

There was my entrance. Not Ritchie, but Ingrid. With Ingrid, she'd be safe. She would convince Ingrid of her silence before the police. Ingrid would convince Ritchie of this. And Prissy would not end up in the desert. *Donde te desmujera,* a nonexistent verb in Spanish, *Where he un-womans you.*

The girl knew. Like I said to Blaze, she knew everything.

But I could not have had this conversation earlier, without the information I now had of the girl's world.

So now I did not need to lie. I could honestly say, *"Yo no sé dónde Ingrid."* This was pure truth: I had no idea where Ingrid was.

"Yo sí," she said. *"San Diego. Pero no a la gran bodega. Te enseño."*

So. We were going to San Diego. But, according to Prissy, not "The Big Warehouse."

Chapter 47

Before we parked in front of the phone booth on a street corner in San Diego, I told her to be careful: According to my lie, Ritchie had sent me, a corrupt cop, to pick Prissy up in the half-way house. Now I was disobeying orders, letting Prissy go to Ingrid first. It was better for Prissy to tell Ingrid that she had simply escaped from the half-way house and hitchhiked her way back here. Something Ingrid could believe, that one of their better trained girls could hitch all the way to the border after leaving a truck driver satisfied. Prissy agreed, so frightened was she of me handing her over to Ritchie. I even made it better: I told her to get on out, and I'd just leave, so Ingrid would believe I had gotten to the half-way house after she had escaped. "I'll take the blame," I said. "I'll just say you were faster than I was." She liked that. "*Gracias,*" she said to me. Quickly, as if unaccustomed to receiving kindness. "*Adios.*"

She walked to the phone booth. I drove away, parked the car around the corner half a block down, took my cell phone and its battery and put them in my pocket, loose, still separate from each other. I got out, walked in shadows back to the corner, and waited. She had already spoken on the phone. Now she was standing just outside the booth, her arms crossed, sometimes looking at the ground, most times looking down the street like a little woman waiting for her ride.

The blue Camry arrived seventeen minutes later. Ingrid rolled the window down, asked if the girl was all right, then ordered her to get in.

Prissy ran to the passenger's side.

I bolted out of the shadow, ran to the open window and aimed, one foot away from Ingrid's head. She made to move; I thrust the barrel against her skull, pushed it against her temple. "Shut off the motor."

She did. I walked sideways in front of the car, my gun still trained right on her, and opened the passenger door. Prissy shook. She said nothing. "*Fuera*," I said. Prissy got out. Without looking down the street, but keeping my eye and my aim on Ingrid, I said to Prissy, "*¿Ves a ese carro abajo? Con un hombre adentro?*"

She looked down the street and in the shadows saw Blaze's car. "*Sí*," she said.

"*Bueno hija, te lo juro que es tu mejor camino. Ritchie no te va a encontrar si andas con ese señor.*" And I left it at that. She would have to choose, whether to go with Blaze or not. "*Corre*," I said. She ran. I didn't see where.

I got in Ingrid's car on the passenger side. "Let's go," I said.

"Where?"

"The warehouse."

"I don't know what you're talking about."

"The one Prissy just told me about. Now." One hand on the gun, the other hand worked with the phone and the battery. Slapped them together again, locked; it beeped. A radio tether back to Fisher, to the Bureau. An L.A. cop behind me. Safety nets.

She said nothing, but slowly reached for the key, turned it and put the Camry into gear.

Chapter 48

We did not go to Mexico. But this did not feel like the United States either. Adobe shacks alongside the road. An abandoned church and its desert yard, overgrown with brush; I could see the cross in the moonlight. An old poster of Jennifer Lopez, posing for one of her CDs, was stuck on a large wall. Then the building, one that could have been a school or a company or any number of offices but at this moment was the warehouse. This could have been either country, the way it was set off from San Diego, the way it lost itself somewhere along the border. Or perhaps this simply was the third country that Officer Saenz had warned me about.

The way I saw it, once we were inside, all I had was my gun and my hostage. Which meant that logistically I was somewhat safer out here, in the dust of the street.

I was wrong. Ingrid turned off the car. She looked at me. She smiled.

"Where do we go in?" I said.

"The front door."

That was too easy. "Where's Ritchie?"

"I don't know."

"Is he inside?"

"He's inside."

"So this is his outfit."

"This is his outfit."

The way she parroted me, she should have sounded like the foolish one. But it didn't work that way; I felt the fool. As if she were more worldly, that her world inside building was much bigger than mine.

She sighed. "Well. I'm going to bed." She clicked open the door.

"Get back in here."

"Why?" Ingrid looked at me, confused. "To wait for your 'backup?' Sorry, but I sure as fuck don't want to be out here when they show up." She opened the door and stepped out. Casually. "Once you get those fuckin' Pezoneros stirred up, they're like jodido wasps. When Ritchie gives the word, you're carne asada." She chuckled.

"Goddammit." I got out, came around the car and put the gun into her back, shoving the barrel into her kidneys. She cursed. I looked around at all the buildings, their rooftops, into all of that silence. "We go in together," I said. "You say anything, I'll kill you."

"And they'll kill you, bitch." But she walked ahead, slowly. She opened the door. We walked down a half-lit hallway, turned right into another hall. There was no one around.

"I have to piss," she said.

"No you don't."

"Yes. I do."

This was once a bilingual public utility. The two words, "Ladies" and "Damas" were still on the door, with the figure of a person in a triangle dress underneath.

Small sinks, low to the ground.

This had been a school once.

Inside Ingrid made to go to one stall. "No," I said, "the next one." For I could imagine she had a gun hidden behind the first toilet.

She pulled down her jeans and sat. The stream was strong. "Where's Karen Allende?" I said. "Is she dead?" Without choking. Not in front of this woman.

She shrugged. "I don't know if she's bled yet."

I had seen the film of young Ritchie. I knew what she meant. I understood her brother more than I cared to.

"Did Marisa Jackson bleed?" I said.

Ingrid merely nodded.

"That why he killed her?"

She said nothing. There was no toilet paper, but there was a glossy women's magazine on the floor, which she used.

"He killed a little girl, because she had her first period?" I wanted to scream the question at her. To rattle her with it.

She crumpled another page. "Girls these days, they're having their menses earlier and earlier. Before you know it, we'll be using eight year olds." She stood up and buttoned her jeans. She was ten inches away from me, in the cramp of the stall.

"So Ritchie kills her," I said. "Why throw her across the border?"

"Ay, Mexican Chota, heads up their asses," she said. "They thought she would have been out of their jurisdiction if she was found in California. Stupid fucks. Scared of their own shadow."

"Ritchie didn't have them throw the body into California?"

"What? No way." Ingrid thought about that. "Ritchie don't care about no borders."

"And there were cops present?"

"Well, yeah."

"Are they . . . the Pezoneros?"

She looked at me as if that made no sense. Mexican cops could be bought off, but their code of honor would not allow them to completely enter Ritchie's world.

"Then who are the Pezoneros? A group of pedophiles? Some kind of cult?"

She looked at me as if I were some pitiful, lost gringa.

"They workers," she said.

I worked the stall door open and backed out. "Alfredo García, the cop. Why did he get killed?"

"He made Ritchie lose the scapular."

That was the word. The religious necklace. Scapular.

She shook her head at her own memory. "Dumb *Viejo*. That's why we use teenagers for workers. Old men, they got too much thought in their head, you know? Alfredo gets all high and mighty. Ritchie was about to put the scapular around a new boy's head. Alfredo runs up, grabs the necklace, throws it, then puts the girl out of her misery. Dumb old fuck."

Too much of an image. An older Mexican cop in a crowd of men, watching Ritchie cut a girl apart. Watching that girl wander about, bleeding on the desert floor. Making a scapular out of the girl, and moving toward some teenage boy, the latest recruit, to crown his neck while the girl stumbles about, naked, torn, still alive. Alfredo lunges, pulls the scapular from the boss' hand, throws it into scrub brush. The rock that we found, bloodied: Alfredo had used the rock on her. Had he come up from behind, so the girl didn't see him? Or did it matter, at that point? Could the girl see anything but all those men around her, and the sun and the desert? Old Alfredo, stone in hand, coming up from behind. Doing a final good deed.

Then Ritchie, approaching Officer Alfredo with his knife. And Alfredo, did he fight? Or did he simply stand there, knowing that all this was inevitable?

Ingrid was smiling at me now. She had caught me, while I stared into my own images of the day Marisa Jackson died. That fucked-up gift of mine. Some have called me an empathic profiler because I can climb into a logical imaginary scene. To put the pieces together, to bring some order to the chaos of not knowing. She had seen that in my face. And now, she was laughing.

"You should see yourself, girl." She laughed a bit more.

"Get me to Karen. Now."

She shrugged her shoulders. Then sighed. Like I was asking too many favors for one day.

Chapter 49

Ingrid took me to a place of many doors. A dark hallway with gray walls that connected with another hallway. No lightbulbs, only moonlight through the windows. We stopped where the two halls made a T. I looked down the first hall, then left and right to the second. More than a dozen doors. It was night. It was quiet in the building, or so I thought, until I stopped and listened.

A whimpering sound. More than one.

"Which room?" I said.

"I don't know. I don't ever come down here."

"Open a door."

"I don't have keys."

"Open a door right now goddammit."

My gun now on her cheek. Meaning to bruise it.

"You cunt," she said. Her voice, perhaps the closest to afraid that I would ever hear from her.

Then there were other sounds: a young man's voice in the distance. Shouting to another man. Orders.

Down the hall to the left a door opened. A man—no, a boy, maybe fifteen—bolted through and headed toward us, small rifle coming up from his side, with a thin buttstock pushed into his armpit—submachine. I pulled my gun away from Ingrid's cheek and aimed it at him. I shot twice. He fell. She fell too, from the report of my gun, right next to her face.

"Get up."

"Fuck you."

"Get up."

"You and that cunt white girlfriend of yours I shot, you'll be dead as her and you can fuck each other in your graves."

I hit her with the butt of my pistol. She screamed. Lay there on the floor of the hallway and bellowed like a cub screaming for its mother. So I hit her again and a third time, a quick pistol-whipping in the name of Nancy Pearl. Then I stood over her and aimed right at her forehead. "I-will-kill-you-you-*puta-chingada.*"

And right then I almost did but chose not to and I don't know why. Instead I shot the handle of the door in front of me. It jarred open. The girl on the inside looked at me. Her cheeks, gaunt like the poverty of an old country but there was a smell in the room, sweet, like honey. She bolted from the bed and stared at me and I wouldn't forget that stare. I asked for Karen, the woman Karen, and the girl pointed down and said, *Abajo*, downstairs. A woman's screams, she explained, have come from downstairs and I wondered when was the last time this little southern Mexican or Guatemalan or Honduran girl heard those screams.

Downstairs. Through the door where the boy with the rifle had come from. I stepped over him. A large pearl of blood grew over his forehead. He wore a thick red string around his neck, the end disappearing into the tuck of his shirt. Behind me Ingrid still screamed and beat the hallway floor with her fists and soles and the hungry girl in the room stuck her head out and stared.

A stairwell. Another dark hall. Other rooms. I yelled her name, Karen, Karen Allende, I screamed it and I knew they would all come after me but Karen must have called out as well. It was her voice I wanted to hear.

I shot doors open. Some rooms were empty, others had girls in them. I yell Karen's name.

A scream. Her scream, muffled. The door to the right. A knob and a deadbolt, loosened by my bullets but still I had to kick and kick to break through.

My girl was in there. Her naked body trembled. She tried to turn to me, away from the mattress. Away from a large knife plunged into the bed next to her cheek.

"It's me, it's me, oh God, Karen it's all right, it's me."

I pulled the blade from the mattress and cut the ropes between her wrists and the bedposts, then cut the rope that had burned a circle round her left knee. The heavy thud of boots moved down the hall toward us. I had just cut her right leg free when he appeared, a tall man, thin, so young with the same black hair from his childhood photo, a man who would be handsome, except for all this. He cursed me from the door and screamed about Ingrid's name and You bitch you hurt my Ingrid my Ingrid. He leapt. No hesitation. No thought. He fell full on me, as if to rape me. He had no weapon, as if he needed none. My arms wrapped around him.

Gun in my right hand now, blade in my left.

It took three tries, like digging in hard ground. First into his backbone like stone, then ribs like thick branches, then the third plunge into the soft matter of muscle and liver and tripe.

He half stood, but then his knees collapsed. His arms reached back toward the hilt. He backed away from me and fell and writhed.

I held my gun to the door, waiting for his Pezoneros to come, but they never did. Above us a war had broken out. The shooting, the helicopters, the sirens. A blowhorn, shouting out demands to Ritchie and his men. Machine guns on one side, the pistols of my Bureau, the rifles of San Diego's finest on the other. They had tracked me. God bless cell phones, GPS systems.

Ritchie was dying in front of me. I held Karen's head to me, pressed her eyes closed against my neck. I would not let Karen see him. I would not, though she felt the rattle go through me as I stared at the door and held the gun up and waited. I had to stare: aiming at the door and waiting for a Pezonero to walk through, or for Ingrid, who surely had picked herself up by now. I held Karen, naked, and shielded her eyes and wished I could cover her body with a blanket. When she lifted her head I put my hand on her skull and pushed it down again and whispered over and again, It's all right, it's all right. All of that authority above, shooting their way in. I whispered about her mother Rigoberta and how this would be over soon. Although I knew that for Karen, none of this would be over, ever.

There were only four young men in the gang of Pezoneros found in the building—only four teenagers wearing the scapulars. All dead, sprawled down the hallways and on the front lawn. My colleagues released the girls in all the rooms.

Mexican girls. Armenian. Guatemalan. Young, some of them as white as my dear partner Nancy Pearl. Others as dark as my Nahuatl Indian ancestors. Forty three in all. Each one of them starving, small, much too thin. Looking at all the SWAT soldiers like refugee children being saved from a war. Some of them looked into the room and saw me, the only officer dressed in civilian clothes, holding a naked young woman. They were confused. The confusion was numbing, though some smiled, realizing this was a rescue. And others who realized this finally cried.

Blaze walked into the room and leaned over me. "It's over," he said. He reached toward Karen and me.

"Shield her eyes. I don't want her to see him, or the others."

"Yeah. Okay."

"Romilia?" Karen's voice was weak.

"Don't worry, hermanita. I'm right here."

Blaze found Karen a blanket and covered her. Medics brought in a cot. They lay Karen on it, injected her with a heavy sedative. They carried her away. I went with her. Blaze stayed behind to handle the scene. I thanked him and crawled into the ambulance, which took us both to the hospital.

Chapter 50

What we learned from Ingrid: she and Ritchie were indeed brother and sister. They were from Mexico. Their parents were illegals, caught by Immigration and sent back to Mexico and never heard from again. Richard Tanner, porn businessman with a specialty in children and a sex slavery ring, had gotten his wife to take Ingrid and Richard from some nuns, which didn't make sense until Blaze and I visited the convent that Ingrid had mentioned. There was once a Sister Adele there, who now had moved on to another job. We called her. Yes, she had remembered two kids, one named Ingrid but the other named Joaquín. No Ritchie. But I didn't doubt that this Ritchie once was Joaquín.

Especially after the report came in from our psychiatrist in the Bureau, after two days of psychological interviews with Ingrid. "She's grieving now," said Dr. Gelson, a woman a decade my senior, who spoke softly, kindly. "She and Ritchie were very close. They were each other's protection."

"Grieving," I said. I must have revealed something in my response, maybe a lack of empathy. "So, how did they go from being victims of Tanner's slave industry to taking it over?"

"Ritchie was not part of the sex trade," said Gelson. "At least, not the business part. Ingrid was. Tanner sold her out to johns. But Ritchie was Tanner's personal play-thing."

"Still, that doesn't answer how the two of them became the head of the business."

"Didn't you say the woman, Seabert, was killed? Run over? And that Richard Tanner disappeared?" Dr. Gelson looked at me, as if waiting for me to figure something out. I was; but I needed her to say it. "I don't doubt that Ingrid here, and Ritchie, well, something happened. They grew up. Tanner may have pushed one of them too hard. Ingrid keeps talking about how Ritchie protected her, and now Tanner's gone. Maybe Tanner accosted her once and Ritchie stepped in."

"But why go into Tanner's business?"

Gelson said something, about your sins being on your children's children.

"What's that?" I said.

"We do what we know." She looked at me. "Why does a man who was beaten as a child grow up and beat his own children? And why does a woman who is the daughter of an alcoholic marry a man with a drinking problem? Why do we repeat the actions of our parents?"

My father's face flashed right through my eyes. Then I thought of my son, and how he may inherit some habits. My habits.

"Ingrid and Ritchie were brutalized in specific ways. It's all they've known, since childhood. All they knew was the world Seabert built for them. I understand from your report that you suspect Ingrid and Ritchie of killing Tanner and Seaburt. I don't doubt that. A way of finally escaping from Tanner. But they didn't escape. They re-entered the only world they knew. And they mastered it."

I wasn't sure I wanted to listen to too much more of this. It meant I had to feel something for the two perps. And I wanted to start choosing where I put my feelings.

⚬⚬⚬

My boss actually hugged me in front of everybody on the floor. "Good to have you home," she said. My colleagues applauded politely.

She ushered me into her office, which was a cue for everyone on the floor to get back to work.

"All the girls in the warehouse are now with Child Protection. Which, by the way, told me they're not going to press charges on you for kidnapping Prissy. You gave them so much more work to do, saving all those children."

"Nice of them."

"Good work, Romilia."

"Thank you."

"Child Protection will work with Immigration and try to get the kids back with their families. Most of them are from Mexico and Central America, though a number of them are from Eastern Europe." She sat back in her chair. "That woman, Ingrid, she got messed up during the raid. Looks like someone took a club, or a pistol butt, to her face."

"Yeah?"

"Yeah," said Fisher. "She's claiming a Federal Agent did it. You, I believe. But you wouldn't have seen it. You were down in the room where they had held Karen, according to the report." She looked hard at me.

"Yeah. Yes, ma'am. Where is she, by the way?"

"Van Nuys Federal. They'll hold her there until her trial."

We were quiet a moment.

"So. How are you doing?" asked my boss.

"I need a drink."

She did not laugh. She nodded. "Yeah, me too." She glanced out her window. "The press are still out there. They want to talk to you. I told them you're recovering from a couple of minor wounds suffered in the line of duty. But they'll be on you soon. This is an international case, and you're the one who solved it."

"I didn't do it alone," I said. "Randall, Shrieber. Nancy." Would my voice forever quake when I said her name? "And Blaze, from LAPD. They were phenomenal."

"Yeah what do you think of Officer Blaze?"

"He's good. Top notch detective. Smart."

She made a note. I wondered if, in the future, Blaze would be joining us here. Our Bureau was famous for looking for the best in other law enforcement groups and taking them for our own.

"What would you like to do now, Romilia?"

I told her. She gave me a month.

⛧

Blaze visited. We walked down the street and bought coffee.

"An honor to work with you, Agent Chacón."

"You too."

"Thanks for putting in a good word for me with the press," he said. "My boss at the Santa Monica precinct was impressed by my name appearing in the *L.A. Times* article."

"That's the way it should be," I said. "Have you uh, received a phone call from Special Agent in Charge Leticia Fisher?"

"Should I?"

I just smiled, knowing I had said too much, and sipped my coffee.

"Well," he said. "I'll wait by my phone."

I looked beyond him, over his shoulder. "We broke up one child sex slavery ring," I said. "How many more are there?" I looked out at Wilshire, as if I could imagine the world of the desert, where innocent women and girls are carried away to die. "Karen got involved in all this because of women disappearing, and getting killed, along the border. Then she and her friends focused on the child sex trade. Then they focused on one man in the trade. It's just a small piece of that world down there . . . no, not down there. Right here. They were selling those children to men in the States." I looked directly at Blaze. "How can people allow that to keep happening? It's not just in some third world country, it's right here, Jesus Christ. How can you not feel so small, compared to all of it?"

He waited, to make sure I was finished, as if knowing that I just had to get it out.

"We do what we can," he said.

We sat, quiet for a while. Which was too bad: the only thing we had in common was this case, and I'm sure he regretted that as much as I did. A case such as this wasn't the best thing to base a relationship on. Friendship, nor any other kind.

Still, he tried. "Listen, I was wondering, if you'd like to get a bite to eat sometime. Just, maybe some lunch, or dinner, my treat, if that's okay?"

He was actually shy. I liked that.

"That'd be nice," I said. "But not right now."

"Oh. Something up?"

"Yeah. My kid." I added, not necessarily out of obligation, "And my mother."

"Vacation?"

"Damn straight." And I actually believed it. Wanted it.

"Well," he said, "I'll be here when you get back."

"It's a date."

⚔

I wanted to do something prosaic. So I checked my email.

Lots of crap, of course. The business dealt mostly with case files, ones that were being sent from DC, or asking for copies of files from our field office to send to Quantico. There were a number of files telling me I had won numerous articles, such as an iPod, a bottle of natural breast enhancer, and a laptop. I deleted those quickly, though I almost opened that herbal one—what root could make my breasts perkier?

Then there was one from someone I didn't know. The subject box said *gracias*. I looked at the sender's address. pmt.gob. What was that?

What the hell. I opened it, hoping our Bureau firewalls were enough to burn up any viruses. *Estimada Agente Romilia Chacón,* it began. The formal way of addressing someone in a letter. The rest of the Spanish prose was as formal as the opening, an old style of letter writing, done in the Spaniard manner.

It is an honor for me to congratulate you on your recent closing of the border case. This is so, as I was fortunate to be there when you first opened it. As I said in our conversation in the cemetery, I am deeply sorry for the loss you have experienced, with the death of Agent Nancy Pearl. I know what such pain does to the heart. It is worsened by the fact that the good people in life are many times the ones who die. Your partner, and I dare say, friend, Nancy, as well as my friend and partner, don Alfredo.

Please know that you will have a colleague on this side of the border. And, if permitted, also, a friend.

Respectfully,
Roberto Saenz
Policía Municipal, Tijuana

I wrote him back,

Sí. Cómo no.

Chapter 51

I'm starting to wonder if one image tries to help you survive another. My father, for instance: he started to fill my head more than usual. And not my drunk father, but my sober one. For I have memories of him sober; and in these days I've been relying on those images.

Maybe it was what Dr. Gelson said, about repeating the sins of your ancestors; or maybe it was because my dead, sober father was trying to stand between me and that other image of a man who hated a woman, hated what a woman is.

Still, I could see it all. Could still feel Karen pressed against me and the ache in my arm as I held my gun up to the door for so long.

And those two remnants of the girls who had been murdered.

Then Nancy. My friend. And my final connection to Tekún Umán.

I had to stop. Especially the images from this case, I couldn't go much further with them. Couldn't make sense out of it. I knew the data, of a young man who as a boy was forced to do horrible things, who ended up doing more horrible things as he grew: who, at eighteen, killed his torturer and took his torturer's place. I could see the facts, could sort out the data. But there was no sense to it, so I abandoned the endeavor. For now.

I visited Karen in the psych ward at the hospital in Santa Monica. They were going to keep her medicated for a while, until they could decide what road to take with her. There was a center for victims of torture in Chicago, which another doctor suggested. Rigoberta was not sure about that, and asked my opinion. I was not sure either. "What did the doctor say?" I asked.

"He thought it would be wise. That Karen is a victim of torture."

"I agree. I think you should do that," I said.

It felt cold coming out of my mouth. But it was clear, and Rigoberta needed clarity.

And I had to choose *not* to help. I needed to get my ass home.

I'd make more decisions. Dry out for a while. But not the way others thought I should. I don't like groups, and I'd be damned if I sat with a bunch of weeping alcoholics banging their heads against one another in a circle-jerk of guilt and remorse. I'd just try to make some choices.

Of course, the moment I got in the car and made my way onto the interstate, the first thought that came to mind was clear ice surrounded by brown liquor.

I thought about Nancy. I missed her. God I missed her. As much as we argued, as much as I got pissed off around her, and as much as she had lied to me in the past year about Tekún Umán—I needed her now.

So I thought more about that shot of Wild Turkey.

I didn't say it'd be easy.

Chapter 52

Mamá paid for the plane tickets. I'd handle the rental car in Oahu.

We had plans. A week in Hawaii. Back home to L.A., then a week in Big Bear, just to mix it up. Then two more weeks for me at home with Mamá tearing out the rug in the living room and polishing the wood floor underneath, something we've wanted to do since we moved in. I actually looked forward to that.

But for now, island beaches.

"And I've got a surprise for you," Mamá said in the airport.

"What?"

"You'll see."

Ten minutes later we were the first in the plane right in there with the families with babies, and sitting in first class.

"You got to be kidding me."

She just grinned.

"How much this cost you?"

"Way too much for you to know."

Sergio hopped into his chair and wowed and laughed and started pushing the buttons on his private television set.

"So, we get a meal?" I said.

"A hot meal. And they give you a hot towel for your face before you eat."

"Damn." I looked at the attendant heading our way, with her smile and her cart full of colas and nuts and a city of bottles. "And aren't the drinks..." oh shit.

"Yes," said Mamá, "they're free." And then that thick sigh.

Fuck. God damn. Son of a bitch. But still, I surprised them both. "How's that coffee?" I asked.

"Just perked," said the perky girl.

I took it black and took a sip and could feel four Salvadoran eyes on me. Yeah. I wasn't making promises, except for this one: a dry vacation. Get back to the old disciplines. Running on the beach. Days in the gym. I was just in my thirties, too damn young to start buying size nines. A week in Hawaii, bone-dry. Then we'd go from there.

And it'd be worth it. By the time we took down the runway, Sergio had hung up the earphones and turned off the television. He snaked his arm under mine and pushed his head against my bicep and closed his eyes and then I knew it, God I knew it: I had not lost him. Nor had he lost me.

A MOMENT FROM THE 5ᵀᴴ
ROMILIA CHACÓN THRILLER

Young Ingrid rests her back against the bars. This has become her favored position to smoke. Not on the bed where the ashes tended to fall on her chest. But here with her head rested back on the iron bars, where she can look across her cubicle and smoke and try not to think.

The smokes are illegal, as this is California. But prison is nothing new. Prison is a place where she can pretend that Ritchie is somewhere in the same building, separated, put in another cell on another floor. She can trick herself into believing that. She can smoke a cigarette slipped to her from another woman in another cell before they brought her down here.

She's earned this solitude. Jabbing two forks into both cheeks of a fellow inmate at lunch got her this opportunity to be alone. She thought solitary confinement would be a box with no windows nor lights. Had she known it was this roomy she would have forked the bitch the day that Latina bitch from the Feds had caught her. The very first day in this cell in Van Nuys. Van Nuys of all places.

They'll move her soon. To a place where she can make plans. Business plans. For there's business to be made out there in the world. So many Johns from all walks of life. Johns who like their pussy young and small and tight. Stupid Johns with money and office jobs. Professors and pharmacists and truck drivers.

She smokes. There are no guards. Too many walls between here and the world. She thinks of Ritchie. She doesn't weep anymore. She doesn't feel him anymore. Ingrid feels little now except sleep. That and a thick towel that slips over the front of her neck.

She drops the smoke and grabs the towel. It's her own towel.

"Let's be quiet," he says from behind.

She turns to the right. On the other side of the bars sits a Panama hat, upside down. She jerks to the left: a wooden cane on the floor. A dark, thin hand picks it up. She can see the light blue veins through the Latino skin. The cane disappears somewhere behind her. She now hears, directly behind her ears, the wood of the cane pushing through a fold in the cloth.

"For the record, that was my daughter you shot out in the desert."

The sound of the twist of wood in cloth.

"But you're not one to feel remorse over such things, are you?" His voice strains only slightly with the twisting. "You don't know what atonement means, do you?"

The muscles of Ingrid's neck constrict and open her jaw and push her tongue out. The tongue stiffens with compacted blood. Her shoe heels leave three hundred streaks upon the concrete floor. Her arms reach for the twisting cane but will never find it and her fingers tear at the towel that will not tear.

One final twist.

When they find her they find the towel bunched and knotted around the cane shaft and the cane hook locked up high around a bar and away from her reach. A cane that obviously no one needed for walking. They find no Panama hat.

Biographical Note

Two-time Emmy Award-winner Marcos M. Villatoro is the author of six novels, two collections of poetry and a memoir. His Romilia Chacón crime fiction books have won national acclaim (named a Best Book of 2001 by the *Los Angeles Times*) and are also published in Germany, Japan, Russia and Brazil.

Marcos holds the Fletcher Jones Endowed Chair in Writing at Mount St. Mary's College. He has performed on NPR and appears regularly on KCET:PBS Television in Los Angeles. Recently he returned from his other home country of El Salvador, where he shot the documentary *Tamale Road*.

Marcos teaches and lectures on poetry, fiction, nonfiction, Latino and Appalachian worlds and tamales. His books are taught in colleges and high schools across the country. He lives with his wife and four children in Los Angeles.

More at marcosvillatoro.net